Benjamin's Field

Book One:

Rescue

A Novel

By

J. J. Knights

The above disclaimer not withstanding, the events portrayed in this novel have happened in one form or another in one place or another at one time or another and will surely happen again. One of our enduring traits as a species is that we never learn from our mistakes.

Never.

For my wife, Dorothy, and our children, Allyson Rochelle, Patrick Marc, and Lauren Bernadette.

i

ACKNOWLEDGMENTS

I am indebted to all those who helped with the creation of this novel. To say this book would never have seen daylight without their advice and support would be an understatement. Regardless, any and all errors and omissions are mine alone.

The following graciously provided many of the technical and background details relevant to their respective areas of expertise to help make this historical novel as accurate as possible: Rabbi Aaron Benjamin Bisno, the Frances F. and David R. Levin Senior Rabbinic Pulpit, Rodef Shalom Congregation, Pittsburgh, Pennsylvania; Robert E. Burtt, author and brother, Harmony Lodge No. 429, Free and Accepted Masons of Pennsylvania; Bethanne Demas, R.N., Senior Regional Director of Public Relations/Communications, Shriners Hospitals for Children, Tampa, Florida; The Very Reverend Lawrence A. DiNardo, V.G., J.C.L., General Secretary/Vicar General, Diocese of Pittsburgh, Pennsylvania; William Green, Jr, M.D.; The Reverend Joseph R. McCaffrey, M.Div., Pastor, and Sister Annie

Bremmer, Order of St. Francis, Pastoral Associate, Saints John and Paul Roman Catholic Parish, Sewickley, Pennsylvania; Dennis Mead, Vice President, The French Creek Valley Railroad Historical Society, Meadville, Pennsylvania.

Authors must have test readers, brave souls who are diligent and committed enough to subject themselves to the lengthy ordeal of reading a new original manuscript with thoroughness and objectivity and then critiquing it dispassionately to sensitive and protective authors. In the case of *Benjamin's Field*, the people who placed themselves in the line of fire were: Robert E. Burtt; Mark Grosher, J.D.; Suzanne Kennedy; Dennis Kissane, J.D.; Arlene Seal, Ph.D. Kerry Neville provided editorial assistance. My wife, Dorothy, who in addition to formatting the manuscript, forgave me the many hours spent writing it.

My thanks to them all.

FORWARD

Jim Knights and I both are pilots, albeit with very different backgrounds. I first met Jim over a decade ago when he was a Special Agent with the Federal Bureau of Investigation and a (very professional) volunteer pilot with the Civil Air Patrol in Pittsburgh.

As for myself, I used a bit of my college scholarship money for flying lessons, and have been flying for 45 years. I've flown light aircraft to Greenland, Iceland, England, Guatemala, Alaska, and Hudson's Bay, and was a crewmember on four U.S. Space Shuttle missions. When I was growing up, I read every aviation-related book I could get my hands on. The best of those used aviation as a way to explore what it means to be human, and to remake yourself while making the future. *Benjamin's Field* holds its own with much of that literature.

The reader could be forgiven for initially believing *Benjamin's Field* is about aviation, as it plays such a significant role in each of the three books of the trilogy. However, such is not the case. For while we use airplanes for travel from one place to another, in the story the author uses them to take the reader on a much different type of journey.

Benjamin's Field is a captivating tale about the journey of life, during which we each experience success and failure, joy and pain, and (if we are lucky) forgiveness and healing.

Especially useful to young readers, but valuable to us all, are the story's lessons about this journey: our greatest achievements are for others, not ourselves; overcoming difficulties makes us stronger; disappointments can be blessings in disguise; help can come from unexpected sources; sometimes one door must close so another can open; it's futile to blame the universe or a higher being for pain that's inflicted by our fellow human beings.

I recommend *Benjamin's Field* for anyone who wants to step outside his or her daily routine for a while and spend some time gaining insight into the indomitable human spirit.

Jay Apt

PROLOGUE

This is not a story about a place, though characters must have a place in which to act out their story. The particular place central to this story became what it was not by design, unless by the hand of destiny, but by chance.

It was not an airfield, or at least one would not have called it that. The place was undistinguished from both the air and ground and, even if a pilot were looking for it, the place was easy - very easy - to fly past without noticing it. No surprise, then, that while it had been there for years, most of the local inhabitants didn't know the place as an airfield. When asked by the rare traveler for directions, the reply was normally, "You must be mistaken. There is no airfield here."

The place could barely be called a landing strip. In point of fact, it was actually a long stretch of rough turf that separated a farmhouse, barn and arable fields on one side from a good-sized pond on the other.

To the west, the grass strip led almost directly toward the setting sun, which often made late afternoon landings literally blinding affairs. In the opposite direction lay the Alleghenies, once called by the old flyers "Hell's stretch" because there was no safe place to put a machine if the engine became troublesome or simply quit, which happened more often than not. In that direction also lay the local cemetery, where, if the pilot failed to handle his machine with care, he would end up one way or another. In the early years, the sight of this sobering landmark always had the effect of making pilots more attentive to the conduct of their precarious machines.

The place was very particular about what type of visitors it would accept. It tended, if grudgingly, to accommodate small, uncomplicated machines with wheels under their tails - constructions that could absorb the bumps, knocks and skids imposed upon them as the price of admission. This was because the place constantly complained about its predicament, as though protesting having been put there against its will by an unseen hand bent on making the patch of grass acquiesce to some malevolent and mercurial will.

The runway sloped down to the east, which meant it had to slope up to the west, and at its eastern end canted, almost imperceptibly to the eye, downward to the north. Its surface wasn't flat and smooth, as one would expect, given its use. Instead, it undulated precariously as it descended eastward and rose westward. Pennsylvania shale filled the length of it, resulting in a million small yet punishing imperfections; it was like an alligator's hide. So, when a machine tried to alight there, it would touch down roughly, careening up and down; if the pilot failed to pay attention, it would slowly slide sideways toward the downhill side. When a strong wind blew across the place, it was like landing on a living, writhing thing angry at the intrusion.

In spite of these conditions, the place did, indeed, speak to those who listened. This place could cast spells. For one standing on the green runway surrounded by hills and trees with a slight wind whispering in the branches, the world outside ceased to exist. If serenity could be said to have weight, it weighed heavily here; a gentle, soothing serenity enveloping the soul like a down comforter on a cold night. So much so, it was a wonder the flying machines could lift themselves into the air. Here, time stopped and magic began; for while the asphalt roads and highways would lead land-bound machines across the surface of the earth like ants negotiating a maze, this few thousand feet of grass was a gateway - for those with the skill and the patience and the time - to anywhere and everywhere. In many ways, it was like the fabled genie's lamp: the right person, at the right time, would get his wish.

The place exists today much as it existed then.

That place is Benjamin's field.

The Benjamin's Field Trilogy

Book One: *Rescue*
Book Two: *Ascent*
Book Three: *Emancipation*

WWW.JJKNIGHTS.COM

That men do not learn very much from the lessons of history is the most important of all the lessons of history.

Aldous Huxley

What experience and history teach is this: that people and governments never have learned anything from history, or acted on principles deduced from it.

G.W.F. Hegel

History repeats itself because no one was listening the first time.

Anonymous

BOOK ONE

RESCUE

Pro parvulus;
Pro posterum

CHAPTER 1

THE FARMER

Distant thunder rumbled. Turning to appraise the threatening sky, the farmer whispered a curse under his breath before leaning into the plow, yet again. It was only early afternoon on this April day, but the northwest sky was already dark with angry gray clouds and heavy with an eerie, preternatural foreboding. Soon the rain would come. Like a stern overseer, the approaching storm looked down upon the farmer, goading him without remorse to complete his task or accept the consequences.

His son would have been a great help, if he were here.

He missed Francis' help around the place, but he missed Francis himself even more. The hired hand was a good worker, a colored man named Hiram who was younger than the farmer, but the farmer missed his son all the same.

A fleeting motion caught his eye. The quickening wind blew something flashing white across the fresh dark furrows to end its bouncing dance trapped by the plow. Looking down, he saw it was his own newspaper that had fallen from his overalls.

He absent-mindedly patted his rear pocket to confirm what he already knew.

"Come here, you rascal. You got away from me."

Bending over to retrieve it, he heard more rumbling from the west and hesitated as he looked up.

He glanced at the headline of *The Pittsburgh Press* for April 6, 1917. To the drumbeat of thunder, he silently read the words "U.S Now At War With Kaiser."

War news filled the front page. Reading further, the words spelled out; "Two million youths will be wanted within the next two years."

The farmer thought, *That many? Two years? How do they know?*

Anger welled up within him.

Young men believing they're invincible, he thought. *That's why old men don't fight wars. They know better.*

This he learned from the bitter fruit of experience.

At the bottom of the page, he read, "Submarines Near U.S is Warning." He recalled the sinking of the Lusitania by a German U-boat two years earlier.

Then, with just a few drops, the rain began, scattering dark spots across the newsprint.

The sting of the cold sprinkle caused him to wonder what it must feel like to be suddenly thrown into the cold sea by a monstrous explosion.

He was wasting time. Knowing he should hurry, he re-folded the newspaper and replaced it in his back pocket.

As he resumed his plowing, the black letters of

the *Press's* headline hung in the farmer's thoughts like a specter: "U.S. Now At War With Kaiser."

It was all a cause for deep concern. He'd heard talk that a draft would soon be started. If the worst did happen at least Francis had an education.

God willin', maybe that will save him from carrying a rifle. Maybe they won't call him at all.

Thoughts of his son going to war pulled Benjamin's attention from the task at hand. Like the ill-fated Lusitania when struck by German torpedoes, the horses and plow abruptly jolted to a halt, hurling Benjamin to the cold, damp ground.

Flat on his face in a spread-eagle position, Benjamin, dazed and winded, slowly pushed himself up. Covered in his own rich, loamy earth, he commenced uttering such a vile string of invectives that both horses turned their heads toward him in unison, as though shocked at his lack of decorum.

In answer to the horses' stares, the farmer continued his enthusiastic diatribe, shouting at the animals, "Well, what in damnation are *you* lookin' at?"

He reached down to check for damage. "Jesus Christ," he said as his callused hand felt the jagged edge of the broken plowshare. It had struck a small boulder, one of many expelled from the local fields every winter due to Pennsylvania's severe freeze-thaw cycle.

He groped through the soil, his fingers becoming black and heavy with damp earth, until he found the severed fragment. He stared down at it, fuming at his own stupidity.

Thick, heavy rain now pelted his head.

From the distance, he heard, "Ben! What are ya doin,' Ben? Can't you see it's startin' to rain?"

Benjamin, still angry with himself, turned to look up toward the barn. A tall colored man dressed in torn overalls covering a well-worn red "union suit" and a floppy, ragged, wide-brimmed hat was jogging toward him.

"Ben," said Hiram Bolt, "stop your yellin.' I don't know what the heck you're carryin' on about this time, but we got to get out o' the rain!"

"The goddamned plow is busted. It hit a damned rock."

"The plow didn't hit a damned rock. *You* hit a damned rock with the plow. It ain't the Lord's fault you weren't payin' attention so stop shoutin' at him."

Benjamin looked down at the broken plow and mumbled, "Damned newspaper, damned government, damned war."

"Ben, I don't know what you're talkin' about, but we both got to get out of the rain. Let's get the horses to the barn. You can finish your cursin' up there, where it's dry."

"Aw, rain never hurt me before."

"Maybe it ain't," Hiram said, "but that lightnin' will sure kick your ass, especially with you standin' out here in the middle of an open field durin' a thunderstorm. What the hell're you thinkin'? C'mon, let's get these horses back to the barn or we won't need no war to kill us."

Benjamin turned toward Hiram and, pointing his finger at him, said, "I don't pay you to scold me." He turned back toward the horses and plow.

"Hell, you don't pay me to bury you, either, but that's what I'm gonna be doin' if the good Lord takes it in his mind to bring you home ridin' a lightnin' bolt.

That's right. Sure. He takes your soul on up through the pearly gates and leaves the rest of your raggedy ass here for me to clean up. Well, *maybe* the pearly gates."

With that, they led the horses to the barn.

The crippled plow was left to fend for itself in the soon-to-be-raging tumult, much like a wounded soldier in a trench.

The rain, falling on the wide backs of the over-heated horses returned to the moist air as sinuous vapors, like smoke rising from the muzzle of a gun.

Benjamin spent a good part of the next day getting the plow repaired at the blacksmith's and, with Hiram's help, digging the boulder out of the ground. All wasted time to Benjamin's practical mind.

At last he was back behind the plow, squinting in the glare of the afternoon sun. Cows were grazing on the nearby shale-filled field. If he didn't get interrupted again he could finish by sundown the next day. As he walked behind the horses and plow, careful to look for other boulders, he glimpsed Hiram on the roof of the barn replacing shingles stolen by the winter winds.

As the minutes passed, he gradually became aware of a strange distant sound. At first he paid no attention, believing it to be a passing motorcar on Fairey Hill Road. The noisy contraptions were becoming more and more common. As the odd sound grew louder, however, he thought he might be getting a visitor, so he stopped the horses and looked down the length of the dirt track leading into his farm. Seeing no Ford or other such vehicle approaching, he expanded his search to Fairey Hill Road bordering his farm to the west.

Nothing.

Turning back to the plow, he caught sight of Hiram standing at the top of the ladder propped against the edge of the barn's roof. Hiram, motionless and staring toward the east, appeared to be transfixed on some distant point. Wondering if he'd caught his hired hand daydreaming, Benjamin shouted, "Hiram! What're ya doin'? Those shingles won't fix themselves!"

Hiram didn't answer.

"Hiram? What the hell's wrong with you?"

Without shifting his gaze, Hiram pointed the hammer eastward.

Benjamin turned to look in that direction.

"Jesus Christ!" He watched with unblinking eyes. "That can't be," he muttered.

A huge buzzing yellow insect was heading directly at him. Benjamin's mind simply could not process what his eyes beheld.

The thing from Hell descended toward the cows peacefully grazing on the long strip of un-tillable land that ran parallel to Benjamin's furrows. They bellowed in terror and surprise as they scattered in all directions tripping and slamming into one another in their panic. The thing arrested its descent and roared down the length of the field, passing over Benjamin so low that he flung himself to the ground to escape being struck and carried away by the beast.

After screaming past the prostrate farmer like a tormented demon, the thing ascended toward the sun in the west. The terrified horses whinnied and rose up on their hind legs, front legs pawing the air, then took off at a gallop. In their panic, they mindlessly dragged the plow bouncing behind them like a mother pulling her helpless child.

For the second time in as many days the farmer found himself facedown in the furrows of his own field.

Pushing himself up out of the dirt, he saw the winged creature continue to climb and then turn south, all the while buzzing like a carpenter bee. As it did so, it leaned to the inside of the turn and Benjamin thought for an instant it might actually flip over. Seeing it from this angle, recognition dawned on him. He had seen pictures of these contraptions in the newspaper, but they were just pictures. Now, there it was for real: a flying machine.

As he struggled to stand, his eyes remained riveted on it. It was difficult for him to comprehend how such a huge thing could hang in the air. Hiram slid down the ladder and came running to stand and watch by Benjamin's side.

"Ben, what in blazes is going on? Is that what I think it is? I never saw one before."

"It sure looks like a flyin' machine," Benjamin answered. "I'm as surprised as you, but I'm gettin' mighty damned mad that some fool just scattered my cows and knocked me into the dirt. Hell, you could 'a been blown off that roof and killed."

Hiram doffed his hat and wiped his forehead with a blue and white-checkered bandana. "Why is that thing buzzin' around here?"

"Hiram, you know as much as I do. But if I get my hands on him, whoever is in that thing'll wish he hadn't come here to show off. Damned idiot."

Together, they watched as the machine flew east parallel to the field. Then suddenly, just as they began to think it would continue on and leave them in peace, the strange craft turned left again - back toward and perpendicular to the field it had just terrorized - and began to drop from the sky. As it neared the end of the field, it turned again, lowering its nose and aligning itself with the field. Just as it appeared to the two men that it would again scream over them, the tempo of the engine's roar slowed. The machine neared the ground and leveled off a few feet above the grass. The cows, now scattered, were no longer a danger to the flying machine.

Benjamin and Hiram stared slack-jawed as the boxy kite-looking thing approached them. They could see it was leaning slightly into the northerly wind that was blowing across the field. The roar of its engine dropped to a murmur and its wheels touched the grass. It bounced along the rough field, wings wobbling, toward the two gawking spectators.

Benjamin, alternately amazed and then angry at what he was seeing, began to allow his anger to hold sway. Resentment was welling up inside him as if it had a life of its own; resentment at this intruder who surprised him; resentment at having to hurl himself to the ground like a frightened fawn; resentment at having no control over what was happening on his own land.

He could feel his hands involuntarily clench into fists and his biceps contract, lifting his arms into a boxer's stance.

Hiram, sensing Benjamin's coiling anger, looked down at his fists. He placed his hand on Benjamin's shoulder and said, "Ben, let's take it easy. We don't know what's goin' on here. It could be he's in trouble."

The quivering, cloth-wrapped machine trundled to a stop a few feet from Benjamin and Hiram. The long, slowly swinging wooden propeller emitted loud *clicks* at longer and longer intervals as it finally swung to a stop and puffed out one last gasp of blue-white smoke from the exhaust pipes on the top of the cowling. The machine had two wings, one above the other, just like in the newspaper photographs. Under the top wing, Benjamin could see two leather-encased heads protruding from the machine's body. One was a few feet behind the other. Both wore goggles that gave them bug-like appearances. For the second time that day, Benjamin was speechless as the bug figure in front lifted his goggles to his forehead, waved at him and with a big smile said, "Hi, Pa!"

Chapter 2

Remembering

Earlier that morning, long before the sun rose, Benjamin lay alone in his bed. Used to rising early, his consciousness began to stir. He could hear the dying remnants of the previous night's fire crack, pop, and hiss as the embers heated errant pockets of moisture hidden among the grains of smoldering wood.

Sounds like infantry attacking, thought Benjamin.

A shiver rippled through his body and he tried to push the image from his mind.

I used to love the sound of a fire.

Suddenly, with a loud *pop,* Benjamin cringed, covering his head with both hands....

"Down, Kyner! Get the hell down!" Screamed the sergeant. The rifle and cannon fire was deafening.

"Everyone, hug the dirt and keep moving forward! Don't give those Spanish bastards a target!"

Corporal Benjamin Arthur Kyner crouched as low

as he could.

I can't get any lower unless I dig a tunnel, he thought.

All around him he could hear men shouting and cursing amidst gunshots. He knelt and brought his hand to his face. It wouldn't stop shaking.

"Keep moving!" shouted the sergeant again. "Get up there and give it to the bastards!"

Benjamin began to move. Then he heard another voice above the din:

"Let's go, boys! We've got the damn Yankees on the run again!"

What the hell? I know that voice, thought Benjamin. Then he remembered: *Wheeler.*

It was old Major General Joseph "Fightin' Joe" Wheeler. An image flashed through Benjamin's mind: a bearded old man working his way down the line of soldiers, shaking each young man's hand before they boarded the ship to Cuba. "Thank you, sir," was all Benjamin could say. Wheeler, the only Confederate General to later wear Federal Blue, had somehow convinced the President to send him to Cuba to help command the American volunteers.

What the hell is he shouting about? We're in Cuba, not Dixie, for Christ's sake. Benjamin worked his way forward, thinking, *We're both goddamned idiots to be here.*

He heard a volley of rifle fire and flattened himself against the Cuban earth, willing himself to melt into it.

Crack. A Spanish bullet passed his head.

Goddamn it. Got to keep moving.

Crack. Another close one.

"It's the one you don't hear that kills you," his drill sergeant told them as young recruits.

If I stay here, I'm dead.

More shouting. He couldn't understand what they were yelling.

Then it dawned on him: *It's Spanish. They're just ahead. Shit.*

Benjamin and his fellow soldiers kept moving forward: rock to rock; tree to tree; hole to hole. Always forward. Each step was terrifying.

He sensed movement to his right. He looked. It was Billy, the kid from West Virginia. The kid with that laughable southern drawl.

The boy looked his way and Benjamin saw the face of real fear.

Do I look like that?

Just then, Benjamin saw something strike Billy in the chest. Flesh and blood erupted from his back and he was lifted off the ground and thrown backward.

Billy!

Stunned, Benjamin froze.

"Move!" Screamed the sergeant, kicking Benjamin in the thigh. The cannon kept exploding. The smell of burnt gunpowder filled Benjamin's nostrils. Keeping low to the ground, he ran to the trunk of a tree severed by artillery. He put one arm around the tree and held on.

Please, God, get me out of this.

He hunkered behind the tree for dear life. He held his rifle close to his chest.

I'll go. Just give me a minute. Please.

As he searched for his next cover, he saw movement ahead.

There they are. I see one.

Shouts and commands in Spanish and English filled the air. Benjamin raised the rifle to his shoulder. The Springfield weighed eight and-a-half pounds. It felt like a hundred.

How can I aim when I'm shaking like a scared rabbit?

Smoke obscured his vision. Sweat stung his eyes. He wiped them with a shaking, grimy hand and tried again to align the sights on the shadowy figure, but couldn't.

Damn this shaking.

He held his breath and pulled the trigger. There was so much noise he barely heard the bark of his rifle as the .30-40 Krag cartridge fired and the Springfield kicked into his shoulder. Nothing. The figure ducked.

Shit! Bolt up, back, forward, down.

The expended casing summersaulted upward and a fresh one took its place.

There. Another one.

Again, Benjamin put the rifle to his shoulder.

I have to do this!

He held his breath, aimed and - fired. The Springfield bucked again. The Spanish soldier dropped.

Mother of God! Did I just kill a man?

Benjamin heard cries of pain. Men were falling all around him.

How many of my friends are dead?

Then Benjamin heard his lieutenant. "Up and at 'em. Let's go!"

Are you a fool? They're slaughtering us. If I go up there, I'll just be one more stiff corpse in the morning. I'm no use if I'm dead.

Benjamin stayed put.

There was more rifle fire, more cannon fire, more screams and cries in both languages.

Benjamin saw the lieutenant run forward waving his pistol and shouting, "Follow me!"

You idiot. You're a target.

Without warning, the pistol flew from the young lieutenant's grasp and he grabbed his throat with both hands. Blood gushed between his fingers and he crumpled to the ground.

Horrified, Benjamin watched the man - or was he just a boy? - drop. Then he felt someone plow into him. Benjamin, terrified, drew back his rifle to bludgeon the intruder....

"Whoa, Ben. Stop! It's me. Jack."

Benjamin checked himself and lowered his rifle. "Billy's dead. I saw it," said Benjamin.

"A lot of 'em are dead," replied Jack. "Ben, you and me gotta get up there. Are ya ready?"

Benjamin looked the other man in the eye. He saw fear there, as well.

"Yeah," said Benjamin. "Let's go."

Benjamin pushed himself up into a crouch and stepped out from behind the tree with Jack at his side.

As he took the first step toward the Spanish position, Benjamin felt a blow to his right arm. At first thinking Jack punched him, he turned and said, "Why...?"

He felt the searing pain and saw the look on Jack's face simultaneously.

"Ben!"

Benjamin fell to the ground.

Jack leaned over him. "Ben, you're hit. I gotta leave ya here. I'm sorry. Somebody'll find ya."

Jack stepped over Benjamin and moved in a crouch up the hill.

Only a few moments later, his right arm in agony, Benjamin heard the sergeant yell, "Everybody back! Move back! Retreat!"

Benjamin never saw Jack again. He also never forgot what he heard old Major General Wheeler shout that day: "Let's go, boys. We've got the damn Yankees on the run again!" It was at that moment Benjamin understood what was happening: an old man was trying to recapture past glory at the expense of young men's lives.

He never forgot it.

Bathed in golden light from the rising sun, Benjamin sat alone in the simple farmhouse kitchen near Athena, Pennsylvania, sipping a cup of strong, black, sugarless coffee. It was almost 20 years ago, the Battle of Las Guasimas. Benjamin rubbed his right arm at the memory of it. He'd been one of 52 wounded Americans. He would be eternally grateful he hadn't been one of the 17 who died.

Later, with his Army "blood money," as he thought of it, Benjamin searched for a farm. Finally, among the rocky hills of southwestern Pennsylvania, he came upon Athena, a small railroad stop. It never occurred to Benjamin, who prayed his son would never experience war, that he chose to raise Francis in a place named for a goddess of war.

Delina, he thought, *you always knew what to do when the dream came.*

She would gently wake him, whispering, "Ben, Ben, you're safe," in her French-Canadian accent. Then she'd hold him until he remembered where he was and the shaking stopped.

They'd met one winter day when Benjamin noticed a young woman he didn't recognize with a child on his frozen pond. The strong-willed little boy of two or three insisted on trying to stand on the ice, though his efforts were only earning him a bruised rear end.

"No, not 'Arter,' my middle name is *Arthur*," explained Benjamin, trying hard not to laugh.

"Dat's what I said," answered the young woman, "Arter."

Unable to control himself, Benjamin laughed out loud.

"It's not so funny," she said, indignant.

"Yeah. It is." He laughed so hard, he was barely able to answer her.

Then she laughed, too.

"Mama," interrupted her little boy, "I wanna try again." He pointed to Benjamin's frozen pond.

"Oh, all right, Francis," she said, "*tu es trop impatient* - you're too impatient."

She had been French-Canadian, a descendant of the Acadians, and, of course, a Catholic. She wasn't from Quebec, which is what most people thought, but from the small Canadian Maritime province of Prince Edward Island.

She told him she was widowed. Her husband was a lobsterman swallowed by the Gulf of Saint Lawrence during rough weather while she was pregnant with Francis. He was never found, so Francis never knew his father. Being a young widow on an island where the main livelihoods were farming and fishing, she left and came south to Western Pennsylvania with her child to visit friends while escaping painful reminders of her loss.

"I'm Lutheran," said Benjamin. "Does that matter?"

"*Non, pas à moi* - No, not to me," said Delina, "but it will matter to da *prêtre* - the priest, Templeman."

"I'll have to convert?"

"*Non*, but you'll have to agree to raise our children as Catholic. Not just Francis, but any we have together." She pronounced Catholic as "cat-o-lik."

"Hell, Delina, I don't give a damn as long as I'm with you. I don't care what Templeman and his pope say. I'll do whatever I need to do to be with you."

"Don't let da *prêtre* hear you say that. Not being Catholic is one ting, being a *Franc-Maçon* - Freemason, is a nutter ting."

"A what?"

"A nutter ting."

"A nutter ting? Oh. You mean 'another thing'." He snickered.

She glared at him for making fun of her accent. Then she laughed.

"And for the record," said Benjamin as he lifted her tiny frame off the ground and embraced her, "you can be a *Franc Maçon* and God-fearin' at the same time. I just think Templeman's a pompous ass."

She put her hand over his mouth to silence him. When he stopped talking, she kissed him.

Benjamin signed the agreement to raise their children in the Church. It was of no consequence, after all. Though Benjamin and Delina tried, Francis remained an only child.

Delina was so moved by Benjamin's acceptance and love of her son that, as part of the adoption proceedings, she changed Francis' middle name to "Benjamin."

He'd made the right decision for many reasons, but he wouldn't fully appreciate it until later, when he realized how little time he was to have with Delina. Yet, it was also only much later that Benjamin would acknowledge an ironic consequence that attended raising Francis in the pope's Church: the restricted confines of their small farmhouse dictated that Benjamin couldn't escape being a reluctant student of the lessons Delina taught their son about her Church and religion.

It had been influenza.

The priest put his hand on Benjamin's shoulder.

"Ben, I'm sorry," he said.

Benjamin lifted his eyes from Delina's still-open grave. He had just watched her coffin, and what seemed like his own spirit, lowered into the ground. He looked at the priest, his expression blank.

Templeman said, "Sixteen is a bad time for a boy to lose his mother."

Benjamin squinted at Templeman, as though he didn't quite understand what he meant.

"Tell me, Father," replied Benjamin, "is there a *good* time for a boy to lose his mother?"

Templeman, shaken and angered, turned red. Benjamin waited for a response so he would have someone to lash out at, someone to punish, but the priest held himself in check. He glanced across the headstones where Francis was being consoled by a small knot of school friends. Then, looking into Benjamin's sad and indignant face, the priest turned and stalked away, weaving between the headstones, his robes flapping in the wind like a pair of giant bird's wings.

Now Benjamin was alone, as he had been since Francis left for Allegheny College in Meadville, almost 80 miles north. In the past two years, Francis came home only at Christmas and during the summer. Thank God he was home in the summer to help with the work. Harvest time was hard without him. At least there was Hiram.

Benjamin glanced up at the Schoolhouse Regulator clock on the kitchen wall, the kind with a red hand indicating the day of the month stenciled around the perimeter of its face. Its pendulum drifted indolently from side to side. It was time to get moving.

For close to three years Benjamin and his neighbors had been helping to feed the armies that were slaughtering each other's youth in yet another war. Now it was inevitable that American boys would soon be on their way to the trenches.

Benjamin thought of Francis.

He stepped onto the porch and surveyed the day. Yesterday's storm was long gone to the east. Hopefully it was making life miserable for the politicians in the state capital at Harrisburg where they so easily spent other people's money. The spring air was clear and sweet, as it usually was after a storm.

His eyes fell upon a long strip of almost useless soil, the one part of his beloved farm that was a disappointment. It always reminded him of an otherwise beautiful child's disfigured limb. All it could manage was grass for grazing his cows. Unlike a bad leg, at least Benjamin got some use out of it.

He headed to the barn to ready the plow and horses. In an hour or so he'd hear the nearby schoolhouse bell sound the beginning of class. Hiram would be arriving soon.

What Benjamin couldn't have known was that Francis would also be arriving, but from a different direction.

CHAPTER 3

OUT OF THE SKY

Dumbstruck, Benjamin could only stare at his son in astonishment.

Francis, making what was without doubt the understatement of his young life, shouted, "Hey, I bet I sure surprised you, huh?"

As though recovering from a sharp blow to the head, Benjamin blinked a few times and said, "Francis? What...?"

By then Francis had jumped down onto the lower wing of the craft. Peeling off his goggles and skin-tight leather helmet, he gestured toward the leather-wrapped head protruding from the second hole.

"Pa, I want you to meet a good friend of mine, Randy Bridgewater. This is his crate."

A young man emerged upright from the rear cockpit. In addition to his goggles and flying helmet, he wore leather gauntlets and a thigh-length brown leather jacket belted at the waist. He also wore a grin displaying numerous white teeth through a mustache that overflowed past the corners of his mouth.

"Good afternoon, sir. Randolph E. Bridgewater, III, at your service and very honored to meet you."

This he followed with a slight but none-the-less theatrical bow from the waist.

Both Benjamin and Hiram looked at him as though he had just harangued them in Mandarin Chinese.

Bridgewater, seeing they weren't impressed, looked with a quizzical expression at the two bewildered men. Then he looked at Francis. Then back at Benjamin and Hiram.

"Of the *Massachusetts* Bridgewaters, sir," he said with his huge grin and with just a hint of condescension. He emphasized the word "Massachusetts" as if doing so would make everything clear to even the most dull-witted.

Francis stepped off the wing and leaned toward his father's ear.

"Pa, Randy's from Boston. That's how they say they're rich without actually saying it in so many words."

"Uh huh. Like flying around in one of these things doesn't already say that? Your friend sure is subtle."

"Well, Pa, subtlety has never really troubled Randy."

With his cocked thumb, Francis gestured toward the machine and said, "Well, what'd ya think of the crate? It's a Curtiss JN-4. They call it a 'Jenny.' Get it? They got 'Jenny' from 'JN'," he proudly announced.

Not caring how the "crate" got its name, Benjamin grabbed his son's shoulders and shouted at him; "Francis, what in hell is going on? What are you doing in this damned thing? Why are you here and not in school?"

Hiram and Bridgewater stared at the pair.

"Pa, please just hang on a bit. There's no reason to be so agitated."

"What do you mean, Francis? Here I am thinking you're up in Meadville when you suddenly come swoopin' out of the sky in this hellatious machine. You scatter the cows to kingdom come, knock me to the ground and almost run me and Hiram down. Then you just up and jump out of it with your rich friend sayin' 'Howdy, Pa,' like it was something you do every day."

"Pa, I'm sorry we scared the cows, but we had to get them off the field so we could land. Randy does this all the time. You come in and do a low pass over your landing spot to scatter the livestock and get a good look for pot holes and rocks and things like that. But, hey, did you like my landing?"

"Your what?" Benjamin said. "You mean to tell me you put this thing on the ground?"

"Sure I did. Randy's been giving me lessons."

"He's been what? Why on earth would you want to learn to operate one of these contraptions? You're gonna be killed before you graduate and...."

Suddenly, a mild, hollow *thrummm* that sounded like gentle tapping on a drum halted Benjamin's tirade. Both he and Francis looked toward the Jenny where they saw Hiram flicking the skin of the machine with his finger. Bridgewater, having dismounted from cockpit, leaned against the fuselage watching with amusement as Francis defended himself to Benjamin. He also heard the sound and looked at Hiram.

Escaping from his father, Francis walked the dozen odd steps to join the hired hand.

"Hiram, can't you say 'hello'?"

Hiram turned around to face Francis and they greeted each other with a bear hug. Benjamin stayed where he was, surprised at being suddenly ignored.

"What's it made of?" asked Hiram. "Some kinda' painted cloth?"

"That's very close," answered Bridgewater. "It's linen. From *lineum*. You know, Latin for flax."

Hiram, looking askance at Bridgewater, responded, "Oh, sure. Everybody knows that." He then glanced sideways at Benjamin as if to say, "What the hell's wrong with him?"

"Good. Well," continued an oblivious Randolph E. Bridgewater, III, "after the linen panels are stitched into place - the frame is made of spruce - they're covered with three layers of dope, a kind of lacquer. The reason it's tight like this," Bridgewater said, tapping the taut fabric, "something like a drum, is because once the dope dries it contracts and tightens the linen. It also makes it practically waterproof."

"Is that so?" replied Hiram, who was listening seriously to Bridgewater's explanation.

"Yes, but the sun and weather play hell with it and it has to be re-covered every few years. You also have to be really careful with the dope when it's wet. It burns like coal oil. *Whoosh*." Bridgewater emphasized the negative connotation of the *whoosh* by throwing both hands theatrically into the air.

Hiram seemed almost entranced by the machine, when Benjamin, his frustration mounting, shouted, "Why the hell are we talkin' about painted cloth?"

Looking at Francis, Benjamin asked, "Why didn't you warn me what you were up to? That you were gonna show up like this?"

"Pa, how about if we just go up to the house? We can talk about it up there. Then Randy and I can come back and bed this thing down somewhere safe for the night. We'll have to stay till morning. It'll be getting dark by the time we're done talking and we can't fly at night."

Benjamin happened to notice Hiram was bent over the rear cockpit where Bridgewater was demonstrating how the controls work. He manipulated some kind of stick that made long panels at the ends of both upper wingtips move up and down. It had the same effect on a wide horizontal flipper-looking thing at the back end of the flying machine.

Taking a long drawn out breath, like a runner who had just finished last in a race, Benjamin said "All right. Christ, at least you're on the ground safe."

Francis called to Bridgewater and motioned to him to come along. As the two headed toward the farmhouse, Benjamin walked over to Hiram; the flying machine still intrigued him.

"What are you doin'? Studyin' to be an engineer?"

Looking up, Hiram responded, "Well, now, you don't see one of these things every day. I just thought I'd take the opportunity to learn somethin' new. That's all."

"Don't you have anything else you could be doin' right now? Like maybe puttin' shingles on the barn roof?"

"Sure, but do you know what all this means, Ben?"

"No," Benjamin replied. "I don't. Why don't you explain it to me?"

"It means you ain't never gonna finish plowin'

that field. Hah!"

Hiram walked toward the barn, laughing out loud at his own joke. Benjamin, exasperated, walked behind his son and Bridgewater. Recalling the previous day's newspaper headlines, he wondered what all this really did mean.

CHAPTER 4

THE DOPE

Benjamin, now calmer, said, "Now tell me what this is all about. You can start by telling me about your friend."

The trio had entered the kitchen of the farmhouse. Francis and Bridgewater carried their goggles, leather helmets and small satchels. They placed their equipment on the kitchen table and hung the satchels from wooden pegs on the wall next to the kitchen door. Benjamin remembered the newspaper in his pocket and tossed it on the table without a thought. Then he started making a pot of coffee while Francis began to explain his unexpected appearance from the sky.

"Well, Pa, Randy here is a classmate at Allegheny College. He started last September. That's where we met, in class."

Francis winked furtively at Bridgewater. They actually met in a Meadville drinking establishment when they were both attempting to impress the same local damsel.

Benjamin, squinting at Bridgewater, uttered, "You look a little old to be just startin' college. And why's a rich Easterner going to college way out here, anyway?"

"Well, sir," replied Bridgewater. "There is a very good reason for that. You see," he said, smiling, "I transferred to Allegheny College from Harvard."

"Now, I might make my livin' workin' the soil, but I do know people like you don't just leave schools like Harvard and Yale to traipse all the way to Western Pennsylvania. You fool around with someone's wife? You kill somebody?"

Bridgewater guffawed, but stopped when he saw Benjamin wasn't laughing along with him.

"No, Pa! It isn't like that at all," interjected Francis, who was absent-mindedly flipping through the pages of *The Pittsburgh Press* that Benjamin had abandoned on the table.

"No. Indeed not, sir. Ha! I know you're kidding," said Bridgewater, though he could tell from Benjamin's expression he was serious.

"Pa, Randy's father is a banker at Whistler and Meeks. That's a big investment firm in Boston. It's part-owned by John Meeks, you know, Senator Meeks from Massachusetts."

"*Was* part-owned by Johnny Meeks," interrupted Bridgewater. "He resigned when he won the election so he could take his seat in the senate."

"Anyway," continued Francis, "you don't have to worry about Randy. He comes from really good stock."

"Well, that just makes me wonder all the more why he left Harvard," answered Benjamin.

"Fair question," said Bridgewater. "You see, Mr.

Kyner, Harvard is a truly exceptional institution, really top drawer in every way. My own father *and* grandfather are proud alumni of the school. However...." Bridgewater trailed off.

"However, what?"

"Randy thinks they're a tad too conservative for his blood," responded Francis.

"Isn't that what your daddy was payin' 'em for?"

"Well, Mr. Kyner, I guess the other side of that coin is that perhaps I was a bit too *anti*conservative for their taste."

Benjamin raised his eyebrows to convey that he expected an elaboration.

"I don't believe I quite met their expectations," confessed Bridgewater.

"Pa," Francis jumped in. "Randy had a unique way of approaching higher education. He just...."

Bridgewater smiled disarmingly and put his hand gently on Francis' shoulder to silence him.

"That's not necessary, Francis. Your father has a right to know about the people with whom you associate." Looking at Benjamin, he added, "Let me explain. You see sir, I may not have attended every class, as is both expected and actually required by Harvard policy. After all, what are the books for?" He chuckled. "I also may have neglected to complete one or two assignments."

"They don't make rich people's kids leave Harvard because they skip class or don't do their homework," Benjamin shot back.

"C'mon, Randy, just get it over with," Francis said impatiently. "Pa, they did expect him to attend class. They did *not* expect him to get his and Harvard's name in the newspaper by driving a Mercedes racing automobile at top speed along Storrow Drive. The Boston Police Department also took offense."

"Now wait," Bridgewater responded with indignation. "That wasn't my fault!"

"How so? Did someone force you to race a car down a city street?" Benjamin asked sarcastically.

"What? No, of course not. But I would not have been caught if that damned electric trolley car hadn't pulled in front of me. Of course, my excellent driving skills did save the lives of that trolley's passengers," Bridgewater boasted. "Sadly, the police did not interpret events in quite the same light."

"And Harvard also expected you *not* to subsequently go roaring under a major bridge in a flying machine," Francis chimed in. "He flew under one of Boston's busiest bridges, Pa, which attracted attention from the authorities, not to mention the people who live on Beacon Hill, who pay lots in taxes in exchange for not having their tranquility disturbed."

Benjamin looked down his nose at both young men. "Is that all?"

"Not actually, sir," Bridgewater sheepishly answered. "Well, never mind. It's not important. The crux of the matter is that Harvard's administration saw some of these harmless exercises in freedom - celebrations, if you will - as a 'pattern of unacceptable behavior.' That's how the dean put it. Donations can only accomplish so much, I'm afraid, especially when the other donors, er, *parents* begin complaining."

"Ultimately, after a long conference with my father and his attorney it was agreed that my 'voluntary' withdrawal from that hallowed institution would result in my record remaining unblemished. Thus, I'd be free to seek admission elsewhere without fear of an unwarranted and misinterpreted reputation haunting me. So, here I am." He finished with a large grin.

"Well, what about Yale?" asked Benjamin. "It's a lot closer to home than way out here."

"Yale, sir? Did you say Yale?"

"Yeah, sure. Why not?"

"Hah! Ha ha ha!" Bridgewater laughed so hard he had to hold his stomach. "You're joking! You're kidding! Francis didn't tell me you are such a card! Hah! You really had me going. I actually took you seriously! Yale! Hah!"

Francis, noticing his father's dour expression, began to explain. "Pa, Harvard and Yale are traditional rivals. Have been forever. Not only would an undergraduate never transfer from Harvard to Yale or vice versa, if they tried it would raise all kinds of suspicion and questions."

"And truth be told, sir," added Bridgewater, "as you say, Yale is close to Boston."

"You're saying they knew who you were," concluded Benjamin.

"Ahhh, well, yes," replied Bridgewater.

"However, for the record, Allegheny College was, after all, started by a Harvard man," Bridgewater explained with a cheerier voice. "So you see, sir, I look upon Allegheny College as a kind of 'Harvard West,' if you will."

Benjamin stared at Bridgewater. Francis stared at the floor.

Every time this idiot takes a breath, he uses up good air, thought Benjamin. He also wondered how anyone could raise a child like this. He decided to keep his opinion to himself.

"Well," Benjamin sighed, "you're someone else's child to worry about and my son seems to think you're worth something, so that's good enough for me."

"Why, I thank you sir, for your kindness and understanding," answered Bridgewater.

Francis grinned with momentary relief.

Benjamin, suddenly struck by curiosity, asked Bridgewater, "Don't you need some type of permit to fly that thing?"

Bridgewater, gaping at him in shocked horror, replied, "Good God in Heaven, no sir! A permit? A license? To fly? I tell you, sir, I rue the day when the government becomes so intrusive into our lives that it dictates a man must possess a license to enjoy the simple freedom of the sky. The very thought, sir, is horrific. Frankly, I truly doubt that will ever happen. There simply aren't any bureaucrats in the government with the competence to assess the flying abilities of men such as myself."

"Well," snickered Benjamin, "lack of competence never stopped the government from intruding before."

Francis returned to reading *The Pittsburgh Press* as Benjamin continued making the coffee. Bridgewater walked over to look out the kitchen window toward the field where they had landed. "Oh, no!" he shouted. He dashed to the door, yanked it almost off its hinges, and ran out of the house toward the field as though chased by Satan shouting, "Stop! Stop! Stop!" at the top of his lungs.

To Benjamin's mid-western ears, the overly

excited Bridgewater's New England accent made it sound as though he was screaming "Stap! Stap! Stap!" It reminded him of a duck's "Quack! Quack! Quack!"

"For the love of God!" shouted Benjamin. "What in hell is that about?"

Francis bolted to the door, pulled it back open, and jumped onto the porch.

"Oh, jeezzz! We forgot about the dope!"

"What dope?" asked Benjamin, striding onto the porch, honestly confused. "Him?" pointing toward the running Bridgewater.

Francis turned toward his father with a look of consternation. "What? Oh, no. Not him. I mean the dope used on the linen. Remember Randy was explaining it to Hiram? Cows love the stuff. They can't get enough of it. Randy told me he once saw what happened to one of those machines when it was left unattended around cows. They ate every inch of linen off it in a few hours. Our cows are down there right now eating Randy's flying machine. I have to go help him."

The next morning Benjamin rose at his usual time. As he prepared breakfast, he looked toward the barn. He, Francis and Bridgewater moved the Jenny into the barn the previous evening before dark, where it had been safe from marauding cows during the night. Benjamin chuckled to himself at the memory of his cows surrounding the rich kid's toy like piglets feeding on a sow's teats, enthusiastically munching on the skin of the machine.

The image of Bridgewater frantically jumping into the air waving his arms and screaming while the dairy cows stared at him almost made the farmer laugh out loud. As he flipped pancakes he thought, *That boy isn't fit to muck out a stall*.

Bridgewater and Francis had gotten to the cows in time. They'd done only a small amount of damage. Bridgewater could easily repair it when he got the machine back to a barn he rented near Meadville.

During supper the previous evening, Benjamin insisted on an explanation as to why Francis and a "spoiled Easterner" had suddenly descended from the sky in "one of those contraptions." Francis explained that learning to fly was a mere diversion. Since he had only one more year at Allegheny College and would probably soon be working at some bank or firm in steel mill-polluted Pittsburgh, his time to just have fun would be limited. Besides, Bridgewater certainly didn't need money, so Francis' lessons and his hours in the Jenny were free.

As to how Bridgewater acquired a late-model flying machine on the eve of America's entrance into the world war, Bridgewater himself provided an explanation. The firm of Whistler and Meeks, where the elder Randolph E. Bridgewater, II, held a significant position, had provided a portion of the financing to the Curtiss Aeroplane Company of Buffalo, New York, for the production of the JN-4, the JN-3 and their less-than-stellar predecessor, the JN-2.

The British bought almost all the newly re-designed machines, which they would use as military trainers, sending many to training bases in Canada. This one had been loaned to Whistler and Meeks, ostensibly as a demonstrator so they could see how their money was being spent. Of course, Randolph E. Bridgewater, III, trained to fly by a Curtiss instructor, was doing the "official evaluation" under contract at a cost to the firm of $1. However, mechanics would soon disassemble it, crate it up, and put it on a British ship that would deliver it to Liverpool. That is, of course, if the ship wasn't torpedoed by a U-boat en route.

"G'morning, Pa," said Francis as he entered the kitchen.

"There you are," answered Benjamin waving his hand in the direction of the steaming coffee percolator, "coffee's ready."

Bridgewater, who was most definitely not the product of a farming family, was still asleep.

Francis took a mug from the cupboard and poured himself a cup of the steaming dark brew.

"Pa," Francis said with some trepidation in his voice, "there's something I want to talk about before Randy wakes up."

"From what I've seen of him so far, you'll probably have till noon," Benjamin replied sarcastically. "Go ahead, spit it out."

The two-day old copy of *The Pittsburgh Press* still lay on the kitchen table, its headline, "U.S. Now At War With Kaiser," plainly visible. Though Benjamin rarely spoke of his experiences in the Spanish-American War, it was always clear they had a profound effect on him and he never had any qualms about expressing his opinion of the military.

Francis took a deep breath and tapped the headline with his finger.

"Pa, we declared war on Germany yesterday. A lot of the guys at school are planning on joining up. I'm going with them."

The newspaper fell to the floor.

Chapter 5

Betrayal

Benjamin froze. He hadn't seen this coming.

"What?" he said in a barely audible rasp as he turned from the wood-burning stove toward his only child.

Then, raising his voice he said, "My God, what are you thinking?" You only have one more year of college left. You're almost done. Then you'll get a good job with a future...."

"Pa," Francis interrupted, "I know...."

"For *what*?" Benjamin now shouted. "You want to throw that away for *what*?" The farmer had not in his worst moments anticipated his son would risk what could be a wonderful future. He felt stupid. He needed an explanation. *"Tell me!"*

"Pa! The whole country is behind this. We've got to stop the Germans from taking over Europe!" Francis was speaking in rapid, staccato bursts. "They think they can sink our ships and kill our people and we won't do anything about it. Do you want me to be the only guy left at college? Everyone else gone off to do the honorable thing and there I am, taking the easy way out?"

"Hell, yes!" shouted Benjamin. "If the damned Army wants you, they can come and get you! Yes! I want you to stay put. You bet I do. Your mother didn't give birth to you so you could go die in the mud before you're even grown up. And die for what? For who? The damned Europeans? It's their mess; let *them* clean it up without dragging us into it. They've been killing each other since the beginning of time. Let them finish it and leave us alone."

"Pa, listen, we're already in it. It's best to get over there and get it done with. That's what some of our professors think. Hell, now that America is in the fight, the Germans'll probably quit, anyway. That's what people are saying. Even if they don't, the war can't last longer than a few months with us in it. If I wait until I graduate, it could be all over. I'll have missed my chance!"

"Your chance for what?" Benjamin shot back. "Glory? Excitement? Medals? What the hell's wrong with you? What good will all those do you if you're in a hole in the ground? Or you come home crippled? And your *professors*?" What in God's name do *they* know about fighting a war? Let them send *their* sons to Europe. Better yet, let your damned professors go themselves!"

"But Pa, you did it. You volunteered."

"You bet I did. That's how I know. I was an idiot and almost died being led by other idiots. When was the last time you heard of old soldiers dying in battle? You haven't because they don't. They don't go to war because they're too damned smart. They leave it to the young dumb ones who think they'll live forever. I've got news for you, Francis," Benjamin said, thinking of Delina and the friends he lost in Cuba years earlier, "none of us lives forever."

Francis, drained, stared at the floor. Both father and son suddenly become aware of an acrid smell. The neglected pancakes were burning in the cast iron skillet. Benjamin, using a dishtowel to protect his hand, pulled the heavy pan off the stove. He looked at it with exhausted disgust. Wasted. *Just like Francis wants to waste his life.*

Benjamin scraped the stinking cremated remains into the sink.

"I guarantee you, Francis. It won't be like you imagine. No glory. No drum rolls. It won't be like that at all. I know. You'll see your friends, wounded, maimed and killed. They could see the same things happen to you. When you're dead tired and scared to death, you won't be able to go running to your mother. You'll have nowhere to turn, nowhere to go. Do you have any idea how many people I saw turned into pieces of meat? Please promise me you won't do this stupid thing."

"Pa, I've given this a lot of thought. I've been thinking of nothing else. I knew how you'd feel. Pa, but I've got to go. I've got to try."

"Listen to me, Francis," Benjamin pleaded, "I watched your mother being lowered into the ground. So did you. We're...you and me," Benjamin stammered, "We're all we have left. You're all I have left of her."

"God, Pa." He buried his face in his hands.

Benjamin watched as Francis wiped away tears. "Pa, I'm sorry. I really am. Pa, I've already signed the papers."

Benjamin felt his blood turn to ice. His son, his only child, had done this without telling him. Without including him. Without respecting him. Other than the loss of his Delina, the farmer had never been so hurt. Not even during the war as he watched his friends, young and mostly good men, die brutal deaths.

Benjamin's only outward reaction was to stare at his son. Francis looked as though he'd been run through with a sword.

There was a sound of shuffling and both men looked toward the source. There stood an embarrassed Randolph E. Bridgewater, III.

"Lord, I'm sorry. I really do apologize. I didn't mean to interrupt a family, ah, discussion," he blurted.

Realization dawning, Benjamin's eyes burned into Bridgewater. He pointed at him, then looked at Francis. "Did this spoiled rich Easterner have anything to do with your asinine decision? Tell me the truth."

"No, Pa. Absolutely not! Like I said, most of the guys are talking about going. Really, everybody's talking about it."

"That sir, is the God's honest truth," Bridgewater added. "Your son made his own decision. *I* had nothing to do with it!"

They both lied.

Benjamin glared a warning at Bridgewater and he shut up.

"Pa, let's take a break from this. I'll tell you everything a little later. Maybe Randy and I should check on the Jenny. The cows may have found a way into the barn," said Francis in a failed attempt at levity. "We'll be back shortly, okay?"

In answer, Benjamin looked at them, his eyes filled with anger. Both young men beat a hasty retreat through the kitchen door.

Watching through the kitchen window above the pump, Benjamin's gaze followed them as they bolted across the yard. Looking at Francis, the farmer recalled all the sacrifices he and Delina made so Francis would have a good life. A life better than theirs. They wanted him to be the first in either family to go to college. They scrimped and saved at every turn. They had old furniture. Their clothes were worn - almost threadbare - but clean. Benjamin had scraped their living out of the ground while Delina kept the home running. He patched together farm equipment his neighbors would have sold for junk. Francis helped with chores of course, but his main job was doing the best he could in school.

Then, when Francis finally began at Allegheny College, there were the bills to pay. Thank God there were scholarships, including one from Benjamin's lodge. Francis had to get a part-time job at a hardware store in Meadville that paid the room and board, but Benjamin had spent every spare dime on tuition and books. Even now, standing in his kitchen listening to the second worst news of his life, he was almost in rags.

After all of that, after all the sacrifice and love, this was his reward. Emotionally winded from Francis' announcement and feeling hurt and betrayed, the farmer sat down at the kitchen table to recover. *This is a nightmare*, he thought.

Cradling his head in his hands, he could hear Delina's French-accented voice: *"Take a deep breath and tink before you talk. He signed da papers and dere's nutting you can do about it. Dere's no way out and you better not say sometink in anger dat you can't unsay later in remorse."*

He blinked back a tear. Squeezing his eyes shut, he pinched the bridge of his nose trying to shut out the terrible reality that had intruded on his world. He had tried so hard to do what Delina would have wanted. He decided there was something he must do later that very day, something he always did when he had to think through a difficult problem. Farm work be damned.

Having decided his next step, Benjamin did the only thing left to him: he finished making breakfast.

Eventually, Francis and Bridgewater returned to the farmhouse.

"Breakfast is getting cold," was Benjamin's cheerless greeting.

The two young men joined Benjamin for a mostly silent and somewhat emotionally chilly repast of pancakes, fried eggs, and slabs of bacon. A farm breakfast.

As they finished, Benjamin toyed with his coffee cup, slowly turning it in its saucer. This ritual was always a prelude to a difficult topic.

Bridgewater, not the insensitive lout Benjamin had taken him for, sensed the tension. He quickly flicked his eyes between Benjamin and Francis, wondering if he should excuse himself for self-preservation as much as sensitivity to a family disagreement.

"So," Benjamin finally asked, "you said you already signed up. What happens next?"

Benjamin's voice was calm and even. Francis unconsciously breathed a short sigh of relief.

"Well," Francis began, "the situation is a little complicated because we're not quite ready for a war. I mean, as a country. It's like a track event back at school. Everyone's going from a standstill to running at top speed, so everyone gets spread out."

"You lost me," Benjamin says with downcast eyes. "I don't care about everyone," he exclaimed while looking at his son. "I care about what happens to you."

"Okay, Pa, here's the thing," Francis explained, "America doesn't have an air force…"

"A what?" Benjamin interjected, confused.

"An air force, Pa," Francis repeated. "We haven't taken the new technology, like the Jenny, seriously. Other countries have. The French, British and Germans are going hammer and tongs at building and improving flying machines. Some Americans, including guys from Pittsburgh, are already flying with the French. Maybe you heard of them? The Lafayette Escadrille and the Lafayette Flying Corps, but they're relatively small outfits…."

"So?" Benjamin interrupted, "What has that got to do with you?"

"Well, Randy and I have signed up with the Army Signal Corps," Francis responded, as though this explained everything.

"*Randy* and you?" I guess I'd be an idiot to be surprised at that. The Signal Corps? That has something to do with flying?" Benjamin was becoming used to feeling stupid. When he was in the Army, what he had seen of the Signal Corps involved soldiers communicating with semaphore flags. It had nothing to do with flying in any form, except maybe using homing pigeons.

"Pa, the closest thing America has to an air force is the Aviation Section of the Army Signal Corps. Our army uses the machines mostly for observation duty. If Randy and I want to fly and not spend the war in a trench, that's where we have to go. All our military machines, except a few the Navy has, are assigned to the Aviation Section of the Signal Corps."

"So, when you said flying was just a diversion, you were lying. You had this planned all along."

"No, Pa," Francis pleaded. "It really started out as just a fun thing to do. Honest. But then the war got hotter and there was more talk about America getting involved on the side of France and England. Since we - Randy and me - were already flying and we could see flying machines were being used more and more, it seemed logical that we go as pilots, if it came to that."

"And it looks like it came to that," Benjamin said bitterly, "and you helped it along by just happening to be ready."

Bridgewater was looking more and more uncomfortable. In fact, he, Francis and several other students at Allegheny College had been scheming about what they would do if the United States joined the hostilities. Some boys had joined the Canadian army, which was now fighting with the British. A few even got themselves overseas and joined the British army.

"Pa, I'm telling you, it's not like that! I wasn't planning this behind your back! I'm not responsible for a war in Europe!"

"No," Benjamin thought, "but you're responsible for taking advantage of the mess those idiot Europeans have dragged us into." The room became quiet. It was clear to the boys that Benjamin could see through their lie.

Benjamin broke the silence. "You still haven't

told me what will be happening to you."

"After we pass our medical examinations, Randy and I and a lot of guys from other colleges and universities around the country will be going to ground school in Texas. After that...."

"*Ground* school?" Benjamin interrupted, "What in blazes is *ground* school? Infantry? I thought you signed up to fly."

At this point, Bridgewater couldn't help himself.

"Hah! No sir, it's not the infantry. Before one is actually allowed to touch a military machine, one must first be properly trained in how they function and operate, not to mention aerial navigation, meteorology, etc."

"Uh huh," Benjamin grumbled, not happy with Bridgewater's involvement in his conversation with his son. "I suppose you won't be skipping out on those classes like you did at Harvard."

Bridgewater appeared stricken at the sarcasm.

"What happens after that?" Benjamin asked, turning his attention back to Francis. "Then they put you in one of those things?" he asked, jabbing his thumb in the direction of the barn.

"Well, Pa, there aren't enough machines for that, or instructors, or mechanics who know how to work on them, or for that matter, not much else. Like I said, America's not ready for this war. Even the machines they do have are too old and unreliable."

"So what's the point of going to school on the ground if you won't be able to learn to fly those things?"

"Like I said, everyone else is way ahead of us. So, once we get through ground school, which should take a couple of months, they'll put us on ships and send us over to England or France, or maybe Italy, for military flight training. Then we'll be assigned to English, French or Italian squadrons."

"You mean to tell me American boys won't be fighting as part of the U.S. Army? They'll be taking orders from Europeans?"

"At least in the air, Pa. America just isn't prepared for aerial warfare. Not yet. The allies are already geared up and running. America will supply the manpower to fight the Germans in English and French machines until we can get our own air force organized and built up and over there."

Sure, thought Benjamin, *our politicians will spend American lives and money to bail out the Europeans.* Again, he kept silent.

"Because we'll be pilots," Francis explained, trying to mitigate the pain for his father, "we'll be commissioned as lieutenants as soon as we get our wings."

Benjamin, experienced at being unimpressed with young officers, continued to hold his tongue on the subject of lieutenants, but asked, "Get your wings? What does that mean?"

"Mr. Kyner," Bridgewater joined in, "military pilots of the various air forces receive flying badges, usually in the shape of stylized birds wings, once they are completely qualified. Even U.S. Army and Navy pilots wear such badges. They are badges of honor."

"Honor. Sure. Do these badges, with all their honor, stop bullets?" Benjamin retorted with acid in his voice.

"Pa, please," Francis again pleaded.

"Sure. All right," Benjamin conceded in a tired voice. "Do you know when you're leaving?"

"Soon. Things are still getting organized, but we have to get through ground school in time to arrive in Europe and finish our flight training before the winter sets in. At least that's what they told us. So, I'd guess we'd have to be in Texas within a month or so."

Benjamin looked into the coffee grounds in the bottom of his cup, as though trying to divine the future in them.

"Well, the Army never moves fast. 'Hurry up and wait.' It's always the same story. You'll learn. At least you'll be able to finish this year at Allegheny. Then you'll have only one more year to go when this is all over," Benjamin said hopefully. "I'll see you before you go?"

"You bet, Pa," Francis said. "I promise I'll get home before we ship out."

Ship out, Benjamin thought. *He's talking like he's already in the damned army. I wonder where he heard that.* Then he remembered. Francis had heard it from *him* on the rare occasions when he'd spoken about his time in Cuba as Francis was growing up. Benjamin felt a brief pang of guilt at the thought.

"Pa. This is going to be all right. I promise. You'll see. This will all be over in a few months. That's why Randy and I have to go soon. Then I'll come back and finish up at Allegheny."

Benjamin had heard this before. He'd said something similar himself before *he* shipped out to Cuba with that idiot, the former rebel General Wheeler. He was angry with himself because he didn't know how to make his son understand what he himself didn't understand at that age. He didn't want Francis to learn the same lessons the same way. The tuition at that particular school was far too high.

"I guess we should get going, Pa." As he and Bridgewater stood and turned for the door, the newspaper fell unnoticed to the floor. It was opened to the page Francis was reading when he told his father his plans.

"Thank you for your hospitality, sir," Bridgewater said while offering Benjamin his hand. "It was a pleasure to finally meet this young rascal's father," he added with his now trademark grin.

Benjamin simply said, "Uh, huh," and then followed both young men out the door.

Halfway to the barn, Francis turned to Benjamin. "Hey, Pa. Would you like Randy to give you quick spin in the Jenny before we go? You might like it."

"Me? In that thing? No. Not a chance. It's bad enough that I know you'll be flying around in that contraption. I'm happy right here on the ground." Benjamin wasn't smiling. They continued walking in silence.

Hiram was waiting at the barn. The four of them maneuvered the Jenny awkwardly through the wide doors toward flatter ground.

After what Francis explained was a "pre-flight" inspection of the flying machine, to include checking for sufficient fuel and oil and ensuring the flight controls worked properly and the tires were still inflated, Bridgewater climbed into the rear cockpit.

Francis walked toward the front of the machine and stood waiting by the propeller.

"These things are able to fly because the air moving quickly over top of the wings creates low pressure that lifts the wings into the air while air deflected off the bottom creates high pressure that pushes the wings up," Francis explained to his father and Hiram, who were standing off to the side.

"The faster the air is moving, the lower the pressure on top of the wings and the higher the pressure beneath them and the sooner we get off the ground. We try to always take off into the wind. That way, the ground speed of the Jenny adds to the speed of the wind and we can take off in a shorter distance. If we took off with the wind, we'd have to go a lot faster before the wings could develop enough lift to fly and that would use up a lot more distance."

Benjamin didn't understand, but nodded anyway.

Bridgewater noted the weather, including the wind direction, and mentioned something to Francis.

Francis turned back to Benjamin and continued, "In this case, since the field has a grade - downhill to the east and uphill to the west - Randy wants to take off downhill so the Jenny will gain speed faster. We'll have a tailwind, but it's so light it won't matter. If we tried to takeoff uphill to the west, it would take us too long to get to flying speed. Plus, we'd have to taxi clear to the other end of the field before we could even start. The Jenny will slide nicely into the air. You'll see."

Benjamin didn't know what Francis was talking about, but he could see his son was proud to display his knowledge of how flying machines worked.

The Jenny had a two-bladed wooden propeller. As Francis faced it, like facing a clock, the two propeller blades were at 10 o'clock and 4 o'clock. Francis focused his attention on the blade at 10 o'clock, which was well above his head. He carefully placed both gloved hands on the blade and steadied himself with his legs shoulder-width apart. "Ready!" he shouted to Bridgewater, who sat waiting in the rear cockpit.

"Contact!" shouted Bridgewater after switching on both spark-producing magnetos.

"Contact!" repeated Francis.

Francis quickly pulled the giant wooden blade straight down and, as the blade reached the bottom of the swing, in one fluid motion he rolled his arms and body away from the moving blade and stepped back and to the side.

Both Benjamin and Hiram jumped as the Jenny's engine coughed to life in a cloud of blue smoke. The speed of the propeller's blades increased and the noise emitted from the awakened machine grew steadily louder.

Francis, now in Bridgewater's line-of-sight, exchanged a "thumbs up" with him. Francis shook hands with Hiram, who also slapped him on the shoulder.

Hugging his father silently, he could feel Benjamin's strong arms tighten around him. Hiram looked on.

After a moment, they released each other. Francis quickly slipped his leather-flying helmet and goggles on.

After pulling the goggles over his eyes, he bounded atop the bottom wing, then into the front cockpit.

Francis fastened his lap belt then waved to the two men while Bridgewater advanced the throttle and the Jenny headed toward Benjamin's field.

Benjamin and Hiram ran after the Jenny. The cows, now awaiting milking, were no longer obstacles. As the flying machine turned onto the field, Bridgewater stepped on the right rudder pedal, swinging the nose of the machine due east.

With a final wave from Francis, Bridgewater

advanced the throttle and the Jenny began speeding along the rough ground, bouncing ever more vigorously from side to side.

Bridgewater pulled the control stick into his stomach in order to keep the Jenny's tail planted firmly on the ground until it reached flying speed. Otherwise, an errant gust of wind could deflect the tail to the point where Bridgewater could no longer maintain control and the machine would spin about it's center of gravity, which was called a ground loop, until it had destroyed itself. He also moved the stick slightly to the left to tilt the wings northward in order counteract the wind blowing from that direction.

As the speed increased, so did the sound of the engine and pressure of the wind. Accompanying the wind was the smell of exhaust and a mist of castor oil from the OX5 engine that was swinging the huge propeller. Bridgewater pummeled the rudder with quickening jabs to keep the Jenny aligned with the long narrow field as the tree-covered hills directly in front of them rapidly advanced. As Francis predicted, the downhill trajectory of the Jenny added to the thrust generated by the propeller and the craft quickly gained speed.

Bridgewater could now feel the control surfaces taking effect as the air pressure on them increased. He released the rearward pressure on the control stick and they felt the Jenny's tail lift into the air. The Jenny was becoming light on its landing gear. The time was *now!* Bridgewater pulled gently on the stick. As the tail descended slightly in response, the nose of the now swiftly moving flying machine pointed upward and the landing gear lifted off the ground. No longer tormented by the shale-filled field, the rumbling and shaking ceased and the flying machine ascended slowly into the cool, clear spring morning sky.

Benjamin and Hiram watched in awe as the Jenny climbed safely above the greening hills to the east and banked gently northward, away from home.

"Well," Hiram, said to Benjamin, both sets of eyes still following his son's aerial steed, "maybe now you can get the plowin' finished."

CHAPTER 6

HARBINGER

Lunchtime found both men headed toward the farmhouse.

With the milking finished, Benjamin had resumed plowing once again. He'd spent the intervening time since Francis and Bridgewater departed in silence.

Hiram, who enjoyed people and needed to be around them, was well aware of his friend's angst and only wanted to help alleviate it. He knew, however, that Benjamin wasn't a talker. In times of stress and worry he detested being around other people. Such times were when he wanted most to be alone. Delina had often told him how unhealthy it was to be that way, but she was unable to change him. So, Hiram kept his own council. Benjamin was happy to find solitude behind the plow.

Entering the kitchen, Benjamin noticed the newspaper on the floor where Francis had dropped it that morning. He bent to pick it up.

Hiram watched Benjamin. He could see the veins

in Benjamin's neck pulsing and his jaw muscles clenching as his eyes darted back and forth over the page.

Whatever he's readin' is really gettin' under his skin.

Hiram could almost feel the trepidation radiating from Benjamin like waves of heat from a fire. He wanted to say something, but knew nothing he could say would help. He remained silent.

In disgust, Benjamin threw the newspaper on the table. Then he turned to lean on the sink and look out the window. Hiram noticed that Benjamin was looking in the direction Francis had flown just a little while ago, as though he was trying to get one last glimpse of his son.

Without turning from the window, Benjamin said, "It's all intended to make young naïve fools run to the nearest recruiting office."

Hiram didn't know if Benjamin directed his comment to him or to himself.

"Go ahead and get yourself something to eat," Benjamin finally said. "There's something I've got to do. I'll be back before dark. I'll see you tomorrow."

Hiram was concerned. It wasn't like Ben to just up and leave in the middle of the day when there were chores to be done.

"Ben, is there something I can do for ya? Ya want me to come along to keep ya company?"

"Nah," Benjamin replied. "I need to do this myself. Nothin' to worry about," he said as he walked out the door.

Wondering what upset Benjamin, Hiram reached for the newspaper.

The *Pittsburgh Press* was open to page six. Hiram's eyes fell on the article he guessed Benjamin had been reading; an article about the American pilots of the Lafayette Escadrille. Reading it, he supposed it caught Francis' eye, as well, since Benjamin told him earlier Francis had mentioned the volunteer flyers.

"War Films Show Yankee Aviators: ...The most skillful airmen...thrilling battles...lost their lives...cited for bravery...killed in action."

Well, Hiram thought, *it worked. They're linin' up to be heroes.*

Hiram's understanding now complete, he looked with concern at the kitchen door that only moments before had closed like a steel trap on Benjamin. His instinct was to go after his friend and try to console him, but he knew that would be futile. Benjamin, locked inside himself, was inconsolable. Hiram felt just as helpless in comforting Benjamin as Benjamin felt in stopping Francis from leaving college and joining the army.

Resigned to spending the rest of the afternoon working alone, Hiram began flipping through the pages of the day-old newspaper. War news abounded. Several articles enthusiastically described recruit honor rolls and new enlistments in the Pennsylvania National Guard.

Talking to himself, Hiram mumbled, "You'd think the country is getting ready for a party rather than a damned war."

As he continued to read, he noticed an article tucked away at the bottom of page seven, next to an advertisement for "Father John's Tonic and Body Builder." "Negroes Enlisting: Alabama Negroes are organizing a regiment of volunteers, which they plan to offer bodily to the war department. Three companies have already been assembled." That was all it said.

Another advertisement followed the brief article, this one promising help for constipation and indigestion.

Well, now, that's perfect, thought Hiram. *Short and sweet. No one's making movin' pictures about the patriotic negroes marchin' off to fight. Nope. Well, at least they can get help for their constipation.*

With a sigh, Hiram put down the newspaper and stood to look out the window. Benjamin was long gone and out of sight. Hiram turned from the window and started looking for something to make into a sandwich. Later, he would have to get home and tend to his honeybees.

Benjamin walked east down the hill off his property and onto Athena-Evangeline Road. He walked until reaching Hutchman, continued to Dobson and finally the familiar dirt lane. It wasn't far. He'd walked this way many times. He could have taken the wagon, but he needed to walk. At last, he arrived.

Athena Cemetery sat atop a small hill just north of the borough and directly east of Benjamin's farm.

Walking past rows of silent monuments, he read the names of old families who had lived in this region for generations: Marburger, Zieglar, Dambach, Frishkorn, Cashdollar, Silbaugh, Kaufman. Scores of Germans among the assorted Irish and English. *Lots of Germans,* Benjamin thought, reflecting upon the hostilities in Europe. *But only one's a Kyner and that one's really a Frenchie.* Benjamin grinned at the thought.

He trudged up the hill toward her until he was close enough to read the stone: *Delina Angeline Kyner. 1871-1912.* Next to her name was chiseled: *Benjamin Arthur Kyner. 1865 - _____.*

From time to time, when his thoughts were troubled, Benjamin would make this trek to Delina's side.

Long ago she told him that her middle name, Angeline, meant "messenger." *That's about right,* he thought. He would come here and turn his problem, whatever it was, over and over in his mind, sometimes speaking to the marble stone. Oftentimes, the mist would part and his path would be clear. Whether this was due to her intervention or not, he didn't know, but someday he would. He did know that coming here always calmed him.

He bent down and pulled a few errant weeds that had taken advantage of the spring rains and warming weather. Then, slowly, he lowered himself and sat next to the grave.

He looked west, in the direction of their farm. He could just make out his silo that peeked above the newly leafed trees. He had chosen this spot for just that reason. Delina, and eventually Benjamin, would be able to watch over the farm from here.

"Well, Delina," Benjamin said softly, "he's gone and done it. Our boy's grown up. I tried so hard to raise him like you wanted. Like I promised you I would. But he's gotten to the point where he wants to make his own decisions without listening to anyone but people who are just as foolish as he is. If I did something wrong, I can't figure out what it is. I don't know what to do 'cause as far as I can tell there's nothin' I *can* do. You can only hold on to 'em for so long. Watch over him, Frenchie. Please make sure he gets home."

He turned and leaned against the stone. He spent a long time there. He used to come and think about what his life would've have been like if she'd lived. He missed the sound of her voice. He once admitted to himself that listening to her talk to Francis about the damnable Catholic Church hadn't been so bad, after all. He'd have given anything to once again hear her voice, even if it meant listening to her talk about the pope. He eventually forced himself to stop because he knew if she could, she'd scold him for torturing himself over something he couldn't change. She was always more practical than he.

Leaning against the stone, he looked off into the distance in the direction of the farm, as if trying to divine the future or recall a past that wasn't. He could do nothing else. As time passed, the setting sun bathed his face in orange light.

As the sun dipped lower in the western sky, Benjamin realized he had to get moving before dark. There would be no moon tonight and he wouldn't be able to see his hand in front of his face. He lifted himself from the cool, moist grass. After looking at the stone one more time, Benjamin began the walk home, past the cold, silent slabs of stone.

Nearing the road leading out of the cemetery, he sensed a motion out of the corner of his eye. Focusing his eyes in the dimming light, he saw a dirty, seedy-looking possum scuttling from stone to stone, in parallel to Benjamin's path, its long ugly tail sliding along the ground.

Unconcerned with a possum, but none-the-less driven by curiosity to watch the only moving thing in a field of the dead, Benjamin looked on as the ugly rat-faced rodent ran haltingly ahead of him, finding temporary concealment as it scurried from stone to stone.

Suddenly, Benjamin was back, years before, when

he ran in just the same way, so low he was almost on all fours, from stone to stone and tree to tree, seeking protection from Spanish bullets, running and hiding, just like the opossum. *Let's go boys. We've got the damn Yankees on the run again!* The memory was so real Benjamin winced in shocked surprise and shook his head to rid himself of the recollection.

Quickly and without warning, the possum ran toward an ancient, dilapidated headstone. It had been broken years before, the lichen-covered slab now propped against its pedestal forming a small tent made of marble. The triangular space between the stone and pedestal was dark and forbidding.

Benjamin watched as the possum deftly disappeared downward into that dark space. He read the weathered and moss-covered lettering on the headstone. A child's grave was host to the possum's borrow. Benjamin couldn't help but wonder how deep the burrow went. Did it reach...? He stopped his wandering imagination and hurried from the cemetery. As he did, darkness closed in on him from all sides.

The sun was sinking lower in the sky as Hiram approached the dirt road leading into the small valley the locals called Black Hollow. As he turned onto the dusty track, his eyes wandered over a familiar sight. Ten small single-story wood frame houses were scattered along the road, many badly in need of paint. Some had flowers planted in small patches just coming into bloom.

Officially named Negro Hollow on county maps, this place was a product of the old Underground Railroad. The simple houses here, most home to extended families representing two or three generations, made up an enclave of descendants of fugitive slaves who escaped to freedom over 50 years earlier. Their clandestine and often dangerous journeys to freedom in British North America, later called Canada, were always exhausting and sometimes terrifying. More than one escaped slave was captured by bounty hunters and returned south of the Mason-Dixon Line. Once they reached a free state such as New York or Pennsylvania, many chose to remain rather than subject their children to further deprivations.

Someday, thought Hiram, *We'll rename this strip of dirt. Someday.*

As he approached his own house, he noticed drying laundry in the backyard flapping in the breeze. Unless she was watching a neighbor's child or having one of her friends over for coffee or lemonade, Sarah spent her days in a quiet house. There were no little hands to throw belongings into disarray.

Walking along the side of the house, he found Sarah hanging a cotton print dress on the clothesline, a half-empty wicker laundry basket at her feet and a few buzzing bees keeping guard. The honeybees that populated Hiram's hives had never been a concern to her. Hiram gave her a peck on the cheek.

Sarah asked, "And how is Mr. Ben doin'?"

"He ain't doin' very well, I'm afraid," Hiram answered.

Hiram's tone of voice was uncharacteristically serious. Sarah stopped what she was doing and turned toward her husband.

"Young Francis has gone and joined up. He's leavin' college for the Army. Thinks he's gonna fly."

"Oh, Good Lord, no. What is that boy thinking? I knew there was something going on when you told me last night he just dropped out of the sky in one of those flying machines. Poor Benjamin must be beside himself, what with his Delina dead and gone and all."

"Funny you should mention her. I have an idea he's up there right now talkin' to her." Hiram nodded his head in the direction of the cemetery.

Hiram's words caused Sarah's features to transform into a look of true sadness.

"What's Benjamin going to do?" Sarah asked. "Did he say anything?"

"You know how he is. When he's in a mood he just shuts down. I reckon he won't do anythin' about it but fret himself to death. Besides, there ain't nothin' he *can* do, unless maybe he breaks both the boy's legs. Francis already signed the papers. Hell, even if Ben did break his legs, the Army would just wait for 'em to heal then they'd come and get 'm."

Sarah frowned and slapped Hiram's shoulder with a towel.

Hiram smiled. "There's nothin' anyone can do, I guess, 'cept pray he comes home alive."

"We can do that," replied Sarah turning back to finish hanging Hiram's shirt. "But tell him I'll be sending some Amish chocolate bread over with you day after tomorrow. I'll start it tonight."

Sarah was well aware of Benjamin's love of any kind of bread. He once told Delina that the only way her bread could be better was if she made it out of chocolate. "Dat's already been done," she said. "It's called cake."

Later, however, when Benjamin and Delina had gone to the Butler County Fair, she was amazed to find the Amish women selling their chocolate bread. Buying some and obtaining the recipe from the obliging

Pennsylvania Dutch woman, Delina surprised Benjamin with fresh chocolate bread one fall day. With Delina gone, Sarah had taken up the chore of making Amish chocolate bread for Benjamin.

"You are a good woman, Sarah," said Hiram. God knows I don't deserve you. Neither does Ben."

"Yes. God knows it and so do I, so don't you forget it," she said, smiling.

"Well," Hiram exhaled, "I've got to check on the bees before it gets too late. They get cantankerous if I trouble 'em too close to sundown." He turned and headed to an outbuilding not far from his hives.

Sarah returned to the house carrying the empty laundry basket. She'd have dinner ready by the time Hiram was done pestering his bees.

CHAPTER 7

GONE WITHOUT GOODBYE

A few weeks had passed since Francis landed the Jenny on Benjamin's field and told Benjamin that he would soon be going to war.

Since then, Benjamin had heard nothing more from his son. Hoping the old adage "no news is good news" was true in this case, the farmer did the only thing he could do. He got on with the business of running a farm.

It was a bright sunny May morning that found Hiram Bolt walking across the field where Francis and Randolph E. Bridgewater, III, landed the Jenny.

Nearing the farmhouse, he spotted Benjamin sitting on the porch bench reading what appeared to be a letter.

"Who you tryin' to fool, Ben? Everybody knows you can't read," he said, chuckling.

Without looking up, Benjamin glumly handed

Hiram the single page missive.

"Oh, it's from Francis," Hiram said as he sat next to Benjamin and began reading.

After finishing the letter, Hiram slowly lowered it, then handed it back to Benjamin.

"Ben, I'm really sorry. I know he promised."

"Yup. My boy promised I'd see him before he left for good, but that's not gonna happen, is it? He and his idiot rich friend are in too much of a rush to be heroes and get their damned heads shot off."

Francis' letter explained that he and Bridgewater had passed their physical examinations for acceptance into the Aviation Section of the Army Signal Corps and had been ordered on short notice to report for an eight-week ground school at the Massachusetts Institute of Technology, of all places. They were assigned to the first class of trainees under the Army's rapidly expanding program. The Army was frantic to train as many pilots as possible as quickly as possible, but didn't have enough facilities or instructors, so it had contracted with several universities to conduct the ground schools. One of those was Ohio State University, a damn sight closer than Cambridge, Massachusetts.

Benjamin's first thought was that the Army hadn't changed since he'd been a soldier. Why train a man close to home when more taxpayer money could be spent shipping him hundreds of miles away? Kids from New England were probably being sent to the University of Texas. As a matter of fact, Benjamin recalled Francis saying he and Bridgewater would be sent to Texas. Then he remembered that Bridgewater was from Massachusetts. *That shiftless rich kid probably had his daddy pull strings to have him and Francis sent to*

Bridgewater's hometown.

Francis had gone on to say he and the others would embark for Europe immediately after completing their initial training at MIT and the other schools. Things were moving too quickly. Francis was sending his unneeded clothes and books home from Allegheny College by rail. By the time Benjamin received the letter, Francis had explained, he and Bridgewater would probably already be headed east, if not already at MIT. If it were at all possible, Francis said, he would get home to say goodbye, but he doubted he could make it.

Benjamin could detect Francis' youthful exuberance from the tone of his letter. It was plain that Francis' excitement had overwhelmed any sense of obligation he had to his father.

Benjamin put the letter down and leaned back, exhaling an audible sigh. Out of a sense of caution, Hiram remained silent.

Benjamin felt absolutely powerless to have even the slightest influence on the most important aspect of his existence - his son's life. He knew this was because he *was* absolutely powerless to affect the choices Francis made. Francis never even bothered to seek Benjamin's advice before he changed the course of his life.

"You know," Benjamin finally said to Hiram. "He didn't even talk to me before he decided to do this. Before he decided to make the biggest decision in his life so far."

"Well, Benjamin," Hiram replied, feeling he was on solid ground, "I guess he knew what you'd say, so he saved you both the grief of arguin' about it. Besides, if he didn't tell ya until he already joined the army, then you couldn't talk him out of it."

"I know," Benjamin said. "I just wanted to say it. I just wanted to hear the words out loud."

Hiram nodded.

"He's so much like his mother. She would have done the same thing."

"Yeah," Hiram chuckled. "She was a lot smarter than you, too."

Benjamin looked askance at Hiram without smiling.

"Cheer up, Ben," Hiram said. "You still got *me!*"

"I know," Benjamin responded. "Things keep gettin' worse." He finally managed a weak smile.

Benjamin stood and walked off the porch onto the pebble-strewn packed earth where grass once grew. Delina would have been furious at how Benjamin neglected the small patch of grass that had been their lawn.

Benjamin turned toward Hiram. "Why don't you start on mendin' the fence along Fairey Hill Road? I'll be along directly." With that, Benjamin turned and walked down the hill.

Hiram went to the barn to collect the tools he'd need to fix the fence.

As he headed out of the barn toward Fairey Hill Road, he looked down the hill. Hiram stopped to consider Benjamin, who was standing on the very spot where he saw Francis fly away. Benjamin was just standing there, looking off into the sky.

Hiram, truly concerned about how Francis' decision would affect his friend, went to fix the fence.

Standing on the impromptu landing strip and looking into the faultless clear sky that had swallowed his

Francis, Benjamin considered that tonight there would be a full moon, which meant there would be plenty of light to travel by. Some members of the lodge would be getting together in Athena. He'd go. Maybe it would help get his mind off his troubles for at least a couple of hours. There. He made a decision. At least he had control over something in his life.

A man of few diversions, Benjamin joined the local Masonic lodge years earlier, well before he met Delina. Harmonie Lodge No. 924 originally met in the small borough of Harmonie, Pennsylvania, the site where in December 1753, an Indian allied with the French shot at a young George Washington who was transiting in the vicinity of the village enroute to Fort LeBoeuf, near Lake Erie. Some believe this was the first shot of the French and Indian War, which set the stage for the American Revolutionary War.

Diminutive Harmonie was situated immediately adjacent to somewhat larger Deutschburgh, which had been founded by a German baron during the previous century. Although of Germanic name and origin, Deutschburgh was quintessentially American in every other possible respect.

By the time Benjamin joined Harmonie Lodge No. 924, it had re-located to Deutschburgh where it met on the top floor of a three-story commercial building located at the corner of West New Castle and Main Streets.

Depending on the weather and season, Benjamin would either walk or take his horse-drawn wagon three miles to the small railroad village of Calvary where he would board the Harmonie Line streetcar for the nearly ten mile trip to Deutschburgh. Athena was closer to Benjamin's farm, but Calvary was closer to Deutschburgh, which meant the streetcar ticket was cheaper.

Since traveling between Athena and Deutschburgh to attend lodge was a time consuming process that was accomplished in the evenings, Benjamin and other lodge members who resided in and around Athena did not attend every meeting of their lodge, especially in the winter when the days were short, the temperatures low and the traveling conditions difficult. They did, however, sometimes gather informally for dinner and conversation at an establishment in Athena, as they would this evening.

Their informal meeting place was the upper floor of a wood-frame building on Clay Avenue, just a short walk from the store where, about once a month, Benjamin would buy supplies. The lodge's insignia, a builder's square surmounted by a two-pronged compass, also appeared on the gold ring worn by the storekeeper.

Once, while passing a few minutes with the man, he asked the meaning of the insignia.

"Why, Ben. I'm pleased you finally asked."

Thus, Benjamin was given a cursory introduction to the Free & Accepted Masons of Pennsylvania - the Freemasons.

Benjamin never before considered becoming a Mason. Actually, he never felt much drawn to join anything. As it happened, he knew a number of men who were members of the lodge, men with whom he'd associated for a long time. The Chief of Police was a member, as was the Volunteer Fire Chief, Mayor and even a minister. Most of the others, including a number of farmers, were good people, though a couple might be questionable in his opinion.

On the other hand, the real SOBs in town were *not* members. While some people voiced suspicions about what went on in the lodge, they were either gossipy fools or fully qualified to be the village idiots. He knew the organization had originated in England and had existed for centuries, so it had to be doing something right. In Benjamin's mind, the scales tipped toward the Freemasons.

Benjamin gave it some thought. While at that time of his life he attended the Lutheran Church a couple of times a month, he thought it might be good to get out more.

Regardless of what the stone-throwers said, he decided that if Freemasonry was good enough for George Washington, Benjamin Franklin, many of the signers of the Declaration of Independence, and President Teddy Roosevelt - a fellow veteran of the Cuban war - it was good enough for him.

Benjamin had always been glad he joined the lodge. While he couldn't make every meeting, especially after Delina passed away and he was raising Francis alone, he really enjoyed the secular fellowship. Part of what made it possible for Francis to attend Allegheny College was a scholarship from the lodge. It would be many years, however, before Benjamin realized why becoming a Freemason was one of the most important decisions of his life.

CHAPTER 8

FREE AND ACCEPTED

Benjamin guided the horse-drawn wagon along unpaved Athena-Evangeline Road, which became Crowe Avenue inside the borough limits.

He looked up as he passed a two-story brick building with a bell tower at the corner of Crowe Avenue and Clarke Street.

The sight of the high school revived memories of those years of Francis' life, years that were all too recent.

From the moment Francis announced he was joining the Army, Benjamin thought of nothing else but his son and how good life had seemed when Delina was alive. When he allowed himself to consider the future his thoughts were filled with trepidation and uncertainty. All that mattered was that Francis got home in one piece. Then maybe Benjamin's life could get back to normal.

He tugged on the reins and the horses turned left onto Clarke Street. A block later Benjamin looked to his right down Grand Avenue and saw a line of gaslights flickering along the small town's main thoroughfare. The wagon creaked and rocked its way across the railroad tracks, which were bordered on each side by West and East Railroad Avenues. Benjamin thought of Delina, who used to say calling the twin streets "avenues" was "grandiose" considering they were each only two blocks long. He smiled at the recollection as he turned the horses south onto East Railroad Avenue.

Approaching the wood-frame building that sat between East Railroad and Clay Avenues, Benjamin glanced at the compass and square mounted over the door.

He dismounted from the wagon, tied the horses to a hitching rail beside of the structure, then walked in.

Standing at the bottom of the stairs, Benjamin hesitated. The muffled sound of several conversations emanating from the room above seemed to make his sense of loneliness and isolation all the more profound. After a moment, he shook off the feeling and climbed the stairs to the second floor where several of his fellow lodge brothers warmly greeted him.

After their meal, Benjamin and the others spent time talking over coffee. The war was the main topic among most of the lodge members, but not for everyone. Benjamin wanted to stay away from the subject of the war.

While deep in conversation with the owner of a neighboring farm, Benjamin felt a firm but friendly grip on the back of his neck. Looking up, he saw the smiling florid face of Frank Zieglar, the lodge's senior warden. Zieglar's ancestors had purchased the village of Harmonie from its founders, German Harmonists, a century earlier.

"Brother Ben, pardon the interruption," he said while looking at the other man in silent apology for intruding. "I heard your son Francis has joined up to fight the Hun. Is that true?"

"Hello, Frank. Nothing stays quiet in this town, does it? Yeah, it's true. Francis and some of his foolish young friends from college have decided it would be a jim-dandy idea to throw away their educations in exchange for rifles." Benjamin was sick of hearing of the war and didn't need to hear Zieglar or anyone else bring it up.

Zieglar grimaced at the bitterness of Benjamin's response. "Well, Ben, is it also true he actually landed one of those flying machines on your farm?" Zieglar pulled up a chair and settled in next to Benjamin.

Benjamin sighed inwardly. He'd come here to try to get his mind off of Francis and the war. The last thing he wanted at the moment was this conversation.

"Yup, Frank, that's true, too. He and a rich Boston friend of his scared the hell out of Hiram and me a few weeks ago with that thing. My cows didn't take very kindly to it, either. That's what they think they'll be doing, flying with the British or French or some such nonsense."

"Flying with the British or French?" Zieglar repeated incredulously. "Not with our own boys? Why in the name of God would they be doing that, Ben? Why won't they be fighting with Americans?" A small knot of men, attracted by Zieglar's tone of voice and the subject of the conversation, was forming around Benjamin and Zieglar.

Benjamin was becoming more uncomfortable.

"I've heard of the Lafayette Escadrille, the boys

who actually joined the French air force, but Francis is joining the U.S. Army, right?" Zieglar continued.

"It's a long story," Benjamin said with a note of exasperation. "There aren't enough of those machines to go around, so they're shipping some of our boys over to help out by flying with the Europeans. You can tell I'm not happy about any of this. Let the Europeans fight their own wars, I say." Benjamin looked down at his coffee cup.

"You should be proud, Ben," someone chimed in, "Your son's doing the patriotic thing. We just can't stand by and let the Germans roll over France. Why, if I had a son…."

His eyes flashing, Benjamin looked in the direction of the voice. It was a younger man who'd been a member of the lodge for only a short time.

"*If* you had a son?" Benjamin replied, his voice filled with bile. "*If* you had a son? Well, you *don't* have a son, but it's really noble of you to be so willing to send other people's kids off to be slaughtered. You were never even in the Army, were you? Have you ever thought of running for congress? That way you could…."

"Whoa, Ben. Simmer on down," interrupted Zieglar, putting both hands up, palms facing Benjamin. "He didn't mean anything and I'm sure Francis will make it home all right."

Benjamin was growing more irate. "How in hell can you be so sure? They're already planting Americans in the ground over there. I've been in a war. People, good people, die. And it's not pretty"

"But Ben," Zieglar said, trying to reason with his upset lodge brother, "people in Washington a lot smarter than us believe we should…"

"*What*?" Benjamin shouted, "Frank, do you hear the words coming out of your own mouth? *Nobody* in goddamned Washington is smarter than the dumbest chicken in my coop. But hold on, I could be wrong. Maybe they're smarter than I give them credit for. You don't see *them* marching off to kill the Kaiser, do you? None of *them* are sending their *own* children into the trenches, are they? Nope, but they're real good at sending other people's kids off to get killed! Do you know how this whole mess got started? Do ya? Some crazy Serbian shot an Austrian Duke, a member of European royalty. So now my boy and other *American* boys have to go and die for it. Does that make *any* sense to *anyone* in this room?" The trigger had been pulled and now Benjamin would not be calmed.

"Ben, please," pleaded Zieglar. "We're all brothers here. Lets just…"

Zieglar was suddenly cut off in mid-sentence by a loud *thud* from outside a nearby window followed by a chilling high-pitched woman's scream that was a mixture of terror and surprise. The whinnying of panicked horses, thundering hooves, and the *arruugah* of an automobile's horn accompanied the scream. Then a dog's frantic bark pierced the night.

Everyone in the room froze, so shocked that, for an instant, they didn't know what to do. Hearing the woman's scream from the street below, Benjamin found himself vividly reliving one of the most terrifying moments of his life.

Years ago, before Francis had started attending the one-room Fairey Hill School, a neighbor's vicious dog had cornered him near the house. Delina, hearing the barking, growling, and Francis' terrified cries, had run from the house to save her son. Benjamin never forgot the overwhelming panic he felt when he heard Delina scream. He was repairing a piece of equipment just outside the barn. Had he actually been in the barn, he probably wouldn't have heard the scream and only God knows what might have happened. He never ran as fast as he did that day. He took in the scene in a glance. Delina was on the ground trying to pull Francis away, the barking, growling shepherd getting closer to them with every snap of its jaws. Benjamin grabbed a shovel that was leaning against the house and ran full tilt at the dog. The dog began too late to turn toward the oncoming threat. Fueled by desperation, Benjamin swung the edge of the shovel down on the head of the animal with such force that it dropped to the ground as though shot.

Then Benjamin began to tremble.

After the three of them recovered, he looked at the dead animal's body. The dog had terrorized the local farms for the past few years, the owner heedless to his neighbors' complaints.

Benjamin tossed the dog's carcass into the wagon and headed toward the owner's house. Hearing the wagon approaching, the dog's owner came around from the back of the house. Benjamin stepped over the back of the seat into the bed of the wagon. Unlatching the back, he jumped down and picked up the dog's heavy limp body.

Seeing his dog, the owner began walking toward Benjamin with indignation in his step, his eyes wide and his mouth opening. At that moment, Benjamin hurled the beast directly at the man's chest sending him sprawling backwards and covering him with the dog's drying blood.

Benjamin approached him, anger seething from

every pore. Pointing a finger at the man's chest as he lay propped up on both elbows, legs splayed in front of him and the dead dog lying partly across his mid-section, Benjamin said "If you even try to stand up, I will kill you now. That animal attacked my wife and child. If I ever hear a word from you or if you are so stupid as to get another animal like this, I will burn your house and barn to the ground with you inside. Try me and see if I don't."

Benjamin then turned and slowly walked back to his wagon. Climbing into the seat, he looked for a moment directly into the eyes of the dog's owner, lying on the ground too fear-stricken to move, the dog's carcass still stretched across his body. Benjamin flicked the reins and guided the horses back to his farm.

The man on the ground never said another word to Benjamin.

Ever.

Snapping back to the present, Benjamin, the adrenalin already pumping into his bloodstream, was the first to respond. He jumped up with such force that he lifted the table several inches into the air, knocking over coffee cups and sending his chair over backwards. He tore down the stairs toward the street, his lodge brothers close on his heels.

The store's door was flung aside and Benjamin burst onto the wooden sidewalk followed by the other men.

Outside the building beneath the open window where the Masons had been having coffee, a young woman, presumably the one who screamed, was kneeling next to a groaning boy who was flat on his back holding his left arm. As she gently probed his arm, he screamed in pain.

Next to her was a small tan-colored mutt with a curled up tail. The dog was in a frenzy and wouldn't stop barking.

Benjamin reached them ahead of the others and knelt down next to the woman and boy. Benjamin was only vaguely aware of the rest of the men crowding around them.

"What happened?" Benjamin asked in a rasping voice having just run down a flight of stairs in near panic.

"I'm not sure," was the woman's confused response. I was walking home when I heard a loud 'thud.' This boy fell off the building's overhang right in front of me. You have to understand, in the dark it all took me totally by surprise. I screamed. I couldn't help myself. I didn't know what was happening." She had her right hand flat against her chest as though she were trying to keep her heart from jumping out. "There was a horse and buggy going by. I don't know what scared the horses the most, this boy falling off the roof and hitting the road in front of them, my screaming, or the dog's barking. They took off like the devil was after them and almost hit a motorcar. It was really bedlam out here."

Benjamin was trying to examine the boy while listening to the girl. The boy lay on his back in the dirt, eyes wide in pain and fear. Benjamin found himself checking the boy for bleeding, an old habit ingrained on the battlefield.

"What are you doing?" the girl asked.

"Nothing. Just seeing what else might be wrong with him."

Benjamin had to get a grip on himself. For just an instant he was back on a battlefield in Cuba. Everything was almost the same; the cooling night air, the noise and confusion, the crowd of men - and a wounded boy.

He squinted as he pinched the bridge of his nose to bring himself back to reality. This hadn't happened in a long time and he didn't like it happening now. He'd never told anyone of these episodes. He'd hoped he'd seen the last of them.

"Hey, mister, are *you* all right?" she asked in a concerned but quavering voice.

Benjamin got up from his knees and stood next to the young, frightened woman who still knelt next to the boy. Some of the others looked after the wagon's driver, who was dusting himself off, apparently unhurt.

Blinking away the memories, or trying to, he nodded.

Peering into a sea of faces, he said, "Someone needs to go for the doctor."

"Already done," was the anonymous retort. "Doc should get here soon."

The young woman looked up from the boy. "Actually, I'm studying to be a nurse. I'm only in my second year, but I'd say that at least his arm is broken. There could be other injuries."

Benjamin removed his jacket and gently laid it across the boy's upper body. He took someone else's offered coat and rolled it into a makeshift pillow. Then he gently lifted the boy's head and placed the coat beneath it to provide some cushioning from the unpaved rock-strewn street. The boy, emerging from the initial shock, began to whimper.

Benjamin and the others turned in the direction of the sound of running feet.

Father James Templeman, now assigned to nearby

Saint Mary's Catholic Church, pushed his way through the crowd. Joining Benjamin and the girl, the priest knelt down next to the boy and held a match to his face.

"I was on the way back to the rectory after visiting a parishioner when I heard the commotion," he explained.

After examining the boy's face, he announced, "This is Patrick Marcs. He's one of my altar boys. He's only14. What the hell happened here? Did someone go for the doctor?" The girl winced at the priest's use of profanity.

After assuring the priest the doctor had been summoned, the girl quickly recounted what she had already explained to Benjamin, including the possibility of the boy having a broken arm.

Looking at the young woman, Templeman asked, "And who might you be, dear?"

"Allyson Rochelle, I'm a nursing student in Pittsburgh. The doctor here was good enough to let me work with him during the summer. You know, for practical experience. I wasn't expecting patients to actually be falling from the sky."

The dog had quieted and was now licking the priest's hand. Templeman, smiling, wiped his hand with a handkerchief. "Well, you did fine here tonight. Most young women in your position would have panicked."

Turning to the others, Templeman asked of no one in particular, "What in the devil was he doing on the roof at this time of night?"

"Your guess is as good as ours, Father," one of the Freemasons answered.

The priest bent down and spoke into the boy's ear, "Pat, can you hear me?"

The boy's only response was another plaintive moan.

At that moment the town doctor came barreling onto the scene.

Giving the boy a cursory examination while the priest explained what he knew of the situation, the doctor announced, "Probably a broken arm. I'll need help getting him back to my office and someone should get his parents. Their house is further up on Clay Avenue."

Looking at the girl, the doctor barked, "Allyson. Good. I'll need help setting the arm and God knows what else. Come with me."

Two men gingerly lifted the boy and carried him off in the direction of the doctor's office with Allyson following. Someone else volunteered to go to the boy's house to give his parents the news.

Frank Zieglar broke away from the crowd and approached Benjamin and Templeman.

Pointing to the spot whence the boy fell, Zieglar issued his hypothesis. "You know, if Pat fell from there," he said, gesturing toward the overhanging roof, "which he apparently did, he would have been standing next to that window," Zieglar pointed upward at the window in question, "which is in the social room. Now what do you think he would've been doing there during our dinner meeting?" Zieglar said slyly.

"Spying on us?" was the simultaneous and indignant response from two or three lodge members still standing nearby.

"That's right," said Zieglar. "That little scallywag was lucky he didn't break his neck."

Turning to Templeman and Benjamin, Zieglar smiled and said, "Well, Father, has it come to this? Are you having your altar boys spy on us? If you want to know what happens at a meeting of Freemasons, all you have to do is ask to join," he said with a grin.

"Oh, sure. You'd love that, wouldn't you?" the priest replied.

"Oh, we certainly would. So would your bishop."

"He can join, too!" someone added. Some of the others joined the laughter while they elbowed each other in the ribs.

Amid the joviality, a couple of Benjamin's lodge brothers slipped to the back of the crowd, out of the priest's sight - or so they thought.

"I notice," announced Templeman, "there are some here who can find the time to attend a meeting of a fraternal association that is *not* the Knights of Columbus, by the way," he paused, interrupted by snickers, "but can't seem to drag themselves to Saint Mary's on Sunday morning."

"Now, Father," said the younger man with whom Benjamin had been quarreling only minutes before, "you really can't blame anyone for that, can you? After all, you have to admit our meetings are a lot more exciting than yours!"

This pronouncement was met with uproarious laughter.

"And the coffee is better!" another of Benjamin's lodge brothers shouted. This was followed by more laughter.

"Careful, Padre, you're surrounded by *fiendish* Freemasons!" chuckled another. More guffaws.

Benjamin recognized what was happening. After responding to a crisis that was now over almost as quickly as it had begun, the men were recovering from the rush of adrenalin in their systems. The laughter and joking were normal responses after surviving a dangerous situation. After all, none of them had been the wounded boy lying in pain in the cold and filthy street.

The crowd began to break up. Amid intermittently uttered "good nights," Benjamin turned to go.

"Ben, wait," said Templeman. Stepping close to Benjamin in the dim glow of the gas lamps along the street, the priest said in a low voice, "I heard about Francis. With Delina gone, I know what he must mean to you and I understand what he did is hard for you to bear."

"Look, Father...," Benjamin began, but the priest put his hand on his shoulder and he fell silent.

"I want you to know you aren't alone in this."

Benjamin looked back at his departing lodge brothers. Templeman followed his gaze.

"Yes, you have them. They're your friends, there's no doubt. Although you're not a Catholic and you belong to that - organization, you would be welcomed back to the same pew you occupied with Delina."

Benjamin couldn't help narrowing his eyes when he heard the priest's negative allusion to the Freemasons. He saw the priest react to his change of expression.

That's right, he thought. *You just said the wrong thing and you know it.*

Templeman continued. "I'm not suggesting you fall prostrate before the cross, Ben. I'm not even suggesting you come every week. Just come. You might be surprised at how you'll feel. I won't even expect you to join the Knights of Columbus," he said with a grin.

"I can't join the Knights, Father. I'm not a Catholic, as you just said," Benjamin responded without a smile, not willing to surrender to the priest's humor.

"The Church's doors are open to everyone, Ben."

Benjamin knew the priest was trying, but he couldn't get it out of his mind that Templeman couldn't know how he felt, regardless of all the well-practiced words he learned at the seminary. The priest had never been married, never made love to a woman, and most significant to Benjamin, he'd never had a child. Even Delina, as devout a Catholic as she was, saw the hypocrisy of it all. "How can da *prêtres* tell me," she once complained to Benjamin in her French-Canadian accent, "how many children to have and how to raise dem when dey don't have children demselves? What do they know of my problems, ay? Let da *prêtres* try it demselves before telling others what to do!" Benjamin laughed when she'd said that, but he wasn't laughing now. Even she understood a priest had no real responsibilities beyond tending to his flock, who, truth be told, were the ones providing for the Church and the Church's priests, or *prêtres*, as Delina would have said. Priests were poor all right; "priest poor." Poor in name only. For Benjamin, hypocrisies such as these were insurmountable obstacles.

Anyone who wears that collar has taken the easy way out and lives in a different world.

Benjamin had been aggravated enough by Templeman. The man was always an aggravation, but for all his education he never seemed to realize it. Benjamin had had enough of him. "Good night, Father," was all he could say. He turned and walked to his wagon.

Templeman watched Benjamin until he was out of sight in the darkness. The priest recalled how devout

Delina had been and considered how odd it was that such opposites could attract. He had heard Delina's confessions countless times. He knew Delina was a good person who loved her husband and Francis was a good son who felt the same way. What force was holding Benjamin in its grip? Why could he not reach him?

The priest had another problem to consider. He noticed at least two members of his congregation among the Freemasons. In a very short time, possibly by the end of the month, the Holy See would, for the first time, issue a Code of Canon Law mandating *ipso facto* excommunication of any Catholic man who was a member of a Masonic Lodge.

He couldn't understand the Church's motivation in doing this. After all, this wasn't the twelfth century. The inquisition was over long ago. Templeman didn't believe a loving and forgiving God would condone *ex parte* labeling as evil any of his neighbors in this small town. These good men would be forced to make a choice between their faith and what was, he was sure, just a harmless fraternal group. Did the Pontiff know any Freemasons personally? Yet, a parish priest could not question Rome.

He caught sight of a sign posted over the door of the building. He allowed his eyes to linger upon the Masonic compass and square. After a long moment, he turned in the opposite direction toward Clark Street and began to walk back to the rectory and away from Benjamin.

CHAPTER 9

UNSAID WORDS

Monday, July 16, 1917, dawned with a high, thin overcast.

Benjamin had simply been marking time since receiving Francis' letter. The summer months were busy ones on the farm. Without Francis, Benjamin was stretched to the limit even with the Hiram's help. With the longer days of summer, he often didn't get more than five hours of sleep in a night. It was just as well, Benjamin often thought. The less time he had to think, the better. He wanted to hold off on hiring a second hand, but come harvest time he knew he wouldn't have a choice if he wanted to get the crops to market.

Though still July, Benjamin and Hiram were working on getting the horse-drawn combine ready. Benjamin had just completed hurling another string of obscenities at a stubborn rusted bolt when Hiram suddenly said, "Ben, hush. Can ya hear that sound?"

Benjamin, not knowing what Hiram was talking

about, stopped what he was doing and listened. In the still afternoon air, there was a distant buzzing, like a motorcar over the next hill. It was a sound he'd heard before.

Both men jumped down from the combine and ran toward Benjamin's field. As usual, the cows were grazing lazily; they looked up as Benjamin and Hiram ran down the slope toward them. Hiram was the first to spot the Jenny in the distance toward the east, the mid-afternoon sun glinting off its pair of wings and spinning propeller.

"Quick, get these cows out of the way!" yelled Benjamin. As the noise from the Jenny's ninety-horsepower OX5 engine grew louder, Benjamin and Hiram herded the baffled cows off the soon-to-be landing strip.

Saved the trouble of doing a low pass to scatter the livestock, the machine descended, more or less gracefully, and touched down at the eastern end of the field. It rolled and bounced to a stop with its unwinding propeller pointing westward.

With the engine finally silent and the wooden propeller still, Francis jumped out of the machine shouting "Hi, Pa!" as he stepped onto the lower wing. "Surprised?"

"Good God," Benjamin shouted, stunned to see Francis wearing the uniform of an army private. "What are you doing here? You said you wouldn't be able to make it home before you left for Europe."

Francis hugged his father. "I said I didn't *think* I could make it home before we left. Well, I was wrong! I forgot to consider the influence of Mr. Randolph E. Bridgewater, III, of the *Massachusetts* Bridgewaters." This he said as he shook Hiram's hand.

"Francis, how in blazes are ya? It's sure good to see ya," Hiram managed to say before Bridgewater burst upon the small group. Bridgewater didn't notice Benjamin's less than enthusiastic expression when he caught sight of him.

Francis continued, "We graduated from ground school on Friday and stopped over in Meadville Saturday and Sunday to see some friends. Hey, MIT's a great place by the way. And *Boston*! Wow! Now *that's* a swell place. It makes Pittsburgh look like the far side of the moon! Anyway, Randy still had the Jenny...."

"Good afternoon, sir," interrupted Bridgewater as he greeted Benjamin. He managed to look dapper in his own drab brown uniform that had clearly been tailored by someone who knew his business.

"You see," Bridgewater continued, "I explained to 'the powers that be' that this machine was merely on loan for purposes of evaluation and had to be remanded to the custody of His Majesty's Royal Flying Corps *poste haste*. They were quite agreeable to Francis and I delivering it to New York, which is actually where the Army wants us. That's where we board the ship for Europe."

"A phone call to Major Bingham from Senator Meeks may have been a deciding factor," Francis added, winking at his father and Hiram while gently elbowing Bridgewater in the ribs.

Benjamin repeated, confused. "Major Bingham?"

Francis explained, "Major Hiram Bingham, III, is a National Guard officer and Yale professor who's in charge of all the army's ground schools around the country. He's not a bad guy."

Major Hiram Bingham, III, Benjamin repeated silently to himself. *Another "third;" another rich man ordering youngsters into the smoke and fire.*

"Yale, huh?" Benjamin said, recalling Bridgewater's vehement reaction the last time that institution's name was brought up.

The insinuation wasn't lost on Bridgewater.

"I will forgive the man his Yale connection, sir, given his superior rank and the fact that he subsequently received his doctorate from *Harvard*. In all fairness, Major Bingham is rather famous for having discovered Machu Picchu."

"Macho what?"

"Machu Picchu, Mr. Kyner. Ancient Incan ruins located in the Andes Mountains in Peru. It was quite an exciting find. He led an expedition there in 1911, just a few years ago. It was in newspapers around the world."

Benjamin was unimpressed. "Uh huh. Well, getting back to what's important, it looks like my field is becoming a regular, what d'ya call it? An 'aerodrome'?"

"And a fine aerodrome it is, sir," added Bridgewater, in a rather fawning tone.

"We'd better move your machine into the barn before the cows remember how good it tastes," ordered Benjamin. The four of them maneuvered the flying machine up the slight hill to safety.

The four men visited for a while. Then, as Benjamin started to put together supper, Hiram said his goodbyes as it was time for him to get home to Sarah. Francis followed him outside on the pretext of saying a longer farewell.

They walked a short distance away. After looking back to make sure they were far enough from the house to prevent Benjamin from overhearing them, Francis turned to Hiram. "I'm worried about Pa, Hiram. I know this is hard on him, but I've just got to do this. I feel terrible about it, but I can't help myself."

"You're a young man, Francis. This is the time of your life when you got to go your own way. It would be different, ya know, if your Ma was still alive. As it is, you're all Ben's got left of her. You're all he's got left in the world. You're right, it's hard on him, but it ain't really your fault. It means a lot to your Pa that you came home to say good-bye."

"Hiram, I know you'll watch him. When I get back after this is all over, things'll be fine. I just need to know you'll be here for him."

"Don't you worry about that, Francis. I'll be here with Ben. You just make sure you keep your head down so you can come home in one piece. Your Pa is a lot more worried about you than you are about him. Remember, he knows what it's like to be in a war. Just get yourself home."

Looking Francis directly in the eye as he offered his hand, Hiram said, "Now, may the good Lord bless ya and keep ya."

The two exchanged grips for a long moment then embraced. Francis returned to the house as Hiram began his walk home to Black Hollow.

Benjamin distrusted Bridgewater. It wasn't simply that he was rich and came from a different world. The boy clearly had never had any real responsibilities. The off-handed way he spoke about his reckless behavior at Harvard was proof enough for Benjamin that Bridgewater didn't know how to take responsibility seriously. Remembering how he and his fellow soldiers depended on each other to stay alive, Benjamin hoped that Francis was never in a situation in which he had to depend on Bridgewater.

Regardless, Benjamin did his best to make sure supper and the rest of his son's stay was amiable. He knew he wouldn't see Francis again until the war was over. He didn't care if he ever saw Bridgewater again.

There was still plenty of light when they finished cleaning up after dinner. Francis said something to Bridgewater and then approached his father.

"Pa, there's something I'd like to do before we leave tomorrow morning," he said.

Turning toward Francis, Benjamin responded, "And what would that be?"

Benjamin and Francis took their time as they walked along Athena-Evangeline Road. Bridgewater had tactfully excused himself by saying he wanted to check on the Jenny and explore the farm.

Walking the same route as they had together and separately many times, Francis told his father what he had studied at the Army's pre-flight ground school at MIT. He explained such things as aerodynamics, how the forces of thrust, drag, lift and gravity affect a heavier-than-air machine, how the machines are maneuvered in flight, cross-country navigation, and ground-to-air signaling.

Francis noticed his father hadn't asked about how the machines were used at the front.

Well, he doesn't have to, thought Francis. *He's read the newspapers.*

As they strode along at a relaxed pace, Frances sensed a strange feeling creeping over him. He had walked these roads all his life, but now, knowing he would be leaving for an indefinite length of time and an uncertain future, it was almost as though he was seeing it all through a stranger's eyes. Everything familiar to him seemed new. He kept this thought to himself.

Reaching their destination, Francis and Benjamin walked past the stones that gave silent testimony to the spent lives of their friends and neighbors. Finally, they approached Delina's grave. Francis had come to say good-bye to his mother.

Benjamin knelt down to once again clear away the weeds that had sprouted since his last visit. There weren't many. Needing some outlet for his nervous tension, Francis began to help him.

"Look, Pa," Francis began, "This whole thing can't last long. Now that America is in the fight, the Germans can't last. I'll be home and back in college before you know it."

Benjamin stood, his eyes downcast. Then, looking into his son's face, he said, "Francis, we've already had this discussion. You're 21 and can make your own decisions. You know I'm not much of a prayin' man, but I want you to know I've prayed for you. I've knelt on this spot - on your mother's grave - and prayed that you come home alive. If you don't, I don't know what I'll do. My world will be over."

Francis felt his throat tighten and his eyes moisten. "I'll get home, Pa."

Nothing else could be said. The two men - father and son - embraced next to the grave of the woman who was their wife and mother.

After a protracted silence, Francis finally spoke. "Pa, there is something you have to know. I've got a girlfriend back in Meadville."

"All right. I suppose that's not a surprise. Do you expect her to wait around for you?"

"She said she would. I think things are getting pretty serious. If it weren't for - *this* happening I would've brought her home to meet you by now. Her name is Eleanor Bennett."

"Uh huh. Does she go to school there, too?"

"No, she's actually one of the college librarians. That's how I met her. She helped me do some research for a history paper at the beginning of the year. She's a great gal, Pa. I know you'll like her."

Benjamin looked at his son. "You just get yourself home safe. There'll be plenty of time for me to like her then." Benjamin turned and looked toward the west.

Francis could see his father wasn't interested in what he probably thought was just another college girlfriend. Given the circumstances, Francis couldn't blame him. There was more he had to say about Eleanor, a great deal more, but being torn between the need to speak and wanting to keep this last night with his father peaceful, Francis held his tongue.

In the distance the sun was threatening to sink below the silo of their farm. With a final look at the headstone, Benjamin and Francis turned and walked away.

After reaching the main road, Francis said, "Pa, if it's all the same to you, I'd kind of like to walk through Athena one more time. I'll see you at home, okay?"

"Sure. There's no moon tonight. Don't get lost in the dark."

Later, as he was climbing the hill to the farm,

Benjamin noticed darkness was falling much sooner than he expected.

The next morning an earlier scene was repeated.

After yet another handshake, another hug, and a final wave, Benjamin stood alone on his field watching the Jenny lift slowly into the air.

Startled by a low rumble, Benjamin turned and saw roiling slate-colored clouds approaching from the west. The storm would follow his Francis. He uttered a quick, silent prayer that he could stay ahead of it.

Turning back eastward, Benjamin watched the fragile Jenny shrink until he could no longer see it against the rising sun. Again, he heard the peal of thunder.

CHAPTER 10

LETTERS HOME

It had been months since Benjamin watched Francis and Bridgewater take off from his field and disappear into the rising Pennsylvania sun.

Since then, Benjamin received a number of letters from Francis describing his training, the places he'd been in England and Scotland, and a few of the new friends he'd made.

According to the letter Benjamin now held in his hand, Francis and his idiot friend Bridgewater had finished - maybe "survived" would be a better word - their training and where now near the front in France.

February 3, 1918

Dear Pa,

Well, Randy and I finally arrived at our new

squadron in France. We're ten miles from the front lines. I have to say our reception was a bit chilly, and I don't mean because of the lousy European weather.

Our new C.O., a Canadian named Card, seems good enough, but the "old-timers" are keeping their distance. By "old-timers," I mean guys who've been here for more than a month or two. One man in particular, a Brit, kept staring at me like I'd done something to offend him. This went on for a while until I decided to introduce myself and ask him what was going on. When I walked up to him and held out my hand, he just turned around and walked away. I thought maybe he was put out because another American was in his squadron. We were warned some of the English feel that way. It turns out his best friend was killed only two days before Randy and I arrived and I got his room. Lucky me. When I found out I was sleeping in a dead man's bed, I got a chill down my spine, but I'm over it now. All of the newer guys are in the same boat.

I know you must be worried, but please don't be. I've been up a few times since I got here. As a matter of fact, Randy and I went up the day we arrived. I was chased once or twice and I went after a few Huns myself, but nothing came of any of it. I think we're doing this to entertain the generals on the ground more than anything else. We've heard all the stories about how bad it is in the air, but so far all that seems to be false advertising. Hey! Do you think I should I ask for my money back? Hah!

We're flying British S.E.5a single-seaters. The British Army mechanics seem to know their stuff and are taking good care of us.

At any rate, the fun times we had training in

England and Scotland are behind us. There was certainly no shortage of distractions in those places, although there are certainly diversions here in France. I hope we can stop at some of the old haunts on the way home and relive "the old days," but now it's time to get down to the real work! At least I hope it is.

The squadron has lost a good number of pilots, but I'm not really concerned. Randy's not worried either. Of course, I've never seen Randy worry about anything. We lost a fair number of friends during training. If Randy and I made it through that, we figure there's not much the Germans can do to us.

I'm sure glad Mom taught me French when I was growing up. It really helps break the ice when I meet the locals around here, but they always want to know why I have a Canadian accent! She always said someday I'd be glad I learned it. How did she know?

That's it for now, Pa. Say hello to Hiram for me. I'll write again soon.

Love,
Francis

Benjamin lowered the letter and looked at the blazing logs in the fireplace. He recalled what it was like to be a young soldier waiting for his first action. Looking down at Francis' signature, he said, "It's only a matter of time, Francis. It's only a matter of time. Then you'll know."

The British sergeant grimaced as he surveyed the battered machine in front of him. "Bloody fookin' 'ell.

Will ya look at that mess! I ain't never seen nothin' near as bad."

"I - I'm sorry, Sergeant," stammered Francis, misunderstanding. "D - Don't worry about it. I'll clean it up." Francis was doubled over at the tail of his S.E.5a. He'd just landed and had only just managed to get out of the cockpit when his stomach turned inside out and propelled its contents not only on the ground, but also all over the olive-drab fabric of the British machine.

"Eh? What's that?" said the sergeant. He spun around and caught sight of Francis. As he walked toward him, he said, "Oh, no. I weren't talkin' to you, Leftenant. I din' see ya there. Ya was curled up into too small a ball pukin' your guts all over the place. I'm talkin' 'bout all the damned Hun bullet holes in ya crate. I gotta patch 'em, me an' the boys, that is if they *can* be patched." The sergeant again looked at the bullet-riddled fuselage. Shaking his head, he muttered, "Sweet Mother of Jesus."

Francis nodded to the man, then turned away and retched again.

"It was ya first time, wasn't it, suh?" asked the sergeant, who was in charge of maintenance for Francis' squadron.

"What?" asked Francis. He looked up and wiped his mouth on his sleeve.

"Ya still new, suh. I'm wonderin' if this was ya first real dog fight with the Hun bastards. Never mind. I can tell it was."

Francis nodded. He didn't want to risk opening his mouth again.

"Well, dunna ya worry, suh. Ya lived through it, that's the thing. Many of the new 'uns don't, ya know. They go out in one of my pretty machines and that's the last we see of 'em. Ya ain't the first to come back and puke ya guts out. A lot of 'em do just that. And ya managed to get out of the machine, first. Many can't. It makes a pretty mess in the cockpit, I can tell ya."

Francis was now wishing the sergeant would shut up and go away.

"And many of 'em soil their trousers. Ain't their fault, o'course. It's the same in the trenches. I can see that you din' do that to yourself, suh. Smell ya a mile away if ya had."

Jesus, man. For the love of God, please shut up, thought Francis.

"Are ya hurt, suh? Any holes in ya? Ya need a medic?"

For the first time, Francis thought to examine himself. He wasn't wounded. It had to be a miracle. "No. I guess not."

"What's this then?" asked the sergeant. He bent down and brushed Francis' right shoulder with his hand.

Francis looked. His padded flight suit had a neat tear across the shoulder. He wasn't aware a bullet had grazed him. He was lucky. Another fraction of an inch and the bullet would have ripped open his shoulder.

"The good Lord smiled on ya today, suh. Did ya get one of 'em, Leftenant? Did ya at least make 'em pay fa' the damages?"

Francis, now thoroughly miserable, only shook his head.

"Ah, well. Next time, then. Well, ya'll have ta 'scuse me, suh. I got to go round up m'boys to take care of all them damned holes."

The sergeant snapped a salute British style, with the palm turned out. Francis only had strength to nod in acknowledgment. The sergeant turned on his heel and walked toward the maintenance hangar.

As he struggled to recover from his baptism under fire, Francis thought of what his father had said when he told him he'd enlisted: *I guarantee you, Francis. It won't be like you imagine. No glory. No drum rolls.... You'll see your friends, wounded, maimed and killed. They could see the same things happen to you. When you're dead tired and scared to death, you won't be able to go running to your mother.* Then the fear he felt in the air returned. He shivered.

"Francis!" someone yelled. "Francis, are you okay?" Bridgewater ran from the other side of the S.E.5a.

"Randy! Over here," shouted Francis, finally able to speak.

Bridgewater ran up to him, but stopped short before he stepped in the remains of Francis' breakfast. "Christ," he said. "Are you're okay? You look like hell."

Francis stood up. "Yeah. How about you?"

"I'm fine. My ship's a little the worse for wear. We lost two, you know."

"Yeah," said Francis. "Did you get off any shots?"

"Oh, hell, yeah," Bridgewater said. "I got off lots of shots. I didn't hit a damned thing, though, if that's what you're getting at."

"Me, neither." said Francis.

"Well," said Bridgewater, "I know Bobby Card got one. At least that's something."

Bridgewater stepped back and surveyed the damage to Francis' S.E.5a. He blanched. "Holy Christ!" That was all he could say. He turned to look at Francis.

Thinking again of his father, Francis said, "Randy, the party's over. We're not in Pennsylvania anymore."

Benjamin reached into his mailbox. It had been weeks since he last received a letter from Francis. He'd been in France for several months and had flown a number of missions against the Germans and he'd seen his new friends die. It worried Benjamin that Francis seemed to be aging quickly. He was becoming more cynical with each letter and the interval between his letters was growing longer.

Benjamin knew that Francis had initially taken pains to shield him from the horror of what he was witnessing. Benjamin had done the same for his parents. But he'd begun to notice that as the weeks and months passed, Francis was, probably unwittingly, allowing Benjamin to see the war though his eyes.

Benjamin examined the pile of letters, flyers and bills. Finally! There it was. He tore it open the letter and began to read.

March 17, 1918

Pa,

Now I understand why the Army paints aviators as glorious aerial warriors and commissions those beautiful Air Service recruiting posters by the thousands. Those posters wouldn't even recruit convicts if they showed how things really are. Flying in this war is hell. If the truth were known, the aerodromes would be empty.

As a matter of fact, I think Hell would be a relief. Maybe I'll find out.

Death is random for both sides. Your fate often rests on chance and chance alone. A Hun may pick you out because the sunlight just happens to glint off your wings or propeller or for no particular reason at all. The same is true the other way 'round.

A short time ago, some Members of Parliament arrived from London to check up on us. Just after they got here a friend's machine was shot to pieces during a patrol and he was killed when he crashed on landing. The politicians attended the funeral, which was fine until one of them started to talk. A Sir Archibald Morus gave a little speech during which he quoted a line from Horace; "Dulce et decorum est pro patria mori," which means, "It is sweet and proper to die for one's country." The man's a fool and a leech. It wasn't his son or brother lying in that grave, nor does he ever risk his own life, but he has no problems encouraging others to fly into the mouth of the devil. Damn him to Hell.

Randy Bridgewater is still among the living, thank God, but even he doesn't smile or laugh anymore, except in hysterical bursts at the strangest times and then he can't stop. He told me the other day that when he was a kid he hated waking up to the sound of rain because it meant he'd have to stay indoors all day. But now when he hears rain on the roof in the morning he's relieved because he knows we won't be flying and no one will be killed, at least not that day. The rain is a blessing.

Would you be surprised to know I've had my ship to over 20,000 feet? Everything is different at that altitude; the air is thin and you become dizzy easily. It's difficult to think and any movement you make is exhausting. In the thin air the motor loses power and becomes balky and the controls lose effectiveness; you can lose several hundred feet in a simple turn, which is not a good thing when you're in a fight with a Hun. At such a height even during the summer it's so cold it can snow and your wings can ice up if you pass through a cloud. Hands and feet go numb and the castor oil from the engine coats any part of you that's exposed, which is one reason why we wear silk scarves - to wipe our goggles. Being given a constant diet of castor oil is why they say pilots are such "regular" fellows! Hah!

Oh, for the green hills of Pennsylvania! The hills here have all been stripped of trees and grass that have been replaced by craters punched into the earth by the incessant pounding of artillery. The world so far beneath us brings to mind a painting by a mad artist who's trying to recreate Hell using only gray and brown paint. It's incredible that human beings - who can't even be seen from that height - are responsible for creating such desolation.

You were right, Pa. This isn't what I thought it would be. I swear that once I get home I'll never leave again! If I ever have a son, I hope he's born with some kind of physical problem that will keep him out of the Army so there will never be a chance he'll have to go through anything like this. It would also stop him from doing to me what I did to you. I'm sorry, Pa.

I hope I can sleep tonight. I'll write some more tomorrow if it rains.

Love,
Francis

Benjamin read the letter again while still standing at the mailbox. Then he folded it, put it back in its envelope, and walked along the dirt track to the house uttering a short prayer for his son.

Meanwhile, in France, it hadn't rained.

CHAPTER 11

THE FREEMASON AND THE PRIEST

As Templeman knew would happen, the hammer fell on Pentecost Sunday, May 27, 1917, when the Vatican issued the Code of Canon Law. As expected, included was an injunction against Catholic men becoming Freemasons: *Those who join a Masonic sect or other societies of the same sort, which plot against the Church or against legitimate civil authority, incur ipso facto an excommunication....*

Although promulgated in May, 1917, the revised law, including Canon 2335, which dealt with Freemasonry and "societies of the same sort," did not take effect until a year later, on Sunday, May 19, 1918.

So, on a Sunday morning in March 1918, as the armies and navies of the world were in the process of tearing each other apart, Father James Templeman stood in the pulpit of Saint Mary's. He looked out over his congregation and prepared to fulfill his vow of obedience.

"Brothers and sisters, our Pontiff, His Holiness Benedict XV, has directed the issuance of a Code of Canon Law, the law which circumscribes the faithful. I believe there are aspects of the law that will have very direct effects on certain members of Saint Mary's parish...."

"Damn it, Frank. I understand the problem. I just don't understand what you want me to do about it. I'm not the pope. I'm not even Catholic. He's not gonna listen to me."

Benjamin and Frank Zieglar, now master of Harmonie Lodge No. 924, were walking the length of Benjamin's field in the waning light of a cool early spring day. America had been at war for almost one year.

"It doesn't matter so much that you're not Catholic, Ben. Your wife was a member of Saint Mary's and your son is a member. Father Templeman knows you. He saw you in Church with Delina every Sunday."

"But still...."

"Brother Ben, our lodge is losing some good members because the pope said he'll excommunicate them if they don't leave on their own. It's not fair and it's not right. It's not fair to those men and it's not fair to the Fraternity. None of us has done anything to the Catholic Church. Damn! The country is at war. Isn't there enough trouble in the world without something like this coming at us out of the blue?"

"Frank, I've got a son in this war. You don't have to tell *me*. But since you brought it up, I have enough to worry about. There's not a day goes by that I'm not scared I'll find a Western Union man at my door with a telegram telling me Francis is dead. With every letter I get from him, I can see he's changing. I'm afraid for him, Frank. I'm afraid he'll be killed and if he isn't, I'm afraid he'll come back so different I won't know him. Either way, I could lose my son. I just don't care about Templeman, his pope or his church. If the Catholic guys in the lodge want to pick the pope over us, then so be it. I just can't worry myself about it. D'ya understand?"

"Look, Ben...."

"Besides, Frank, what do you want from Templeman? He's just a priest in a small church in a small town. He can't do anything to change what's happened. Even if he could, why would he? He works for the pope. You and I both have better things to do than go crawling to him."

"How do you know until you ask him?" said Zieglar. "It's been a few weeks since Templeman made the announcement. Maybe something's come up we don't know about - some way those guys can stay in the lodge. I don't know, maybe if they light enough altar candles? At least get him to explain why this is being done. *Catholic* law? *Jesus!*"

"Frank, I...."

"Please, Ben. I'm asking as a brother. Just give it a try. Talk to Templeman just once. I'm not asking you to grovel on the floor of the church. Just ask him. What can it hurt?"

Benjamin heaved a sigh of exasperation. "All right, Frank. You win, dammit. I was hoping never to have to talk to that damned priest again, but I will if you want me to, for all the good it will do."

"Thanks, Ben. Drop by afterwards and let me know what he said, will ya?

Benjamin watched as Zieglar climbed up into the seat of his wagon. Zieglar turned and gave Benjamin a wave, then flicked the reigns and headed the horses toward Athena.

Benjamin pondered this new situation.

After everything that's happened, now this. The pope wants to kick dues-paying members out of the Church, so now I have to talk to that damned priest. Could things get any worse?

The sound of the main door opening and closing brought Templeman out of St Mary's sacristy at the rear of the church. He saw Benjamin in the center aisle walking toward him. He knew why he was there.

"So, you're their emissary?"

"Whatever you want to call it. It's not my idea. Frank Zieglar came by my place a few days ago and asked me to talk to you. You scared off all the Catholics in the lodge and he figured I was the best choice since Delina belonged to Saint Mary's."

"Well, I expected they'd send someone, but I have to admit I never considered you, Ben, not considering your obvious attitude toward the Church. I thought they'd send one of your members who's a minister at one of the protestant churches."

Damn, thought Templeman, *Why him of all people? Could this get any worse?*

"I suppose we're not that clever, Father - or that sinister. We're honest, simple men. We'd make poor politicians. I suppose they thought you'd see a minister as a rival. To Frank it seemed reasonable for me to speak to you since my wife was a member of your parish. That's all there is to it."

"I see. Well, a couple of parishioners who are, or *were*, lodge members dropped by when no one was around to make sure they understood correctly. I told them what I expect I'll be telling you."

"Which is?"

"Which is, Ben, there's nothing I can do about it. The Holy See - the pope - has promulgated a Code of Canon Law, which includes a prohibition against Catholics becoming Freemasons. If they do, they're automatically excommunicated. As you just said, 'that's all there is to it.' Your Catholic lodge brothers have to make a choice: Freemasonry or the Church. It's just that simple."

Templeman noticed Benjamin clench his jaw.

"That's what I told Zieglar you'd say. I told him I'd be wasting my time talking to you. You people have made up your minds. It doesn't matter that those men are successful hardworking citizens. It doesn't matter that they're businessmen and farmers who contribute to this town and put money in your collection basket. None of that makes a difference to you and your Holy Roman Catholic Church, does it? You don't see a man. All you see is a Freemason, or what you think a Freemason is. Nothing else about him matters."

Templeman was surprised Benjamin was still there. He'd fully expected him to turn around and walk out of the church once he'd gotten the answer he must have known he'd get.

Why is he still here? Who is he really angry at, the Church or me?

"Why is this happening now?" Benjamin continued. "How old is your Church? 1,900 years? You'd think this would have come up before now, in the middle of a world war. Don't they have anything more important to do in Rome?"

Templeman gestured toward the front pew. "Let's sit down, Ben," he said with a note of resignation, "we're going to be here for awhile."

They sat down and turned to face each other in the pew.

"Ben, this isn't 'coming out of the blue,' as you put it. Catholics have been forbidden from becoming Freemasons for almost 200 years. Simply because we haven't gone around hitting people over the head doesn't mean they shouldn't have known about the prohibition against joining a Masonic Lodge. One reason the Knights of Columbus was created was to provide Catholic men with an alternative to Freemasonry. That's no secret."

"It still isn't right to throw a man out of his church because he joined a fraternal group. That seems more like something the Kaiser would do or maybe those Communists in Russia we keep reading about in the papers."

"Ben, there's a misunderstanding, but it's a common one. No one is excommunicated *from* the Church. Being excommunicated simply means a Catholic can no longer receive the sacraments, such as Communion and absolution of sins. That means he can't fully participate in the life of the Church. Excommunication is either formal or informal. There are a number of offenses that automatically incur informal excommunication without any action being taken by a Church official. Becoming a Freemason is one of them."

"Are you saying the Catholics in my lodge have already been excommunicated?"

"Yes," Templeman said. "They were excommunicated the moment they took their first Masonic oath. But all they have to do to have the excommunication lifted is to resign from the lodge and confess to a priest. Organizations have rules, Ben. Men who join your lodge and become Masons agree to follow your rules, don't they? So do Catholics."

"Maybe it's not that simple," replied Benjamin. "This doesn't seem to be about religion, Father. This isn't about worshiping God or Jesus Christ. This isn't about compassion and forgiveness. This is about *control*. This is about the Roman Catholic Church maintaining as much control as it can over its members so the pope and his cardinals, bishops and priests can keep their fat cat jobs. Without your so-called *faithful* to do the working and the earning and the paying, all you priests would have to go out and get real jobs. You think Freemasonry is a threat to all that because you have no control over it. Hah! That's what really going on!"

Templeman struggled to maintain control. *This man is sitting in my church and attacking my faith. What gives him that right?*

"Ben, you're making my next point for me. What you just said is both anti-Catholic and anti-Papist. *That's* the issue my Church has with your Freemasonry! That's why our pope and other popes before him have condemned it! Maybe you're the one who's ignorant and prejudiced!"

Benjamin rose from the pew and walked toward the altar rail a few feet away. He turned to face Templeman. His arms were crossed and his back was to the altar. The scene struck Templeman; the crucified Christ, suspended over the altar, appeared to be looking down at Benjamin in sad contemplation as though listening to his every word in judgment. For a few seconds, Templeman was rattled by the image.

"That's idiotic, Templeman. The Catholic Church threw the first punch. For as long as I've been a Mason, I've heard no one, I repeat, *no one*, utter a single word against Catholics or the pope. We're not even supposed to talk about religion in the lodge - or politics for that matter. Masonry allows men of different faiths and politics and backgrounds to get together as equals. Politics and religion are sources of too many differences that can lead to arguments. We leave it all alone. To be a Mason, a man just has to believe in God. Period. We don't care what religion a man practices or if he even practices one at all, as long as he believes in God."

Templeman looked down and took a deep breath. He then he lifted his eyes and looked at Benjamin.

"Ben, we believe the Roman Catholic Church is the one true faith. By stating a man's religion is irrelevant for admission to Freemasonry, that in the view of Freemasonry all religions, or even lack of religion, are viewed as *equal*, Freemasonry is heretical. The Masonic concept of religious equality is viewed as proof that Freemasons champion the downfall of *all* religions, specifically Catholicism. Not only that, but if religion is held to be irrelevant, justice and morality will follow."

"I can't believe I'm hearing this from an intelligent and educated person," said Benjamin. "Even Delina never spoke like this, and she was a devout as they come. We never said religion doesn't matter in a man's life! We only hold religion doesn't matter as far as *joining a lodge* is concerned, not that we want all religions eliminated! You've twisted the meaning of a rule that was meant to bring men together as equals."

"Ben, please listen to me. There's no doubt in my mind your lodge isn't *explicitly* anti-Catholic in that you aren't consciously conspiring against the Church or the pope. But you have to understand that the idea that a man's religion is irrelevant is heretical. Therefore, Freemasonry is *implicitly* anti-Catholic and that makes it an enemy of the Church. Now you can see why no man who is a Freemason can be accepted as a Roman Catholic."

"No," Benjamin said, "I can't see that. When I was a young man in the Army they told us that just because we have to take orders doesn't mean we don't have to think. That was one of the few things I learned in the Army that made any sense. I realized that on a battlefield my only defense against stupidity was thinking. That lesson was driven home when I left Cuba alive. A lot of my friends didn't. I remembered that lesson, Father. Ever since then, I've made it my business to give a lot of thought to what's important to my family and me. And just because I'm a dirt farmer, doesn't mean I don't read. I do. I read as much as I can. I do it in self-defense."

"Look, Ben...."

"No. Let me finish. The reason I got back from Cuba was because I refused to swallow anything on blind faith. I don't believe in it. I suppose that's why I'm not so religious. Just because someone I'm supposed to be able to trust says a thing, doesn't mean it's so. That includes you, Father. What I see here is ignorance and prejudice. Considering us heretical just because we don't care about a man's religion is pretty paltry stuff. There has to be some other reason why the Church would be so hell-bent to vilify a fraternal organization. What I see are church bosses condemning a group of men they don't know anything about and don't want to know anything about. Why? I still think it's because the pope is terrified of losing control over the members who pay the bills."

Templeman's anger was rising. He stood up. "Ben, we can have a reasonable discussion or we can have a shouting match. You came to me and you're in God's house. Please respect that or we can't continue."

"If you want me to respect you, then you respect me and my organization - an organization of millions of good men who have done a lot of good for a lot of people." Benjamin kept his arms crossed over his chest and looked at Templeman.

"Ben, I'm not making any of this up. To answer your question, over 30 years ago the pope at the time, Pope Leo XIII, issued what is known as a papal encyclical. It was titled *Humanum Genus,* the Human Species, but that's not important. What *is* important is that it detailed the objections the Church has to Freemasonry. It still applies today."

"Really? So what other heinous and heretical beliefs are we guilty of?"

Templeman could see the veins in Benjamin's neck were pounding.

I wonder if the veins in my neck are bulging like his?

"Please, Ben. Listen to me. You aren't going to like this, but please be calm so we can have a rational discussion."

Benjamin's expression changed from one of anger to suspicion.

Chapter 12

Lille

Francis, Bridgewater, and four others were assigned to an afternoon patrol along the front near Nieppe, northwest of Lille. The area had once been known as the aerial hunting ground of the infamous German ace Max Immelmann, killed almost 18 months earlier, in June 1916.

They formed a wedge-shaped flight of six Royal Flying Corps S.E.5a's at 12,000 feet. As they approached "no man's land," all six pilots, most now veterans, continually twisted and craned their necks to see above, below, and behind them as they kept formation with their flight leader, Captain Robert Card, R.F.C., a Canadian hailing from Nova Scotia.

Their instructors back in Ayrs, Scotland, persistently pounded into them the life-saving maxim: "Beware of the Hun in the sun."

A favorite German tactic was to fly far above the allied patrol altitudes. After spotting the enemy, the

Germans would maneuver to place themselves between them and the sun. Diving with the sun behind them, they were all but invisible until the first fusillade of machine gun fire raked the allied machines.

Francis was flying ahead of and to the left of Bridgewater, who occupied the rear of the formation. The rear was the most dangerous position because that's where the enemy was most likely to strike, for he could do so unseen by his quarry.

At 12,000 feet the temperature was well below freezing and the relentless sound of their engines combined with the rushing wind created an ear-deadening cacophony.

The pilots grew tense as they approached the front lines. They knew that after crossing no man's land they would be in enemy territory and could expect to be met either by enemy fighters or air defense fire, nicknamed "archie" by the British. The largest projectiles weighed 40 pounds and were able to devour sky at almost 3,000 feet per second. They could easily shred the fabric-covered machines - and the men of flesh and blood within.

When they finally arrived over the front, Francis looked down and saw the long stretches of segmented lines that were the trenches. Scarring the earth as far as the eye could see, Francis saw each slit as a separate Hell in which the damned were confined. In each miserable hole soldiers awaited yet another order, given in French or German or English, to go "over the top" and into oblivion.

Francis shook his head to clear his mind. He couldn't allow himself to be distracted by such thoughts. He continued scanning the sky.

Looking to his left, he saw Winters, one of the newer replacement pilots. Francis had made a conscious effort not to get to know Winters, nor any of the other newer arrivals, since the chances were they wouldn't be alive for long.

As they each searched for the enemy, their eyes met. Winters waved a greeting. Recalling that when he was new and naïve he'd been as cheerful as Winters, Francis lifted his arm and gave a short wave in return. Without warning, as though Francis had given a signal, Winters was engulfed in a sudden storm of splintered wood and shredded fabric. As machine gun bullets passed through him, the man burst like a balloon filled with strawberry jam. Flames and smoke erupted from the engine cowling as the S.E.5a banked sharply to the right, directly toward Francis, and then dove almost straight down.

The destruction of Winters' machine seemed to have taken only a split second. In that same split second, as Francis watched yet another squadron mate die, his own S.E.5a began shaking violently. Before he could react, massive holes appeared in both upper and lower left wings and bright red German tracer rounds flew within inches of his face.

Almost simultaneously, a German Albatros D.III passed over him and pulled up from its strafing run, the roar of its engine adding to the tumult around him. Another Albatros, presumably the one that killed Winters, dove through the formation of British S.E.5a's and followed Winters down.

At least half a dozen multi-colored Albatros D.IIIs, possibly more, dove out of the sun. Some passed through the formation while others pulled up rolling and turning like sharks in a feeding frenzy. All began to turn back toward the British machines, which had begun to scatter in pursuit of individual foes.

Francis frantically spun his head around looking for more Albatroses. He saw only Bridgewater's S.E.5a maneuvering violently. He couldn't tell if Bridgewater had been hit.

In the distance ahead, Francis saw an Albatros in a climbing right turn. He slammed his motor's throttle forward and aimed his S.E.5a at the German. If the enemy pilot were successful, he would have the advantage of "the high ground" and thus be in a position to dive swiftly down on Francis. Francis willed his machine to climb faster.

Francis' S.E.5a had two machine guns. A belt-fed Vickers was mounted ahead of him on the cowling and was synchronized to fire through the spinning propeller. A drum-fed Lewis gun was mounted atop the upper wing and placed just forward of the cockpit.

Following suggestions from more experienced pilots, he had rigged the firing mechanisms of both machine guns together so the pull of one trigger fired both weapons. He had only to capture the enemy in the sight of the Vickers gun and pull its trigger and both machine guns would send converging streams of bullets exactly where Francis wanted them.

In the months since he'd arrived at the front, Francis had accomplished this, more or less as planned, on four prior occasions. This would be his fifth kill, thus making him an ace.

Francis looked rapidly around to ensure he wasn't being "jumped" by one of the Hun's friends. Seeing none, he applied all of his concentration on his target.

The Albatros had reversed course and was now about 500 feet above Francis and several hundred yards distant. Francis was still climbing. The enemy pilot could choose either to elude Francis now and find another target, or press on with his advantage of altitude and resulting speed. If he chose stay and fight, he could attack Francis while retaining the option to rapidly peel off and get away. He chose to fight.

Francis concentrated on the bullet-nosed plywood missile hurtling at him with the two flickering, cowl-mounted, Spandau machine guns. Tracers from the Albatros flew between the wings of the S.E.5a, but Francis didn't notice them. His entire world consisted only of the enemy in his gun sight. He was only vaguely aware of the Spandaus' 7.92mm rounds slamming into the wood and canvas around him. Francis didn't waiver.

When the moment was right, without thinking, without any conscious calculation he was aware of, but based purely on instinct borne from experience and desperation, Francis pressed the trigger. The angry roar of both machine guns overpowered the tormented scream of the 200 horsepower engine as it flung the huge four-bladed propeller in a frenzied arc.

Charging upward either toward victory or extinction, an adrenaline-fueled primal urge deep within him suddenly burst through Francis' consciousness. Just as countless numbers of his brothers-in-arms below had done when they poured over the top of the trenches and charged into to fire-breathing enemy guns, he began to scream; *Eeeyaaaaahhhhhhhhhh!*

The deranged rush toward the unknown lasted for an eternity - and for an instant.

Without warning, a blinding flash and thunderous

roar told Francis his engine had exploded. *This is finally it,* he thought. He would either burn to death as he plunged toward the ground or, if he crashed and miraculously lived, he would be a prisoner of war. The fight had drifted over the German lines.

But he flew on. The sky ahead was empty. The German was gone. Removing his finger from the trigger, thus silencing his guns, he pushed the control stick forward and to the right and banked the S.E.5a into a steep arc.

After reversing direction but seeing nothing, Francis banked to the left and searched the void between himself and the earth.

Far below, he saw a swiftly diminishing ball of flame at the end of a long trail of swirling smoke. It was like looking at a falling meteor.

Thanks, Mom. The words appeared in his mind unbidden.

Searching the sky around him for another target and to ensure no German was "bouncing" him from the rear, Francis instantly absorbed what he saw. It was a maelstrom. He hovered on the edge of a swirling vortex of screaming machines of war. The roar of his engine assaulted his ears. His face was frozen by the propeller blast. Adrenaline coursed through his veins heightening his senses and blinding him to much of his physical discomfort. Multi-colored craft decorated in red, white and blue roundels and black Maltese crosses dove, swooped, and rolled around each other like furies in a tempest. The air was filled with glowing red trails of tracer rounds reaching from one craft toward another and dark arcing trails of smoke from burning engines. Francis was in a pilot's Hell.

The fight had carried Francis higher, but his squadron and the Germans were all around him. Below, Bridgewater, who had successfully shaken off an attacker during the Albatroses' first assault, was engaged with another Hun.

Flinging his machine at the Albatros, Bridgewater fired relentlessly as he banked left in a shallow dive to keep the enemy in his sights. The Albatros suddenly lurched straight up and seemed to be climbing insanely before stalling. Then it slid backwards, finally dropping into a spin that carried it and its dead pilot to the waiting earth below.

Exhausted by the two encounters yet exhilarated at being alive, Bridgewater committed a fatal sin.

At that moment, Francis chanced to look down and recognized his friend, who had just killed his third German. Francis couldn't believe what he saw. Into the din, he shouted uselessly, *"Randy, what the hell are you doing?"*

CHAPTER 13

HUMANUM GENUS

Looking Benjamin squarely in the eye, Templeman began. "In addition to the Masonic tenet that men of any religion may join, *Humanum Genus* specifically condemned Freemasonry for supporting the concepts that civil law should be uninfluenced by Catholicism and governments should be formed without regard to the Church; that children should receive secular educations without the influence of religion; that rulers govern only with the consent of the governed and that that consent can be rescinded by the people; and people have complete equality in civil matters and are, in fact, equal in all ways."

Benjamin unfolded his arms and put his hands in the rear pockets of his overalls. He turned and took a few steps away from Templeman, then turned and faced him. The look on his face wasn't one of anger or suspicion, but of perplexity.

"The pope, or the Church, has accused us, as Freemasons, of believing in equality, separation of church and state, the secular education of children, and government controlled by the governed. Is that really what you just said?

"Pope Leo XIII did so in his encyclical, yes."

"And the Church still abides by all that?"

"Yes, Ben. The encyclical is still in force."

Benjamin's eyes narrowed as he looked at Templeman. Then, in a low voice devoid of anger but laden with accusation, he said, "But those ideas helped form the very bedrock of American liberty laid down by the founding fathers. Men like Jefferson, Franklin, Madison, Adams and Washington. Those ideas are some of the foundation stones of our way of life."

"Ben, two of the men you mentioned were Freemasons."

"I know. At least nine of the signers of the Declaration of Independence were Freemasons. It could be there were more, which is most likely how those anti-Catholic ideas of 'separation of church and state' and 'all men are created equal' got into the Declaration of Independence and the Bill of Rights."

"Benjamin, those ideas were the ideas of the founding fathers. They weren't the ideas of the Roman Catholic Church. They were *their* ideas, not *ours*."

Benjamin looked perplexed. He repeated the priest's words.

"*Theirs*. Not *ours*. You mean to say they're not *your* ideas, the Catholic Church's ideas?"

"Yes, Ben."

"As I recall, Father, God was mentioned in the very first sentence of the Declaration of Independence that was signed by those Freemasons and I believe it also said our rights are endowed by our *Creator*."

"I don't see what that has to do with the Church's position on Freemasonry, Ben."

"You said those ideas aren't Catholic, they're Masonic. But they're also *American*. Every school child learns them during his or her *secular* education. And by the way, keeping your Church out of public school isn't the same thing as keeping God out of school. No one's doing that. No one's keeping God out of school. The very ideals you and your Church criticize are part of our Constitution. Sure, many of our founding fathers were Freemasons. Maybe back then the freedoms we have today were too revolutionary. Maybe those men did use their influence and their skills as *Masons* to cement those freedoms into the foundation of American liberty. If that was the case, then thank God they did. Remember, Father, the purpose of the Constitution is to keep Pandora's box closed."

"I think you're stretching the facts, Ben."

"Do you? It's sort of funny when you think about it, Father. You can sit here and run your Church as you like and criticize our rights and freedoms without fear of retribution from the government, while also slandering the very organization that helped guarantee you have the very freedoms you condemn. How would someone describe that? What's the word I'm looking for? Ironic? Is that it? Yes. I think this is all very *ironic*."

Templeman thought, *I hope you're finished waving the flag in my face.*

"I didn't realize you were so well versed in history, Ben."

"I read about it, Father. Maybe you should, too.

It's not complicated. Delina taught Francis about being Catholic, but she wasn't raised here. I taught him - and her - about being Americans. Are you an American, Father?"

Templeman sighed audibly, no longer caring if he offended Benjamin.

"Yes, of course. However, Ben, I'm a Catholic first. A person's first allegiance is to God, not man - not to a secular nation."

"How in God's name can you be both after what you've just told me?"

"Well, Ben, so far, it's worked."

"Maybe that's because you've never been tested. If that day ever comes, then it'll be your turn to choose between your country and your Church."

"I can't imagine that happening, Ben, but if it does, there would be no question which I'd chose. Think about it."

A slight smile crossed Benjamin's features.

"Oh, of course. I guess I forgot. The very country whose concepts of equality and freedom you condemn also protects your right to condemn them. We call that freedom of speech."

Now it was Templeman's turn to remain silent.

Well, Ben, aren't you the self-righteous secularist?

The look on Benjamin's face didn't change, but he put his hands behind his back and looked at Templeman. Benjamin took just a few steps toward the priest. In a calm and even voice, he spoke. "But, yes, *Father* Templeman, I'll think about it. I'll think about how I stood in a House of God, in the Church of my dead wife's faith, the faith in which my son was baptized, and listened to a priest of that faith condemn the American ideals of equality and freedom laid down by our founding fathers."

Benjamin's speech was so calm and deliberate that Templeman was unnerved. He actually wished Benjamin would start bellowing at him. He knew how to handle that, but not *this*.

"Ben...."

"Just a minute, please, Father. I have a serious question."

Templeman bit his tongue - almost literally. It seemed to him the farmer was intentionally refusing to anger, as though he was taunting him.

"Go ahead, Ben."

"I was just wondering, since you and your fellow priests seem to know more about my organization than I do...."

"Yes?" Templeman interrupted with impatience.

Remaining calm, Benjamin said, "You know, Father, Delina loved the Church. She really did. But there was something that troubled her. Something she couldn't understand about the Church she loved so much."

Templeman said nothing as he tried to imagine what was coming.

"Father," Benjamin continued, "isn't it true the Holy Roman Catholic Church caused Catholics - its own people - to be tortured and burned at the stake? Weren't Jews and Muslims forced to convert, and then tortured because pope didn't believe them? Weren't they tortured until they 'confessed?' And how many Jews were burned because they refused to convert? Wasn't that what they call 'The Inquisition?' Oh, wait. There was more than just one inquisition, wasn't there? Oh, sure, it was all a long time ago. Maybe the Church has forgotten about the whole thing. You see, Father, I'm not very smart, but Delina was. I learned a lot from that little French Canadian about her religion. All I had to do was listen to her while she taught Francis."

"How *dare* you..." Templeman stood.

"How dare I? How dare I what? I only asked a question." Benjamin raised his voice, but only slightly. His question actually sounded sincere, not accusatory, which Templeman knew it was.

"I've had to sit here in this Catholic Church and listen to you parrot your pope about the imaginary heresies of one of the finest organizations that ever existed. One so excellent and so well considered that other groups, including your own Knights of Columbus, have copied it. The fact is, Templeman, no matter what lies you spin about Freemasons, thousands upon thousands of people were never murdered and tortured in the name of Freemasonry. No, *never*. If you want to point the finger of blame for being heretical, Templeman, look in the mirror! How many of the faithful has your own beloved Church tortured and burned to death or banished into exile? I don't care how long ago it happened. The point is *we* never did anything like that, but *you did* and you have the hypocritical gall to accuse *us* of heresy because we believe in separation of church and state and providing children with a public education and government of and by the people? The Catholic popes condoned the torture and murder of Catholics, Templeman, how anti-Catholic is *that*? *Jesus Christ!*

"You have no right to come into my Church...."

"*Your* Church, Father? Isn't this God's House?"

Now Templeman shouted. "You've twisted the facts! The Church never tortured or burned anyone!"

"Maybe not, but the Church *caused* it to be done! Your popes and cardinals and bishops *knew* what would happen to the accused, and they let it happen!

Templeman exerted a huge effort to regain control.

"Again, you're misrepresenting the facts! Every organization has a few bad people. Christ warned of that very threat. The Church is no different, but the foundation of the Church is indestructible and pure!"

Benjamin said nothing. The two men looked at each other in tense silence for a moment.

"Do you understand what all of this truly means, Father? It means that we - the Catholic Church and Freemasonry - will never resolve our differences. I should say the *Church* will never resolve its differences with Freemasonry. I've said it before and I'll stick by it: We have no problem with the Roman Catholic Church. It's sad, really. There will never be a reconciliation."

Templeman, finally calming down, sat down in the pew and replied, "No, Ben. There won't be."

"Because, Father, the Roman Catholic Church doesn't *want* a reconciliation. The Church is happy with things just as they are."

Benjamin stared at Templeman. He didn't know what to expect next. For a brief moment, he thought Benjamin might actually spit in his face. Templeman started to rise, but stopped when Benjamin put up his hand, palm out.

"All of this wrangling and fighting won't help. It won't change anything. I've come here for answers and you've told me what I need to know, just not in the way you thought you would. I suppose I should be grateful."

"What in God's name are you talking about?"

"I'm a farmer. I know crops need both sunlight and rain. Good days and bad. There can't be good without bad, can there, Father? Just as there can't be day without night or white without black. The Church needs Freemasonry to be the enemy. You paint us as anti-Catholic and anti-pope so you'll look 'white' compared to our 'black.' You need us to be the devil so you can play the saint. The Church can never allow Catholic men to become Freemasons because that would prove there *can* be reconciliation, then you'd have to find someone else to play the devil."

"I bet you think you're brilliant for coming up with *that* idiotic theory."

"No, Father. I'm not brilliant. Far from it. But I *do* know Freemasonry doesn't attack the Catholic Church. It's the Catholic Church that attacks Freemasonry. Freemasonry can exist with or without the Church, but the opposite isn't true, is it, Father? I guess I was right about the Church being ignorant and prejudiced. If you didn't have us, you'd be forced to find someone else to accuse of heresy."

"That's absolute nonsense, and you know it is."

"What I know, Father Templeman, is it's now clear to me why Catholic Churches always have a statue of Christ nailed to the cross hanging high over the altar. It's so He can look *down* on you."

Templeman rose out of the pew. His face was burning red. His eyes were wide. As he began to speak, he sprayed spittle into Benjamin's face, causing him to step backwards and wipe it away with his sleeve. Templeman jabbed his finger toward Saint Mary's doorway.

"Get *out*! *Damn* you! *Get out of this church*!"

"Damn *me*, Father? Did you just say that? I don't believe you have that authority. Maybe you're the one who should be damned."

Benjamin turned toward the door and walked with a straight back and determined gate out into the sunlight. The double doors banged closed with a loud echo that resonated throughout the small, empty, church. Empty, save for one person.

I have never in my life thrown anyone out of a church. My God! What in the name of Christ just happened? That man took control in my own church. What's wrong with me?

In the darkened sanctuary, among flickering candles, Templeman, breathing hard, took out a handkerchief and wiped the perspiration from his forehead. As he did, he happened to turn toward the altar. Catching sight of the crucifix, he looked up. There, above him, hung a figure forever nailed to the cross. To Templeman, Christ appeared to be looking directly at him, His sad eyes filled with accusation.

CHAPTER 14

VALHALLA

In an open invitation to attack, Bridgewater had failed to keep maneuvering his S.E.5a. He was flying straight and level. He was easy prey.

From his perch above, Francis saw an Albatros banking steeply to come up on Bridgewater's tail, like a hyena sneaking up on a stranded gazelle.

Half rolling to his right and shoving the stick forward, Francis dove on the Albatross.

Too late, Bridgewater realized his blunder. As he banked left, the German's tracers shredded sections of his upper and lower wings.

Concentrating on his quarry, the German failed to see Francis descending upon him.

Francis tried to put the German in his gun sight, but they were converging at too steep an angle. Taking the risk to save his friend's life, Francis fired as the needle of his airspeed indicator raced upward. His tracers arced uselessly behind the German.

With no time for another attempt, Francis heeled his machine hard left above the pair.

Banked at over 60 degrees, he was pressed into his seat as centrifugal force made him feel more than twice his weight and his arms became heavy and sluggish. He gauged the turn and his descent carefully, but he overshot and had to continue banking left to come up on the Hun's tail. This was made more difficult because Bridgewater was maneuvering frantically while the German matched his every twist and turn in his drive to kill him.

There! Finally! Francis closed on the German machine. He had to gauge his fire so as not to shoot down Bridgewater.

A quick burst. Then another. Tracers whizzed past the Albatros, some punching holes into the wings and fuselage.

The German pilot was aware someone was on his tail, but in his single-minded drive to destroy his prey, he refused to break off the chase. It was a mistake.

Bridgewater broke to the right and dove. Francis saw this and, anticipating the German's next move, gently nudged the S.E.5a's nose to the right and down.

The German unwittingly obliged and slid neatly into Francis' gun sight. Francis, the propeller slipstream beating him with screaming, freezing air, pressed the trigger. Both machine guns erupted. Tracers stretched out and seemed to gently touch the Albatros. Francis watched the German pilot jerk convulsively then slump forward, forcing the Albatros' control stick against the instrument panel. The Albatros nosed straight down trailing white water vapor from its punctured radiator. Building excessive speed instantly in its near vertical dive, both sets of the Albatros' wings folded neatly back against the fuselage as though hinged.

Francis managed a brief sigh of relief. He looked for Bridgewater and saw him in ahead of him. Not wasting time, Francis quickly searched for enemy machines. Seeing none, he began to reload the depleted upper machine gun. He lowered he gun on its mount, then, with speed and efficiency resulting from both practice and desperation, he removed the spent drum and tossed it out into the air. He snapped in a fresh drum, chambered the first round, and slammed the gun's mount back home.

As Francis began to search the sky prior to checking the ammunition supply of the second gun, his world exploded around him.

Bullets buried themselves in his wings, fuselage and instrument panel. His small windscreen shattered, sending razor-edged shards hurling past his head, some embedding themselves in his leather flying helmet.

An avenging Hun had slipped in behind Francis while he was reloading.

Francis broke hard to the left in an attempt to bring the murdering Albatros past the sights of Bridgewater's guns. The German stayed with him peppering his machine all the while.

Bridgewater witnessed Francis' plight, but was unable to maneuver into position to fire on the Albatros.

The German pilot obviously wasn't new. Francis couldn't shake him regardless of how severely he twisted and turned the S.E.5a.

Suddenly fighting for his survival, Francis' mind reeled as he frantically sought a way to escape. Then a thought struck him: the Albatros was known to have weak lower wing. It might be possible get out of this by tricking the German into maneuvering so violently that he would tear off his own wings.

Francis rolled inverted and pulled the control stick into his stomach causing his machine to fly a crescent-shaped path downward. He felt his body being pushed into his seat as he watched the earth rush toward him. Keeping the stick back, the nose of the machine, now pointed in the opposite direction, floated up to meet the horizon. Francis relaxed the pressure on the control stick and allowed it to move forward to keep the S.E.5a in level flight. He had just executed a "Split S," a common maneuver to escape a dogfight.

For a moment it worked. There were no more German tracer rounds dancing around the cockpit of the British machine.

Then more bullets arced past Francis' head.

Bridgewater had been gaining on the German, but his machine guns failed to find their mark. He tried to get closer, but the Albatros was too fast. He watched as first Francis then the Hun performed a Split S and sped past him in the opposite direction. Bridgewater, not needing at this late stage to perform the maneuver himself, banked hard to the left and nosed down to increase airspeed. He had to catch the German.

Now speeding back toward the main body of the aerial battle, Francis realized he had to perform yet another Split S. He did it again hoping against hope the German's desire to destroy him would cause him to push the Albatros beyond what it could endure.

Bridgewater was amazed by what he saw. Followed by the Albatros, Francis completed a second Split S. As they pulled out of the maneuver, the German, his lower wing still intact, again opened fire.

To keep up, Bridgewater now had to perform the maneuver himself. He was closer to the Albatros, but not close enough. Screaming in frustration, he was powerless to intervene in the drama he could only witness.

In spite of the freezing propeller blast, Francis was drenched in sweat. His face was numb and his shoulders and thighs ached from forcing his machine to dance through the sky. His neck was sore from constantly twisting his head in search of the enemy and he was inhaling freezing air in deep rapid gulps.

More tracers from the twin Spandaus threatened him.

He was out of ideas and near panic. He was gyrating all over the sky to throw off the German's aim, but realized doing that would ultimately prove futile. His only realistic chance of living was to perform yet another Split S.

Understanding the German would be expecting him to try the maneuver again, Francis decided to first zoom into a steep climb. He would slow down, but if he were lucky, the surprised German would hesitate before climbing after him. Then, Francis would roll inverted into a last Split S and finally escape this relentless Hell.

He did it. At full throttle Francis pulled the S.E.5a straight up. No more tracers. He continued until he felt the wings about to stall, then he pushed the rammed stick forward and the nose began to drop. As his airspeed increased, Francis pulled the nose up to meet the horizon, then rolled into another Split-S. He hoped against hope that he had confused the German enough to escape him. Praying, Francis pulled out of the Split-S. Nothing. No tracers assaulted his S.E.5a. Had it worked? Was he finally...?

Francis felt an odd sensation. It was as though someone was pounding on the back of his seat with a sledgehammer. How could that be? It was impossible. In the freezing air, Francis felt an unexpected warmth flowing across his chest. He placed a mittened hand on the front of his padded flight suit and looked down at it. His mitten was covered in a dark fluid. His world had become black and white. He raised his heavy eyes and saw the same slippery stuff all over his instrument panel. All of the gauges were smashed, leaving jagged slivers of glass in the round bezels. His compass was gone. As the fog in his mind thickened, he thought, *How will I find my way home?*

His vision was narrowing as blackness advanced from the edges of his sight. It was as though he were looking through a long narrow tube. The roar of the engine was fading. He didn't understand why he suddenly felt so warm.

He was back in Pennsylvania. He was playing in the front yard when that big mean dog began snapping and barking at him. His mother ran to him, screaming, reaching out to hold and protect him.

As the darkness became complete, Francis Kyner of Athena, Pennsylvania, heard his mother's voice: *"Francis, don't be afraid. I'm here."*

Bridgewater stared wide-eyed in nightmarish disbelief as he watched Francis slump forward against the instrument panel his S.E.5a, sending the smoking machine into a vertical dive. The only real friend he had ever known was dead and it was his fault. If he had only kept his wits and been more careful after killing that first Hun bastard, Francis wouldn't have had to rescue him and none of this would have happened. If he had not relaxed for those few seconds, Francis would still be alive!

The German, in a fever fueled by hubris and stoked by adrenalin, dove after the disintegrating British machine. As the pilot nosed over to chase his dead enemy and bask in triumph as the S.E.5a fell burning to the ground, both lower wings of the Albatross slowly folded back, separated from the fuselage, and fluttered away into the blue sky as victor joined vanquished in a double funeral pyre on the altar of Valhalla.

Chapter 15

Western Union

The episode with Templeman weighed on Benjamin's mind, but only for a time. He told Frank Zieglar what had happened and that there was no way around what the pope had done. The Catholic members of the lodge had to make a choice. They chose to leave Freemasonry.

Benjamin also made a choice: not to dwell on the situation further. He had a son in a war and a farm to run. He couldn't afford the luxury of contemplating on problems he had no power to resolve.

Entering the town, the stranger noticed dark clouds on the horizon. He hoped he could get home before the rain came. If not, he'd be soaked riding this damned motorcycle.

At 60, he was too old to be drafted. He was also too old to be on this motorcycle, but there he was. At least he wasn't learning close order drill at Fort

Indiantown Gap near Harrisburg, as was his predecessor in this job.

Riding slowly through Athena, he spotted what he was looking for: a church. Any church would do and this was the first one he happened to see.

As he entered the building, he doffed his billed cap with the blue and gold Western Union emblem on the front. He stopped in the vestibule for his eyes to adjust to the dim light.

It was a weekday afternoon and the simple wood frame building was empty. Streams of sunlight not yet halted by the approaching storm shimmered through the stained glass windows. Thousands of dust particles were cast in shades of blues, greens and yellows. It was a peaceful place.

He was cautious. Stepping into the nave of Saint Mary's, the messenger called out in a tentative voice, "Hello? Is anyone here? Hello?"

He heard a muffled stirring in the back of the church, then footsteps.

"Hello!" said Templeman, slipping into his black suit coat as he emerged from the sacristy.

"Father, I wonder if you could help me?"

"Well," the priest responded, smiling, "That's why I spent all those years in seminary. What seems to be the problem?"

"Oh, no, Father! That's not what I mean. It's not like that!"

"Oh," Templeman said, still smiling at his own attempt at humor. "What is it, then?"

"Well, Father, I'm with Western Union. I have a telegram to deliver and I'm having trouble finding the place. I thought maybe you know the people. Maybe they're members here?"

The smile faded from the priest's face. More and more telegrams were being delivered since the United States entered the war. "Maybe. Who are you looking for?"

The messenger pulled an envelope from his pocket and looked down at it. "Benjamin Arthur Kyner, Father. Do you know him?"

Good Lord, no.

"Yes, I know him. Can you by any chance tell me...?"

"Father, I'm sorry. I can't. It's against company regulations. You know, privacy and all. I could get fired if I told anybody what's in this telegram."

"Of course. I understand. I'm sorry I asked."

"No problem, Father, but look. Just between you and me - you're a priest, right?" He didn't wait for an answer. "I don't mind telling you that delivering these telegrams is really beginning to wear on me. You know, I'm beginning to have nightmares. People used to get excited when they saw me coming. Now, I scare the hell out of them." Reacting to his slip of the tongue, he gasped, "Oh, God. I'm sorry, Father."

Templeman was only half-listening to the man. Now he knew without a doubt what news the telegram contained.

"Forget it. This is hard on us all. Let me get my hat. You can follow me to Ben's place."

"Gee, thanks, Father. Oh, by the way, do you know him pretty well?"

The priest, who had been heading to the sacristy at a clip, stopped. He looked back at the Western Union messenger and nodded his head. Then he turned his back on the man and hurried on.

Behind the wheel of his black Model T, Templeman turned onto the long road leading to the Kyner farmhouse. The Western Union messenger followed on his motorcycle.

The messenger was relieved to have the priest with him. Truth be told, he never even tried to find the Kyner place. He'd made a beeline for the first church he could find.

Since these telegrams started coming from the War Department he learned pretty quickly it was best not to knock on a door alone; it was better to have a priest or minister with you.

Not long after the war began he'd delivered a telegram to a family who lived in the northern part of the county. The man of the house opened the door and stared at the messenger. He was the soldier's father. Before the messenger could utter a word, the man grabbed the envelope, tore it open in front of his wife, and read it. Instead of signing the receipt offered by the messenger, the man threw it to the floor and began to pummel the messenger for bringing the news that his son had been killed.

Searching for a way to avoid having grieving parents take their anger and frustration out on him, the Western Union messenger finally hit on the idea that people, even people getting the worst news of their lives, were more likely to restrain themselves in the presence of a pastor of some kind. It would, he had reasoned, be even better if the family were members of the pastor's flock. That way, the priest or minister or what-have-you could step right in and start doing his job and deflect attention away from the one who delivered the bad news. The messenger had been mostly right.

Benjamin was in the hayloft of the barn when the vehicles pulled up to the house. He didn't hear them approach, but he did hear the distant rumbling of the approaching thunderstorm. Hiram was splitting wood between the house and barn, but also didn't notice the Model T until it was close to the house.

Hiram looked up to see the priest's car, but didn't immediately see the motorcycle, which was blocked by the automobile.

Hiram approached the Model T as Templeman stepped out. He stopped when he caught sight of the Western Union uniform.

"Hiram," Templeman asked calmly, "is Ben around?"

Hiram, a look of apprehension spreading across his features, nodded and answered, "Yep, Padre, he sure is. He's in the barn. I'll go fetch him."

Templeman nodded in response. The Western Union man hovered behind him.

After entering the dark barn, Hiram looked up in the direction of the hayloft.

"Hey, Ben!" He looked back toward the house where the two visitors were waiting. Then turned and again shouted into the dark cavern of the barn, "You got company! Someone's here to see you!" A moment later, Benjamin emerged from the barn wiping his hands on a rag. He heard more thunder and glanced in its direction, noting the clouds rapidly moving toward his farm.

Recognizing Templeman standing next to the Ford, Benjamin mumbled under his breath in an exasperated tone, "Oh, God. Now what does he want?"

As he began to walk toward the automobile, Benjamin caught sight of the Western Union messenger standing just beyond the priest, as though trying to hide. Benjamin froze. A telegram accompanied by a priest can only mean one thing. He forced himself to take the last few steps to the waiting men. Hiram stepped up behind him.

With some hesitation, the messenger stepped forward.

"Mr. Kyner? Benjamin Kyner?"

Benjamin nodded.

"I...I have a telegram for you, sir. Please sign here."

Benjamin took the offered pad and absent-mindedly scrawled his name. He handed the pad back. The messenger held out the telegram. Benjamin simply stared at it.

Hiram reached out and took the telegram from the messenger. He offered it to Benjamin.

A loud peel of thunder broke the silence.

The messenger quickly turned away. His job was done and now it was time for the priest to do his. As he moved toward his motorcycle, he mumbled a quick "Thanks, Father," to the priest, then whispered, "Good luck." Templeman, his eyes locked on Benjamin, ignored him. The messenger mounted the motorcycle, kick-started it, and rode off.

The fading roar of the motorcycle's engine emphasized the silence that had befallen the trio of men for whom time had stopped.

Templeman took a step toward Benjamin. The movement jarred Benjamin to consciousness. He slowly tore open the telegram and began to read. As he did,

Hiram moved closer. Benjamin looked into Hiram's eyes, then back at the paper in his hands.

April 15, 1918

To: Benjamin A. Kyner, Athena, Pennsylvania
"Dear Sir, the Secretary of War deeply regrets to inform you..."

Benjamin's eyes quickly absorbed the terrible words on the paper - dark blue letters burned into a buff-colored background. His first sensation was intense denial. His eyes went wide in disbelief, as though he could push the truth away if he stared hard enough.

Benjamin, holding the telegram with both hands, raised his eyes slowly and allowed his arms to drop as though the weight of the paper in his hand was suddenly too great to bear.

Looking past Templeman and Hiram, Benjamin seemed to be focusing on something a mile away, or perhaps far in the past.

In a flat, lifeless voice, Benjamin said, "I warned him this could happen. I told him. He wouldn't listen to me." As his eyes dropped to the telegram, he continued, "Now this...."

Templeman raised a hand, intending to place it on Benjamin's shoulder. Before he could, the farmer looked up.

"I want you to go. Both of you."

Templeman began to try and reason with him, "Ben, you need...."

"Don't tell me what I need. I know what I need. I need to be alone. Now go."

Both the priest and Hiram hesitated.

"Please. This is private. Don't argue with me. Just go."

The Western Union messenger stopped halfway to the road. Out of morbid curiosity he looked back at the scene behind him. He saw the priest and the black man watching as the farmer walked to the farmhouse as though he were walking through thick mud, the telegram clutched in his right hand. Then the Western Union messenger continued on his way.

As the motorcycle turned onto Fairey Hill Road the heavens opened, accompanied by the simultaneous flash of lightning and crack of thunder. The storm had arrived.

Templeman and Hiram stood next to one another and watched Benjamin walk through the kitchen door and close it slowly and deliberately behind him. The sound of the latch sliding home was eerily clear and distinct. The rain was now falling heavily on the farmhouse roof.

"God, he's a tough case," the priest said. "Come on, Hiram. I'll give you a lift back to the hollow."

They rode in silence. There was nothing that could be said.

Arriving at Hiram's front door, he stepped out of the Ford into the hard rain. Turning to speak to Templeman, rain flowing from the brim on his worn hat, Hiram said, "Father, he shouldn't be alone now. It's bad for him."

"I know."

Hiram hesitated, waiting for more. The priest only looked at him in silence. Hiram closed the car's door, pushing it until he heard it latch.

Templeman shifted the Model T into gear. Hiram stepped back and watched as the black car disappeared like a ghost through the curtain of heavy rain.

Sarah heard the car and was waiting for Hiram at the front door. Her concern over his early arrival home doubled when she saw the Catholic priest's car.

"Baby, is something wrong?"

Hiram looked at her for a long moment, unintentionally heightening her fear, then answered, "Benjamin's hurting. This time Amish chocolate bread won't help. Francis is dead."

Sarah gasped. Her open palms flew to cover her mouth, leaving her wide brown eyes to follow her husband as he walked slowly past her into the house.

Back at the Kyner farm, Benjamin was kneeling next to Francis' bed. With both arms he held his son's pillow tightly to his face as he sobbed into it.

CHAPTER 16

TEMPEST

The thunderstorm was a harbinger of melancholy weather that showed no sign of diminishing. The storm itself had abated, but several hours after nightfall a steady rain still drenched the fields, streets, and rooftops of the town.

Templeman was kneeling at the altar railing of St Mary's. To an observer, he would have appeared to be deep in prayer, but he was actually consumed with memories - memories of other young lives lost and chances wasted. Perhaps his was simply another form of prayer.

The stillness was disturbed only by the sound of the ceaseless rain falling beyond the walls of the church. It was as though Heaven itself was in mourning over yet another young life squandered.

Templeman's mind finally wandered to the confrontation he and Benjamin had had in this very spot only a short time ago.

He forgot how long he had been on his knees. In the darkened church, the only illumination of the crucified Jesus suspended above the altar was from the ever diminishing votive candles lit by the faithful for their intentions. The Savior's face reflected the candlelight in a manner that gave it a soft glow against the dark; a serene disembodied specter floating hauntingly above the priest.

Finally, looking up with weary, bloodshot eyes into the perpetually tortured face hanging above the altar, the priest whispered, "Benjamin Kyner accused your Church within these very walls. Would your Father want one of his priests to help such a man who has just lost his own son?" Then he rested his head on his folded hands and took in the sound of the rain.

After a moment he rose. He looked up at the figure of Jesus. The priest knew what he had to do. He'd always known.

He stood and walked with purpose to the sacristy where he left his hat and coat. Exiting the sacristy, he considered Benjamin's state of mind, as well as his own, and detoured to the rectory next door on his way to the Model T.

The thunderstorm had downed a number of trees, some of which blocked the roads. The roads not blocked by trees were virtual rivers of mud.

The conditions made it impossible for Templeman to drive to the Kyner farm the usual way; he had to pick and feel his way along a dark, muddy maze in search of an alternate route. Twice he almost drove into ditches because the darkness and driving rain obscured approaching bends in the road.

Benjamin's farm was due north of Athena. Forty-five minutes into a drive that should have been less than ten, the priest had driven in a jagged circle around the farm and was several miles out of his way to the north. He was physically and mentally drained by the exertion of attempting to find a passable road that would take him south to his destination. After an ungodly expenditure of effort, the man of God was finally southbound on Fairey Hill Road passing the one-room schoolhouse.

Rain continued to pound the Ford's canvass top and windshield, obscuring the priest's vision. As he finally turned onto Benjamin's property, he could see the farmhouse was dark.

"No lights," he mumbled absent mindedly. "But he's got to be here. Where would he go on a night like this?"

The Model T crossed the shale-filled field that was the daytime province of grazing cows. Unbeknownst to the priest, he drove across the very spot where Francis and Bridgewater had taken off in the Jenny eight months earlier.

As the Ford turned toward the house, its headlamps swept over the field. Templeman did a double take at the sight of a figure standing in the rain and looking up into the dark, weeping, sky.

My God.

Templeman straightened the automobile and carefully maneuvered to within ten feet of Benjamin, keeping him in the beams of the headlamps.

He jumped from the car and ran through the downpour to Benjamin. His every step caused small geysers to erupt from the sodden ground.

"Ben," he shouted over the noise of the rain. "Are

you all right? What in God's name are you doing out here at night in the pouring rain?"

Benjamin seemed not to hear him.

"Ben, can you hear me? Have you been drinking?"

"No, not yet," Benjamin finally answered, still looking up, allowing the rain to wash over his face.

Templeman put his face close to Benjamin's, "For the love of God, Ben...."

Turning toward the priest, Benjamin said, "You know, for a priest, you sure make a habit of invoking God's name. Did you know that?"

Templeman, now drenched by the storm, was taken off balance by what he just heard. "What?" It was all he could think to say. But Benjamin was looking back into the black, mournful sky. He staggered forward half a step, then turned.

"This is where I saw him for the last time. This is the last place I saw my son alive. It was right here. This is where he took off in that damned flying machine."

The priest looked up, finally understanding. He put a hand on Benjamin's arm.

"Ben," he said, water streaming from the brim of his black fedora, "why don't we get in the car and I'll drive us up to the house."

"No," responded the farmer with determination in his voice. "I need to be here right now."

A flash of distant lightning split the darkness. A few seconds later, the sound of thunder followed. Another thunderstorm was building.

Templeman looked in the direction of the lightning, then back at Benjamin.

"All right, Ben, if that's what you want. If you

don't mind, I'll just stand here with you."

"My wife is dead. Now my son," Benjamin croaked. It seemed to the priest that he was talking to himself. "She couldn't help it. It wasn't her fault that she got sick. I don't blame her. Not now. Not anymore. I did then. I was angry with her because she left me - left me alone with our little boy. Then I felt ashamed because I knew she didn't have a choice. I knew she really didn't want to leave. But Francis, he did have a choice. He didn't have to go. He could have stayed in college. He could have lived his life."

Templeman said nothing. He stood listening to the farmer in the middle of an empty field in the middle of a dark night in the middle of a storm.

"I must have done something to drive him away. He should've wanted to stay home. Instead, he wanted to leave. This is my fault! I tried. God knows I tried. I don't know what I could have done that would have made a difference…."

"No, Ben," Templeman shouted over the din of the storm. "Francis made his own decision. This wasn't your fault! Thousands of boys like Francis volunteered to go. There was nothing you could have done to stop him. Ben, you've got to believe me!"

Benjamin turned and glared at the priest, shouting, "But he didn't have to do it! Don't you understand? None of this *had* to happen. He could be here right now," Benjamin screamed, pointing toward the farmhouse, "sleeping in his bed instead of rotting in his grave somewhere in goddamned France!"

Ben!" shouted the priest. "You've got to listen to me! Stop torturing yourself. Would Francis want this? Would Delina? You owe it to them to pull yourself together."

Benjamin spun to face the priest. He raised both hands and, with fingers spread, held his head as though trying to keep his skull from rupturing. "Don't you *understand*?" Benjamin shouted in the priest's face. "My son is *dead*! I want my son *back*!" Benjamin was illuminated in the yellow glow of the Ford's headlamps. His face was contorted with grief and his eyes were squeezed shut. His tears were invisible in the rain.

Templeman grabbed both of Benjamin's arms and shouted, "Listen to me. Ben, I know how you feel…!"

Upon hearing those words, Benjamin's eyes flew open and he fixated on the black and white collar in front of him. He knocked the priest's hands away.

"You? You know how I feel? A priest? How can *you* know how I feel, you arrogant son of a bitch? I had a *wife* and a *son*. I watched her being lowered into her grave. Then I raised that boy alone only to get a telegram telling me he's dead. That's it. A telegram. A piece of paper is all I have left of him. Now *you* with no wife and no son have the gall to stand here in the last place I saw him alive and tell me *you* understand? *You can go straight to Hell!"*

Anger spread across Templeman's features. This was the second time in only a few weeks that Benjamin had driven him to such outrage. Once again he had ceded control of his emotions to another person - to Benjamin.

Lightning flashed again. The thunder crashed. The rain intensified to a deluge. The storm had arrived in force.

Templeman grabbed the Benjamin by the front of his shirt and shook him.

"Now you listen to me, you self-righteous

bastard! You don't think I understand what's going on inside of you right now? You look at this collar and you think you know who I am and what I've endured? I'm a man the same as you, you pompous fool!" With that, Templeman shoved Benjamin backwards. He stumbled, shocked, but he didn't fall.

Looking Benjamin in the eye, the priest said in a subdued, threatening voice, "Do you think you're the first man to ever lose anyone, Ben? I had a family. I had a wife and a daughter and a son."

Benjamin raised his arm to shield his eyes from glare of the Model T's headlights. Incredulous, he peered at Templeman as the rain created rivulets across his features.

"They're dead, Ben."

The priest took a few steps toward the farmer. Again, lightning flashed and thunder resounded around them.

"It was over 20 years ago. I was a businessman. My biggest concern was making money when it should have been my family."

Templeman took a few deep breaths.

"We lived in a house outside of Philadelphia. I traveled much of the time, leaving my wife to care for our children and the house. Then, one day while I was in New York trying to convince a client I deserved his money, I received a telegram, just like you did, Ben."

Benjamin and Templeman stood facing each other in the rain.

Finally, the priest continued. "The telegram said my family was dead. It was a house fire. My family burned to death one night while I was sleeping in a New York City hotel. Later, the fire chief said there had most likely been a problem with the gas lights in the house."

He continued, "You see, I should never have been away as much as I was. I should never have left my wife to take care of that house and a seven-year old boy and his 12-year-old sister. If I had been there, Ben, they'd still be alive today and my wife and I would be grandparents. So yes, I do know how you feel."

"I didn't know...."

"No one knows," Templeman interrupted. "At least no one around here knows. Only you, now."

The two men were startled when the Model T's headlights were suddenly blocked and a shadow fell across them.

"If ya'll don't keep your damned voices down, pretty soon everyone around here's gonna know."

Templeman and Benjamin turned to see Hiram Bolt standing behind them silhouetted by the beam of the Ford's headlamps, his hat, limp from the rain, had collapsed around his ears and his black poncho glistened.

"Ya know, Padre, I knew Ben had a penchant for standin' around in fields during thunderstorms, but I gave you more credit."

CHAPTER 17

REVELATION

The thunder and lightning finally ebbed. The rain was again reduced to a steady tattoo against the roof of the farmhouse.

The three sodden men were gathered around the fireplace. Their eclectic collection of clothes were draped on any available corner or fixture around the fireplace to dry: worn coveralls, a black shirt with white clerical collar, and a red union suit, among other things such as socks, trousers, and hats. The men themselves were wrapped in blankets and huddled on chairs trying to steal as much warmth from the flames as they could.

Templeman stood up and began to search the pockets of his long overcoat that was hanging on the edge of the mantle. When he turned around, he was holding a bottle containing a dark fluid.

"Where are the glasses, Ben?"

Benjamin pointed to a cupboard over the sink.

The priest returned with three glasses. He gave

Benjamin and Hiram each a glass. Then, after setting his own on a nearby table, he uncorked the bottle and poured the dark fluid into each one.

Benjamin picked up his drink and sniffed. "Whiskey,' he pronounced.

Hiram sniffed his and added, "I'd bet this is actually the Irish variety?"

Templeman smiled and lifted his glass in a salute to Hiram's astuteness.

"I grabbed it from the rectory on my way out. I thought it might be useful tonight," the priest said.

"You sure thought right," responded Hiram.

Templeman, standing in front of the fireplace with his face half illuminated by the orange and yellow flames, looked up. "If you don't mind, Ben, I think it would be proper to toast Francis. Francis and all the fine boys the war has taken from us."

Benjamin, who had been looking into the fire, looked up at Templeman. He nodded and stood, followed by Hiram.

Together, the three raised their glasses.

"To Francis," they each whispered, though not quite in unison. They took a sip of whiskey.

Benjamin looked down in the glass deep in thought. Hiram and Templeman slowly returned to their seats.

"I suppose I was acting like a fool," Benjamin said. "I won't apologize. This - isn't easy. I don't know if I can get through it. He was all I had. It never mattered to me that he wasn't my natural son. I never thought about it. I couldn't have loved him more even if he had been."

Hiram was the first to respond, "Ben, no one

asked for an apology. We don't expect one. You're hurting. You got a right."

"Ben," Templeman began, "Like I said out there," he waved his glass toward the kitchen door, "I know how you feel. A lot of people do"

"I still dream of his mother - of Delina. I know I'm not the first man to wish I could turn back the hands of the clock or put the pages back on the calendar. I would give anything for none of this to have happened."

"I know that feeling, too," uttered the priest.

I've got to be careful, Templeman thought, *he's walking a tightrope and could fall either toward or away from me.*

"There's nothing anyone can say, Ben, to lessen the pain you feel."

From his chair, Benjamin looked at Templeman and said, "Don't start talking about Francis 'being in the arms of the Lord' or 'he's with his mother' or any crap like that. If you do, you know where the door is. You can take your whiskey with you."

"No, Ben, I won't say anything like that. If I thought it would help you, I would, because I believe it. But you see, Ben, saying things like that would comfort some people, but not you. I know that."

The priest paused for a few seconds.

"Not long ago, an elderly parishioner passed away. It was just his time to go. It was no surprise to anyone. Well, his wife - his widow - was, or rather, *is* a very devout woman. I sat with her for hours talking about heaven and the words of Jesus. She loved hearing how Jesus could calm people by using simple parables to illustrate common problems. I think she had them all memorized. I believe what she found in the parables and the way Jesus used them was proof, at least to her, that love is eternal. If love is eternal, then our souls must be eternal. For her, that was proof that one day she would again be with her husband."

He paused again. Both Benjamin and Hiram remained quiet.

"But all that won't work with you, Ben. I'm not going to try to force something on you that won't fit. That's not a judgment of you; it's just the way things are. We're all different and we grieve in different ways. I'm not saying you're right or you're wrong. I'm not sure what you believe, but I'm not here to preach. I'm a man of God, but I'm not here as a man of God. I'm here simply as a man who has suffered a loss much like yours. We both had children taken from us violently and without warning. We both lost the women we love."

Benjamin looked into the flames and allowed the dancing light to allow other thoughts to form in his mind, if only for a moment. Hiram took another sip of the dark liquid from his glass as he watched his friend.

"There's something else," Benjamin said. "I fought in a war. You both know that. I know what men are capable of doing to each other in combat. It can be ugly and cruel - hideous. It's difficult to think that Francis did those things and that others tried to do them to him. I gave him my name. I carried him in my arms. I taught him to swim and played catch with him. After Delina died, it was just him and me. When he was sick, I took care of him. I took him to church every Sunday because his mother couldn't. I stood there alone and watched him graduate from high school. It all wears on me."

"Ben," Templeman said, "take a look sometime at

the Old Testament, and I don't mean to pray. You'll see that throughout history good men have been called upon to do unholy things for a holy cause. You were called upon, and so was Francis. Neither of you started the wars you fought in, but you answered the call and did what you both felt was the right thing. You both acquitted yourselves well. Don't despair on that count. Be proud of your son."

Templeman looked into his glass. "I hope that doesn't sound trite."

The room went silent, only the snapping and crackling flames in the fireplace could be heard.

Hiram, breaking the tension in the room, suddenly said, "Who'd a thought it. A priest with a wife."

"That was before I became a priest," corrected Templeman, in a more animated tone of voice.

"All the same," Hiram continued, "I never considered it. I'm not a Catholic and I don't come to your church, but I just can't picture you married and with kids."

"Well," answered Templeman, "life is full of surprises."

He looked at Hiram, "And you and - Sarah, is it? - are welcome at Saint Mary's any time."

"Sure," Hiram said, grinning, "I bet your congregation would be really happy to see a couple of folks from Black Hollow just stroll in one Sunday morning." Hiram then chuckled.

"Give them...give *us*, some credit, Hiram. I said you'd be welcome and I meant it."

"Padre, we may just take you up on that some day. Just remember you asked for it."

Benjamin suddenly spoke up. He spoke to Hiram,

but he looked at Templeman, "Hell, Hiram, if they let in Freemasons, they won't even notice *you.*"

Templeman looked at Hiram. "Just don't try taking Communion. We just had the roof replaced and I don't need any lightning bolts punching holes in it."

"Hah," snorted Hiram. He took a sip from his glass and said, "What a sight we are. A Catholic priest, a Freemason and the Baptist grandson of slaves, dripping wet, wrapped in blankets like Indians sitting around a campfire, and sipping Irish whiskey!" Then, with a big smile, he raised his glass and added, "Only in Athena, Pennsylvania, truly heaven on earth. Hallelujah!"

Templeman wanted to keep the conversation away from Francis' death for just a little while longer to give Benjamin's grieving soul some respite.

This might cost me something, but it's now or never.

"I would appreciate it if you would both keep my revelation to yourselves."

"It doesn't matter to me, Padre, I'm not one of your flock, but why keep it a secret?" Hiram asked.

"It's like you yourself said, Hiram. You can't picture me married with children. Well, neither could my parishioners. I've worked hard to maintain the image they expect of a Catholic priest. I don't want that image altered. If it were, it would also alter my relationship with the people to whom I minister. They have an idea of who and what a priest is and I don't want to put them in the position of having to try to absorb a reality that doesn't fit that idea."

"But also," he continued, "my loss is very private to me. If anyone found out, they'd start asking questions, as much out of out of compassion as curiosity. It's just human nature. When I put this collar on, I made a conscious decision to put worldly things behind me. Don't misunderstand, I loved my family dearly and I remember and pray for them every day, but only in here," he said, lightly tapping his chest over his heart.

Benjamin spoke up. "Isn't that called a 'lie of omission'?" After a pause, Templeman answered, "Ben, are you thinking of Francis?"

"Yes, without telling me, he learned to fly with every intention of getting in the war. Then he went ahead and signed up behind my back."

"Ben, at some point you'll forgive Francis. But to answer your question, yes by keeping my past in the shadows, I'm committing a lie of omission. I won't deny it. In this case, however, I believe the truth would be more detrimental than keeping my past life private. If you would prefer a Biblical precedent, which I'm sure you don't, I've got one. When the Pharaoh of Egypt saw how strong the Hebrews were becoming, he ordered the Jewish midwives to kill all newborn Hebrew males. Of course, they didn't. When the Pharaoh found out, he asked them why they didn't carry out his orders. They lied. They said the Hebrew women were delivering their babies without the midwives. For lying to the Pharaoh, God rewarded the midwives. That's all in Exodus 1:19 and 1:20, if you'd like to verify it."

Templeman took another sip, and then said, "I don't expect God to reward me in this case, but there's something else you both can relate to. The one weakness we priests have in common is that we're human. We all have our secrets, including me."

"As secrets go, Father," Hiram said, "I've heard a lot worse. After all, it's not like you robbed the poor box."

"Your past is safe with us, but there is something I'd like to know," Benjamin added.

"Oh? What's that?"

Benjamin put the glass to his lips and took a sip. "A lot of people would curse God for doing to them what he did to you. Yet you seem not only to have forgiven him, but you became a priest. Why?"

Templeman saw Benjamin had just opened a window on his inner struggle. It was open just a crack, but that was enough. Bringing the whiskey had been divinely inspired.

"This isn't easy to talk about," he began. "Benjamin, Hiram," he said looking at them both in turn. "I did curse God. At the time, I believed I hated him. After my family's funeral, I stood over their graves and cursed him."

Hiram was spellbound. He had never heard a man of the cloth speak like this. Benjamin, more cynical after having seen the worst of humanity during his time at war, remained stoic, but respectful.

Continuing, Templeman said, "I slid into depression; not just sadness, grieving and guilt, but a real, deep, smothering depression. I had never been a stranger to a bottle, but I began to drink in earnest, to dull the agony, I suppose. The agony caused by grief and guilt. I came very close to losing my business, which would have been another tragedy since my wife and two children had literally died for it." He looked into the whiskey glass he held with both hands

"There had been fleeting thoughts of suicide soon after the fire. Those thoughts became more concrete the further down I slid. I even planned what I'd do. Nothing elaborate, just a bullet to the head. After what I'd done to my family, or failed to do, I deserved to die. That's how I felt."

Benjamin and Hiram exchanged a furtive look. Neither had expected this.

"I felt the time was getting close, you know, to do it. I began feeling an odd sense of relief, believe it or not. I needed to visit my family one last time. So, one late spring evening as it was getting dark, I made my way to the cemetery and stood there looking down on their headstones and became overwhelmed with grief. I'd brought a bottle with me, of course, so I began to try and drown my pain. The relief would only be temporary, but anything was better than suffering like that, so I continued to drink."

The priest paused to take a deep breath and settle himself. Benjamin and Hiram waited.

"Eventually, I passed out. When I finally woke up with the sun in my face, shivering from the cold and drenched with dew, I didn't remember where I was and then realized I was lying on my wife's grave. To top it all off, I had managed to piss myself during the night."

Templeman looked into the faces of Benjamin and Hiram. They were expressionless.

"So, there I was. Lying on my family's graves stinking of piss and booze with a hangover that made me feel I'd already shot myself in the head. That was the low point of my life, that very moment. As bad as I felt - both physically and spiritually - there was one thing that was very, very clear to me. There was nothing else left to me in my existence except God and me, like two boxers in a ring. Really. That's just how it seemed. Lying there on my wife's grave, I felt like I was lying on the mat all bloodied and bruised and defeated and there was God standing over me with gloved fists knowing he'd won and saying, "Okay, you fool, now what? It's your move."

He paused again to take a few breaths and think about how to phrase what he next had to say.

"I'd rented an apartment while my house was being repaired. I managed to get back to it without getting arrested for vagrancy, but not without some stares and blunt comments from passersby. Thoughts of self-destruction were replaced by a need for answers. I needed to understand why my family had been taken and why everything after that had happened. I could think of only one place to look. I got myself cleaned up then went to the bookshelf and pulled down our family Bible, which had been among the things not destroyed by the fire, and began to read. After some time, I don't know how long, days probably, my path became clear."

Looking at the two men, Templeman said, "You see, everyone I loved had been taken from me because of my own hubris; my own pride and conceit and vanity. Now all that had been stripped away. I'd been put through a clothes wringer and it had all been squeezed out of me in a very painful way. I'd gone through a dark tunnel and emerged at the other end. My purpose, as I saw it, would be to help others going through the same thing, and maybe, God willing, to stop other fools from making the same mistake. I felt the call, sold the business and my house and I became a priest. Thank God they took me. I truly believe if I had not gone to my family's graves that night, I'd be dead today. I like to think they had something to do with my decision."

For a time, the three men remained still.

Hiram spoke first, "God a-mighty. Padre, I ain't

never heard anythin' like that before."

"I expect not," replied Templeman.

He looked at Benjamin, who took another sip of whiskey and appeared to be contemplating the flames.

"I didn't really mean to drag you both through all that, but 'in for a penny, in for a pound,' I suppose. Now you know the whole story."

After pausing for a few seconds, he continued, "Ben, it was important I use myself as an example, so you'll understand that I've been where you are. I had to establish my credentials, so to speak, so you will believe what I'm going to tell you now, and it's got nothing to do with religion."

With tired eyes, the farmer gazed at the priest.

"I will never get over the death of my family, Ben, nor will you ever get over the deaths of Francis and Delina. I will promise you this, however; you will grieve for your loss in your own way and the pain will be real. You think now it will never pass and your life, for all intents and purposes, is over. I know. I felt the same way. But time will pass and, little by little, the pain will dull. The pain will never truly leave you, but it will lessen. I know it seems impossible now, but one day you will laugh again, you'll be able to enjoy a beautiful sunset and the smell of wet leaves in the autumn. You see, I wasn't there when my family needed me. I am responsible for their deaths, yet I am able to carry on. You are *not* responsible for the loss of Francis or Delina, no matter how you may feel now. It's natural to feel guilty after losing someone close to you but neither Francis nor Delina would want you to suffer that way. You know that. You are a good man and they loved and respected you. Your task is to honor that love and respect, move past the grief, and have a good life. Not to do that would be to dishonor both their memories. Every day I draw breath is in honor of my wife and children. I try to be the best man I can be for *them*." The priest put the whiskey glass to his lips and upended it.

"Now I'll shut up," he said.

"You make a lot of sense, Father," Hiram said. "Thank God that's one road I haven't traveled."

Templeman simply nodded in agreement and then added, "I think after all that's happened you should both call me Jim when no one else is around."

Benjamin said, "Well, Jim, you didn't tell us what you did before all this happened. How you made your living. What business where you in?"

Templeman sat silently for several seconds looking into his empty glass, then answered without looking up, "Ben, I owned a company that distributed residential and commercial gas lighting equipment. Lamps, fixtures, pipes, things like that. It was my equipment that malfunctioned and caused the fire that killed my wife and children."

Hiram exhaled a long breath and then whispered "Jesus Christ."

"That, all of it, is a terrible burden to bear," Benjamin said. "If I were you, I wouldn't want people asking questions about it, either."

"No, sir," added Hiram. "Padre, I'm taking that story to my grave, and that's a promise."

"Thank you. Both of you."

"You came out here in this storm to tell me that?" Benjamin asked him. "You know, it's normally the sinner who confesses to the priest, not the other way around."

"Ben, I came out to make sure you were all right,

or as *all right* as could be expected. I also wanted to make sure you understood that you aren't alone, that others have gone through what you're going through and survived. I never intended to tell you about my family or how I came to the priesthood. That just happened. God's will, I suppose."

"Thank you."

"You're welcome."

The priest had willingly removed his collar both literally and figuratively, if only for a short time. He allowed Benjamin to witness the man within. For the first time Benjamin was seeing not Father Templeman, but Jim Templeman. Until now, he didn't know Jim Templeman existed.

Ben looked at Hiram. "Hiram, I'm also indebted to you. You're a good friend to come back out here on a night like this." Benjamin hesitated a moment, then said, "Just don't expect any overtime pay."

"Ben, that's the kindest thing you've ever said to me." Snickering, he added, "Actually, I only came back because I forgot my top hat and cane."

Templeman smiled and refilled everyone's glasses. As he did, he noticed the relentless rain had finally relented.

CHAPTER 18

AFTERMATH

The day after receiving the telegram, Benjamin, in what he knew would be a vain search for solace, once again made the trek up the hill to Delina's grave. As he stood in the cool spring air contemplating her headstone, the forgotten minutes stretched into forgotten hours as he tried to assimilate this irreversible alteration to his existence. The cold stone before him remained silent. No answers came forth.

Finally, after the sun had etched its path across the sky, he asked his wife to find and look after their son. "He's your responsibility - again. I love you both."

The days blended into weeks as Benjamin did his best to accommodate himself to the fact he would never again see Francis.

As word of Francis' death spread, the requisite stews, pies, and various German potato dishes appeared from sympathetic neighbors. Benjamin was stopped on the street by well-meaning souls intending to provide some comfort, but who instead only reminded him of his loss. His lodge brothers, knowing him better, offered brief condolences, adding only that it would be good to see him back at lodge.

Rest came hard. At first, it was almost impossible for him to get more than a few minutes of sleep at a time. On those occasions when he actually managed to fall into a deep slumber, he sometimes awoke forgetting Francis was dead. Then, after several seconds, he remembered his son was gone and felt as though he'd been punched in the gut. As though cursed, he relived the nightmare of realizing his son was dead over and over again.

Benjamin had closed the door to Francis' room and hadn't entered it since the day he received the telegram. He ignored its existence as best he could, though he realized one day he'd have to deal with its contents.

Several weeks after receiving the War Department telegram, Benjamin found a letter with a foreign military postmark resting in his mailbox. Not waiting to return to the house, he opened the letter and began to read as he walked along the long dirt drive.

April 8, 1918

My Dear Mr. Kyner,

By the time you receive this letter, you will have been officially informed of the loss of your son, Francis, during aerial combat over enemy lines on April 4, 1918.

I was Francis' squadron commander. I am writing to inform you, as best I can, of how Francis died that day.

Our squadron was flying at 12,000 feet very near the front in the vicinity of Lille, France.

A German squadron composed of approximately eight machines suddenly attacked us from above. While the situation immediately became very confused, I can tell you I did see Francis heroically engage and destroy a German Albatros. This was Francis' fifth kill, which qualified him for the status of "ace."

As the fight was soon spread over many miles, I did not witness your son's second engagement, but a squadron mate reported that Francis had been assisting another squadron member who was being pursued by the enemy. Francis successfully destroyed the enemy machine, but in the process was himself attacked.

I must regretfully inform you that while Francis valiantly attempted to outmaneuver the enemy, he ultimately succumbed to enemy fire; however, due to Francis' outstanding skill as an aviator, the enemy pilot was required to subject his machine to extreme maneuvers that resulted in its structural failure and ultimate destruction.

Accordingly, I have credited Francis with a total of three victories. Added to the four he had from previous actions, his total is seven enemy machines destroyed.

I impressed upon my wing commander Francis' skill, bravery and self-sacrifice in coming to the aid of a comrade. On my recommendation, Francis' name was mentioned in dispatches, which qualified him to receive the Distinguished Service Order from His Majesty, King George V.

I trust you will find some comfort in knowing Francis' bravery and sacrifice has been acknowledged by the official awarding of the DSO. This will be forwarded to you through official military channels in the very near future.

Mr. Kyner, Francis was an excellent aviator, a good man and a good friend to his squadron mates and me. He gave his life for a friend and a holy cause. As the Bible says: "Greater love hath no man than this, that a man lay down his life for his friends."

I was proud to know your son. The world is diminished by his loss.

It is my sincere hope this letter provides you with some measure of comfort in this time of grief.

Respectfully,
Robert Card, Capt.
Commanding

As Benjamin approached the house, he finished reading the letter a second time. It was from someone who knew Francis and it made him feel closer to him.

As Benjamin passed Hiram he stopped long enough to hand him the letter, then he returned to what he was doing before he checked the mail.

Benjamin turned back to face Hiram, "I hope the man he died saving was worth it."

He turned and walked away.

After reading the letter, Hiram found Benjamin working on a piece of equipment in the barn.

Returning the letter to Benjamin, he said, "It was decent of the Captain to write to you, Ben. It's good to know he thought so well of Francis."

Placing the letter in a pocket of his overalls, Benjamin said, "Don't forget I spent my time in the Army. The commanding officer always has to write a letter to the family and he always has to tell them what a fine fellow their son or husband was. He can't very well say, 'Dear Sir. I'm sorry your son was killed, but he was a real horse's ass,' can he?"

Hiram looked at Benjamin with a crestfallen expression.

Benjamin said, "Hiram, we both knew Francis. This Captain Card is right."

On a cool day in May, Benjamin and Hiram were just finishing their mid-day meal when they heard an automobile approaching.

Benjamin went onto the porch and saw a green Dodge pulling up to the house. The car came to a stop and a young girl of about 25, her brown hair in a bun and wearing a military-style uniform, stepped out of the car and closed the door. As she approached Benjamin, she smiled and said, "Mr. Kyner?"

"That's right, young lady. What can I do for you?" Noticing a small red cross pinned to each shoulder strap of her uniform, as well as to her billed cap, Benjamin asked, "Looking for a donation?

"No, sir. That's not why I'm here. My name is Bernadette Chevaliers. As you can probably see, I'm with the Red Cross out of Pittsburgh. Actually, I went to school in Athena. My parents still live here."

"Didn't you used to skate on my pond in the winters?"

"Yes, I did," she answered with a smile.

"Sometimes with Francis. That's why I wanted to be the one to visit you today."

"I thought you looked familiar. You've grown into quite a young lady. Why the sudden visit?"

"Mr. Kyner, first, let me offer you our condolences for the loss of Francis. I'm with the Red Cross Home Service. We work with military families. We've received some information from the International Red Cross in France. I'm here to provide it to you. Is there someplace we can sit? This won't take long."

Benjamin froze upon hearing the girl's purpose in coming to his farm. Information about Francis? What information could the Red Cross have about his son? He's dead. The envelope she was holding now registered with Benjamin.

Sensing a sudden change in Benjamin's demeanor, Hiram, who had remained out of sight in the kitchen while listening to their conversation, opened the kitchen door and stepped out. The girl from the Red Cross was startled to see a black man dressed in worn work clothes suddenly appear unannounced.

Hearing the squeaking spring of the kitchen door and noticing the surprised look on Bernadette's face, Benjamin looked over his shoulder at Hiram, then back at her.

"This is Hiram. He works here. We were just finishing lunch. Why don't you come in and have a seat in the kitchen."

The emissary from the Red Cross mounted the stairs. Hiram held the kitchen door open for her and Benjamin. Hiram pulled out a chair for her, and Benjamin sat opposite. Hiram remained standing.

"Mr. Kyner," she began, "the Red Cross has

confirmed your son, Francis, went down behind German lines near Lille in northern France, quite close to the Belgian border. We hope you will find some comfort in knowing his body was immediately recovered by German soldiers and he was given a Christian burial in the Lille Southern Cemetery, just south of the city. A French priest conducted the ceremony. A soldier's religion is stated on his identity tags - his 'dog tags'." She paused.

Benjamin nodded in acknowledgment of what she said. Hiram shifted his weight.

She had spoken from memory. She handed Benjamin the envelope.

"The report is here. It's quite short, but we thought you should have it."

Benjamin said, "I appreciate your driving out here, but you came a long way to say something you could have sent in the mail."

She thought for a moment before answering. "To be honest, Mr. Kyner, I do this a lot, lately. You see, you and a great many others have received what must be the worst news of your life and it was delivered by an impersonal telegram. Maybe because of the war the government can't pull people away to deliver such news in person, but that doesn't mean we have to follow suit. When we have any additional information, we always deliver it personally."

"Well, thank you," Benjamin said. "I do appreciate the effort."

"It's the least we can do, Mr. Kyner," she replied. "We'll certainly be in touch if we learn anything else. God bless."

With that, she nodded to Hiram, stood up and walked to the door, which Hiram again opened for her.

Then she walked down the porch steps toward the Dodge.

As Benjamin and Hiram watched her from the porch, she stopped and turned around. "Also, my fiancé is in the infantry in France. I pray every day we won't have to do this for his parents." She then slipped behind of the wheel of the Dodge, started it, and drove away.

Benjamin and Hiram returned to the kitchen. Sitting back down at the table, Benjamin looked at the envelope in his hands and said to Hiram, "first the telegram, then the letter, now this. I know they're just doing their jobs, but I wish they'd leave me alone."

As he finished speaking, he looked toward the mantle of the fireplace. On it sat a photograph of Francis that Benjamin had framed not long after receiving the telegram. It had been taken during Francis' senior year in high school shortly before he graduated. Though Francis was smiling from behind the glass, the black and white image couldn't do justice to his flaxen hair and penetrating blue eyes.

"Well," responded Hiram, "according to the letter you got from that Captain Card, you can expect that medal to show up anytime."

"Yeah, I know. I sure hope that'll be the end of it."

The two men cleaned up the detritus from lunch and returned to work.

Several days later Benjamin was outside when he heard yet another vehicle approach his front door. A young U.S. Army First Lieutenant very politely and correctly introduced himself. Benjamin listened patiently as he was consoled yet again. The young man, who was wearing thick wire-rimmed eyeglasses, very solemnly explained that he had come from Pittsburgh to present

Benjamin, as Lieutenant Kyner's next of kin, with the Distinguished Service Order awarded by the King of England. Benjamin thanked him and, as he was about to leave, Benjamin looked at the young man's thick glasses and understood why he was in Pittsburgh instead of France.

"There's something I'd like to ask before you leave."

"Yes, sir?"

"The War Department sent me a telegram to tell me my son was killed in action, but they send an officer to deliver his medal. You'd think it would make more sense to do it the other way around."

To give himself time to think, the lieutenant removed his glasses, pretended to clean them with a handkerchief, and replaced them, carefully and deliberately adjusting each wire hoop behind his ears.

"Mr. Kyner," he finally responded, "It's a sad case there are so many of those telegrams. We just don't have the personnel to deliver them in person. That's very regrettable; however, please understand, there are very few decorations of this nature," he said pointing to the case in Benjamin's hand. "We thought the very least we could do was make the presentation in person by someone equal in rank to your son. Doing so has been an honor."

"Thank you."

The young officer turned and left.

After the Lieutenant was gone, Benjamin looked down at the medal. The citation that accompanied the medal essentially mirrored the words contained in Captain Robert Card's letter.

So, my son goes off to fight their war and this is

what I get back, and from the King of England, no less. Damned Europeans. Well, maybe now I'll be left alone.

Walking toward the mantle with the medal in hand, Benjamin's eyes rested on Francis' framed photograph as he considered what to do with the medal in its beautiful satin-lined case. He thought for a moment, then turned to a nearby desk, slipped the case in a drawer, closed it with a bang, and went about his business.

The following week, Benjamin was in Athena picking up supplies for the farm. Walking between stores, he heard himself being hailed. "Ben, Ben!"

Looking around, he saw Templeman behind the wheel of his Ford pulling up beside him.

"Ben, I'm glad I caught you here in town. I was planning on coming out to see you later today."

"Is there a problem, Jim?"

"You could say that," responded the priest. "Why don't you jump in so we can talk?"

CHAPTER 19

THE CARDS WE'RE DEALT

Templeman and Benjamin were in the sitting room of Saint Mary's rectory. Benjamin was seated on a Victorian sofa while Templeman slowly paced the carpeted floor.

"This is hard to swallow," Benjamin said. "On top of everything else that's happened, I wasn't expecting anything like this. Not remotely."

"I know you weren't," the priest said. "News like this would shock anyone."

Benjamin looked up at Templeman, "You know, Jim, I don't think I can take any more shocks. I'm not kidding." After a pause, he continued, "You say she just had the baby?"

"Yes, about three weeks ago. Ben, I hope you understand why I felt I had to notify Allegheny College about Francis. They were expecting him to return after the war and finish his degree and I'm sure he had friends still enrolled there. So, after you received the telegram, I went ahead and contacted the campus chaplain and explained everything. He was grateful and said he'd make sure the news would be in the school newspaper."

"If you hadn't, he never would have gotten back in touch with you and we never would have found out about this."

"It wasn't hard to believe," Templeman went on. "Francis came to see me last July the night before he left. He told me he'd been seeing this Miss Bennett and that things had gotten serious."

Benjamin, his head dropping and his shoulders slumped, nodded. "We'd gone to the cemetery after supper so he could say good-bye to his mother. On the way home, Francis told me he wanted to take a walk through town one more time. I guess I'm not surprised he wanted to say good-bye to you, too."

"To be honest, Ben, I also heard Francis' confession. He wanted a clear conscience before he left for Europe. That's really why I'm not surprised about the baby. I can't say more than that without violating the sanctity of the confessional, but you can guess the rest."

Benjamin nodded. "I never really thought of that. I should have, I guess. Then, lifting his head to look at Templeman, he said, "Growing up, Delina made Francis go to confession every Saturday. He got his religion from her. He sure didn't get it from me."

It was Templeman's turn to nod, but he didn't.

Benjamin added, "He told me he'd been up to Meadville to say goodbye to friends. I suppose that's when it happened."

"The baby was born in April," Templeman said, "so July would be right."

"You said the girl's parents didn't take it well?"

"No," Templeman said. "The Bennett's are a prominent family up north. Their only daughter's illegitimate pregnancy wasn't exactly announced in the local society pages. I was told her father was furious and may have disowned her."

"I bet those rich folks are really thrilled that the father of their grandchild is a farmer's son," Benjamin interjected with bitterness in his voice.

"They shipped her off to relatives out west as soon as she told them," Templeman said. "With Francis overseas, she felt nearly suicidal, I'm told. Before she left, she poured her heart out to the campus chaplain and kept in touch while she was gone. Her mother apparently went out to help with the delivery. I'm told the girl - Eleanor - won't be going back home with a babe in arms nor will she be resuming her position as a librarian at Allegheny College with or without the baby. Her parents wouldn't tolerate it. It fell to the chaplain to write her about Francis."

Benjamin said, "I'm not trying to be an ass, but I don't know anything about her. Is this chaplain sure the baby belongs to Francis?"

"Actually," Templeman replied, "he addressed that issue without any prompting from me. He told me he's known Eleanor and her family for years. Her father is a significant financial supporter of the college. She and Francis were inseparable for the last few months before he left for the army. The chaplain told me there is no doubt Francis was the only one. She loved Francis, Ben, and she refused to give up the baby for adoption. She feels the baby is all she has left of him. That's what I'm told."

"So, now what happens to her? It'll be hard for a

woman in that - *situation* - to find someone to marry."

"That's the real problem right now," Templeman said. "The chaplain and I had a long discussion about that by telephone."

Benjamin nodded. He had never used a telephone.

"Ben," Templeman continued, "we might have come up with a solution, if you agree."

"If *I* agree?" Benjamin responded, "What have *I* got to do with it?"

"Ben, you've lost your wife and your only child. You're alone. This young woman and her baby - your grandson - are also alone and need help. They can't go back to Meadville. According to the chaplain up there, she and Francis were planning on getting married. Francis didn't mention it to you, did he?"

"The night before Francis left - when we went up to the cemetery - he mentioned her to me then. He told me her name was Eleanor. I thought she was just another girlfriend. Thinking back, I guess there was more he wanted to tell me about her, dammit, but I was too wrapped up in my own feelings to pay attention. He probably thought I was ignoring him. I'm such a damned fool."

"Yes, he did want to tell you and yes he did feel you weren't listening and yes you are a damned fool."

With a calloused hand Benjamin rubbed his forehead.

Templeman said, "Francis told me about it that night. He didn't force the issue because he didn't want to ruin your last night together."

Benjamin took a slow, deep breath, then sighed.

"Ben, that's over and done with now. We all make mistakes. Your only child was going off to war, so of course you were wrapped up in your own feelings."

He gave Benjamin a moment to let what he said sink in.

"There's something else," the priest finally said.

"What else could there be?" Benjamin asked sarcastically.

"Ben, the child was born with a problem." He paused to soften the blow, "The boy has a clubfoot, I'm afraid."

Benjamin looked up at Templeman. "Clubfoot? The baby's crippled?"

"That's right, Ben. Your grandchild - Francis' son - is crippled. Eleanor's mother took one look at her grandchild and said his deformity was 'God's vengeance for her sin of lust,' if you can believe it."

"And you want *me* to take them in?" Benjamin asked, incredulously. "A crippled bastard baby and its unwed mother? Her own parents don't want them."

"*Your* grandchild and the woman who loved *your* son, Ben," retorted the priest.

"My God," exhaled Benjamin.

"You're better than that, Ben. Before you start judging, take a good, long look. This is hard on you, Ben, I know. Too many blows at once. I'm sorry. I truly am. Your wife and then your son are cruelly taken from you and before you can catch your breath, there's this."

Templeman walked to the sofa and sat next to Benjamin.

"But now the page has turned and you've been given a new chance. Part of Francis has been returned to you. At the risk of sounding trite, one door has been closed to you, but another has been opened. As your friend, if I can presume to call myself that, I'm asking you not to make a mess of this, Ben. The three of you can help each other. You've all lost the same thing. That young woman who loved Francis, and that crippled baby, need help and, frankly, you're the best one to give it to them. Honestly, Ben, you need help, too, and they're the best ones to give it to you."

Benjamin waited a few moments before he looked up and said, "I just told you I don't think I can take another shock, and you lay this at my doorstep."

"Ben, I don't run the universe. We all take our cards as they're dealt to us. I know this is a hell of a thing to drop on you, but I honestly believe that, in the long run, taking the child and his mother in will be the best thing for everyone. I can tell you without a doubt that if I were given a chance like this, I'd pounce on it. Besides, it wouldn't be the first time you brought a child into your home that wasn't of your own blood."

"Jim, I just can't handle this now. I know I'm being a son-of-a-bitch, but I feel all dried out inside. I've got nothing to give anyone. Everyone I love is dead. They're in the ground and my life is in the past. I'm sorry, I know you mean well, but I've got to go now."

Templeman watched Benjamin stand and walk to the door. He ran his hand through his hair, picked up his black fedora, and followed him to the Model T.

The ride back to Grand Avenue was silent. Benjamin remained deep in thought and Templeman left him alone, hoping he'd find the right course of action on his own. The priest had done all he dared do for the moment. To say anything else at this point would only aggravate Benjamin and force him deeper into recalcitrance.

CHAPTER 20

THE COUNSELOR

The next morning, Hiram arrived to find Benjamin walking the length of the field that had twice been used as an impromptu aerodrome by Francis. The still spring air was cool and there was enough ground fog to hide Benjamin's shoes and create the disturbing illusion he had no feet. The misty hills appeared to be far in the distance and the trees lining the field looked like ghosts standing sentry duty. The effect was ethereal.

Benjamin neglected to acknowledge his hired hand and friend. Hiram considered that since returning from town yesterday afternoon, Benjamin had been moodier and more withdrawn than usual. Something surely must have happened.

"Ben," Hiram asked as he ambled toward Benjamin, "what's going on? You ain't been the same since you got back yesterday. You've gone and crawled inside yourself. I know it's none of my business if you want to sulk, but I just thought I'd let you know I noticed."

Benjamin stopped walking and looked at Hiram. He had a worn baseball and was nervously passing it from one hand to the other and back again. Hiram watched as Benjamin passed the baseball back and forth with the regularity of a metronome.

Benjamin responded, but he was looking off into the distance. That, plus his tone of voice made Hiram wonder if he was simply thinking out loud.

"There's no grave," he said.

Hiram was confused. "What? No grave? Here?"

"Sometimes when I feel the need, you know, when I need to think, when I need answers, I can go on up the hill and at least pretend to talk to Delina. At least I know where she is."

"I know that, Ben," Hiram said, beginning to understand.

"I can't do that with Francis. He's somewhere in France - in Europe. Where they can't stop killing each other. Where they killed *him*.

Hiram said nothing.

"You see, Hiram. This field is all I've got left. This is the last place on earth I saw Francis. This is where he last set foot on the land where he grew up. You remember when I told you about the time he and Delina were attacked by that miserable dog?"

"Yeah, Ben. I remember you told me about that and how you killed it."

"That happened right over there," Benjamin said as he pointed to the spot near the house where the attack occurred.

"And down there," Benjamin pointed to the pond on the other side of the field, "is where Delina and I taught him how to swim so he'd be safe in the water. Maybe he'd still be alive if he'd joined the Navy."

Hiram watched and listened.

"And this is his baseball. Sometimes after church we'd play catch up there near the barn with this very ball." Benjamin turned and took in the long narrow field. "And this is where he left his home to go to war. This is what I have instead of a grave. Goddamn it."

"No, no, Ben, that's not right. If you want to talk to Francis, all you got to do is talk. That's all. It's almost like praying. Wherever Francis is, he'll hear you. You don't need a grave to talk to your son, Ben."

Benjamin was quiet for a moment. Then, without looking up, he said, "Our good padre told me yesterday that Francis had a girl up there in Meadville."

"Oh, well, that isn't a surprise. Francis was a good lookin' boy. He took after his mother," Hiram said, trying to lighten the mood.

Benjamin didn't take the bait. He nodded, but didn't smile, "You're right about that. He was blessed with her looks."

Then he continued, "Templeman also told me the girl just had Francis' baby." He then looked Hiram in the eye to see his reaction.

"Good, Lord, Francis had a child?

"No. Francis never had a chance to have a child. He never had a chance to be a father."

"But his child's been born," persisted Hiram, "and you have a grandchild."

"Looks that way"

"Boy or girl?"

"Boy."

"There's no doubt it belongs to Francis?"

"None, according to the college chaplain."

"Ben, there's something else going on here. What is it?"

"Oh, nothing much. The girl's family have disowned her and sent her away. They won't acknowledge their grandchild and...oh, yes, the baby's crippled."

"Crippled, Ben?" Hiram ignored the rest of Benjamin's explanation. "How is the baby crippled?"

"Clubfoot."

"Lord almighty, on top of everything else, the little boy is crippled. Are you ever goin' to get a chance to see the baby, Ben? Your grandchild? Is that what's got you down?"

Not realizing the irony of Hiram's innocent question in relation to his dilemma, Benjamin answered his hired hand.

"If the good Father has his way, I'll be seeing plenty of him."

"Ben, stop talking in riddles. What do you mean?"

"Jim Templeman thinks I should take the girl and baby in since her highfalutin' rich family has thrown them both into the gutter."

"Good God, that's a lot to have heaped on a man at one time, especially after – well, you know, everything else that's happened," Hiram said, alluding to Francis' death.

"Yep, I agree with you there," said Benjamin, still handling the baseball.

"Sounds to me like you're arguing with yourself about what you're going to do. Am I right?" Hiram asked.

"How the hell am I supposed to know what to do?

Of course you're right," snapped Benjamin. "Why do you think I'm wandering around this field? I have to think."

"Ben, I know this ain't none of my business and you can tell me to go to Hell and you probably will, but it's always seemed to me that the answers to life's important questions are all really simple, when you get right down to it."

"Now who's talking in riddles?"

"Well, you say either 'Yes' or 'No'."

"God in Heaven, you're a genius, Hiram. Why didn't I think of that? Have you thought of running for Congress?"

"Now hear me out, Ben. Why would you say 'No'? Because you don't want to be bothered?"

"The baby's my grandchild, Hiram," Benjamin said, his eyes flashing anger.

"Ah," said Hiram, his white teeth gleaming. "So let's put a checkmark on the 'Yes' side of the ledger."

Benjamin scrutinized him.

"Is it the money?"

"No. Delina and Francis and I got by. It wasn't milk and honey, but we got by."

"That's another checkmark in the 'Yes' column. Now, would you say 'No' because the child's crippled?"

Benjamin, his eyes downcast, hesitated before answering. "It's not what it seems. That's a lot of responsibility. I don't know if I'm cut out to handle it."

"If Francis had some kind of problem when you first met Delina and him, would you have been able to handle it?"

"That would've been different," responded Benjamin indignantly. "Delina would have been there."

"Well," Hiram answered, "the child's mother

would be here."

"I don't know her, Hiram. How do I know what kind of person she is? Does she have what it takes to raise a crippled child?"

"Would Delina have?" replied Hiram.

"Of course she would have," Benjamin answered angrily.

"Why?"

"She was Francis' mother!"

"Oh," Hiram said, allowing Benjamin to draw his own conclusion.

"Yeah, yeah. I see what you mean. But I still don't know what kind of person she is. I don't know if we'll get along."

"Well, you've got a pretty good clue."

"What do you mean?"

"Francis loved her. Francis learned about love - about women - from you and Delina."

Benjamin nodded in agreement as he looked at the ground.

Hiram continued, "She's a rich girl who probably had the world by the tail. Now she's got nothing but a crippled baby. A lot of girls in her position would have given the baby away, especially a crippled baby. I bet if she did that, Mommy and Daddy would take her back. Instead, she kept him not knowing what the future holds for either one of them. You said her family's thrown her out. She doesn't even know how she's going to feed him. I'd say those are pretty damn good clues about who she is, Ben."

"You're right," Benjamin said softly.

"Seems to me like you're chalkin' up a lot of 'Yes's,' but there's one other thing, to my mind," Hiram quietly said, almost to himself.

Benjamin looked at Hiram with expectation.

"Sarah and I have been trying for a long time to have a baby. It just ain't happenin'. You should see the look on her face when she sees someone else's child. Sometimes, just once in a while, I hear her off in some corner of the house, crying. I stopped a long time ago asking her why."

Hiram paused for a moment. "If Sarah and I had the chance the good Lord's given you, Ben, there ain't any doubt about what we'd do. That child is all you have left of your son and your wife. They're both in him. The Lord won't give you more than you can handle. He's taken a lot away from you. Now, He's finally giving you somethin' back."

Benjamin was reminded of Templeman's words: *one door has been closed to you, but another has been opened.*

"Ben," Hiram says.

"Yeah?"

"Don't make a decision you'll regret. Don't mess this up."

Benjamin didn't respond, but considered that Templeman also said much the same thing, but he was less direct.

It's like they got together and planned their strategy before they talked to me. But, Hiram, it's my life, not yours - or Templeman's.

Later in the day Templeman was in the sacristy of Saint Mary's when he heard the main doors of the church open and close. When he stepped out to see who'd entered the church he saw Benjamin standing in the center aisle of the nave.

Without so much as a saying hello, Benjamin said to the priest, "Call your friend up in Meadville. Tell him to send them down."

Templeman nodded and said, "All right, Ben, I will."

CHAPTER 21

ELEANOR MATILDA BENNETT

"It's certainly a beautiful day for Eleanor to see Athena and your farm for the first time, Ben," said Templeman. "I've never seen June look so good."

"To be honest, I haven't noticed, Jim," replied Benjamin, stifling a yawn.

"Trouble sleepin', Ben?" asked Hiram, grinning.

"Well, wha' d'ya think, Hiram? In a few minutes, my life's gonna change forever. I don't have a clue what I'm getting myself into. So yeah, I had trouble sleepin'. I didn't sleep a damned wink all night."

Templeman ignored Benjamin's cursing and looked up and down the train station's platform.

"Quite a few people are wearing a face masks," he said, "even this far out from Pittsburgh. This influenza epidemic is putting the fear of God into them."

"I still think she shouldn't have come," said Benjamin, "especially with the baby. She'd be safer back in St. Louis instead of travelin' half-way across the country cooped up with a pack of strangers."

"Well, Ben, she had her reasons," said Templeman. "According to the chaplain up at Allegheny College, Eleanor felt that not only had she overstayed her welcome with her relatives in St. Louis, but she believes, with good reason, that she and Jeremy would be safer on a farm in the country than in a large, congested city. I suppose she thought the train trip would be worth the risk. I can't say I disagree. After all, heavily populated areas are being hit hard."

"Ya know, Ben," said Hiram, "if you and Miss Eleanor are already buttin' heads, I think I like her already."

Templeman smiled. Hiram guffawed. Benjamin fumed.

Unbeknownst to Templeman and Hiram, Benjamin had prayed, in his own way, that Eleanor's decision wouldn't result in another catastrophe in his life. Afterwards he felt selfish. *I should be worried about Eleanor and the baby, not about himself, but I can't help it.*

"By the way," said Hiram, "I wonder why she named the baby Jeremy?"

"The chaplain didn't get into it," replied Templeman, "and I didn't ask. It's not as important as getting her here safely and that's something she should talk about with Ben privately."

"Well," said Benjamin, "I'm curious, but I've got bigger things to worry about."

The train's whistle interrupted their banter.

"There it is!" said Benjamin.

Looking in the direction of the distant shriek, they saw smoke billowing from behind the trees as the train approached the curve that would lead it into Athena. As the train slowed and pulled into the station, steam vented from the engine, obscuring the platform. The three men craned their necks to see over and between the heads of others who were either meeting passengers or were themselves departing.

"Will ya look at that?" said Hiram with a note of incredulity. "Every passenger getting' off that train is wearin' a face mask."

"What did I tell you?" said Templeman. "People aren't taking chances. The Red Cross is warning everyone to wear those masks on any type of public transport. I've heard that in some cases, a person will come down with the flu in the morning and be dead by sundown. In some parts of the country there aren't enough priests for all the funerals. It's a nightmare."

Benjamin spoke up, "All the more reason to find her and the baby and get them back to the farm, where it's safe."

Just as he spoke those words, a young woman carrying a baby, but otherwise alone, appeared at the top of the stairs two cars down from where the trio was standing.

She was dressed in a lightweight, white cotton dress with pleated bodice and skirt and a high collar adorned with a dark blue ribbon tied as though decorating a gift. She stood beneath a straw-colored, broad-brimmed summer hat, her dark eyes searching the crowd. Like many of the other passengers, a white surgical-type mask concealed her lower face, but her eyes revealed an air of uncertainty.

Responding to the press of the anxious passengers behind her, she descended into the milling sea of people and out of sight.

Benjamin pointed as he shouted, "Is that her? It has to be. She's dressed the way she described. Damn! She just disappeared."

The three men began pushing their way through the throng of humanity. Suddenly she reappeared a few feet away, holding her baby and looking around in all directions. She was searching each face for some sign of recognition.

Her brown eyes fell on the priest's collar and she stopped, eyes flitting from Templeman to Hiram to Benjamin. She raised her hand to her face and removed the mask, revealing a tentative smile.

Her attention returned to the priest, "Father Templeman?"

"Yes, dear. That's me. You must be - Miss Bennett?" Benjamin picked up on Templeman's hesitation; he also felt it was awkward to refer to a young mother as "Miss."

"Yes, Father. I'm Eleanor Bennett," she curtsied as she looked with apprehension at Hiram and Benjamin.

"Let's move over there out of the way of all these people so we can at least hear one another," Templeman suggested.

After leading them to a quieter area, Templeman made introductions.

"This is Hiram Bolt," he said as he gestured toward Hiram who was already in Eleanor's line of sight.

"I'm very pleased to meet you, ma'am," Hiram said while removing his hat.

"Hello, Hiram," Eleanor Matilda Bennett responded, confused as to why she was being introduced to a colored man.

"And this," Templeman continued, "as you may have guessed, is Benjamin Kyner."

Benjamin could only look at Eleanor. She stepped toward him and curtsied with a smile. She surprised him by putting one arm around his neck to hug him lightly as she held the baby in her other arm.

With some hesitation, Benjamin slowly placed his arm around Eleanor's waist, and then dropped it.

"I'm very happy to finally meet you, Mr. Kyner," Eleanor said. "You're very kind to help us like this. I don't know what to say."

"We'll have plenty of time for all that later," Benjamin responded. "Just call me Pa. You're - family."

Templeman and Hiram looked at each other, slight smiles on both their faces.

"Do you mind if I take a look at the baby?" Benjamin asked with some trepidation.

"Oh, of course not!" Eleanor stammered. "What am I thinking? You're meeting your grandson for the first time!"

Looking around to make sure they were away from the crowd, Eleanor removed the small gauze bandage covering the baby's face. He fussed at the intrusion.

"O, Lordy," Hiram exclaimed as all three men crowded around Jeremy, "will you look at that, Ben? He looks just like Francis!"

"He sure does," Benjamin agreed, and then he bit his lip to keep from crying.

"He even has Francis' blue eyes," Eleanor added. "You'll see when he wakes up."

"Father, would you mind blessing Jeremy?" Eleanor asked.

"Of course not, Eleanor," replied Templeman.

The priest made the sign of the cross on the baby's forehead.

"Thank you, Father," Eleanor said with a smile.

Amidst the noise and bustle produced by the train station, Benjamin said loudly, "Well, we'd better start looking for your baggage and get you to the farm."

After bidding Templeman good-bye, Benjamin helped Eleanor up onto the seat of the wagon. Hiram jumped in the back with Eleanor's baggage.

It was obvious to Benjamin and Hiram that Eleanor wasn't used to riding in horse-drawn wagons over rough country roads. Although clearly uncomfortable, she bore up well, uttering not one complaint. For her part, Eleanor noticed that Benjamin kept stealing surreptitious glances at Jeremy, who was cradled in her arms and hidden beneath layers of blankets

After turning onto the dirt road leading to the farm, Benjamin guided the horses to the crest of the hill overlooking his property.

"Well, there it is," he said. "That's home."

Eleanor took it all in for the first time: house, barn, silo, outbuildings, garden, plowed fields, and grazing dairy cows. A gentle breeze, redolent with the scent of newly turned damp earth, blew softly against her cheeks. After several silent moments spent examining the place that would be her and her child's home, she said, "Why, it's lovely. I can see why Francis loved it so."

Francis never told me he loved this place, thought Benjamin.

Benjamin flicked the reins and the horses

continued the familiar route to the house.

After arriving at the front door, Eleanor handed Jeremy to Benjamin while Hiram waited to help her to the ground. Upon alighting from the wagon, she turned to take the baby back. She stopped at the sight of the tall, rough, weathered farmer enveloping her baby in his arms.

Hiram tactfully cleared his throat causing Benjamin to look up.

Embarrassed, he said, "Oh, I'm sorry. Here you go." With obvious reluctance, he tried to return the baby to Eleanor.

"No, Pa, why don't you take the baby into the house?"

Benjamin smiled his gratitude. Holding Jeremy, he led Eleanor toward the house as Hiram began unloading the baggage.

Benjamin mounted the stairs and held the door open for Eleanor and Hiram. Eleanor stepped into what would be her home for years to come. Her eyes roamed over everything as she followed Benjamin to her room.

"There are three bedrooms," Benjamin explained as Hiram manhandled the luggage into the room. "I've been using this one for storage. I just finished emptying it out for you."

Eleanor looked around the room as Jeremy, still held by Benjamin, began to squirm, signaling his feeding time was approaching. The single wood double-hung window was partially covered by thin muslin curtains that may have once been striped blue and yellow. The plaster and lath walls were covered with fading flowered wallpaper. The bedstead was dull brass. There was a simple chest of drawers with a small mirror affixed over it and a matching armoire. They appeared to be made of maple. The floor was laid-on unpainted pine boards.

Hiram left to fetch the remaining luggage.

"The other room belonged to Francis," Benjamin continued. "You can have that one, if you want, but I haven't cleaned it out, yet. I thought you might like to see it the way it was - before. Also, I haven't really felt up to it, if you understand my meaning."

"Of course I understand, Pa. This room will do just fine for Jeremy and me."

"I thought, you know, later, little Jeremy could have Francis' room. When the time is right and all."

"I think that would work out just fine," Eleanor replied.

"Look," Benjamin suddenly said, clearly uncomfortable, "this house hasn't seen a woman since Francis' mother, Delina, passed away during a flu epidemic years ago. First it was Francis and me, and later, just me. Hiram, well he lives over at Black Hollow a few miles away on the other side of Calvary."

"The house is fine, Pa. Really, it is. I'm lucky to be here," replied Eleanor, trying to put Benjamin at ease.

"What I'm trying to say, Eleanor, is that I'm not a foolish man. I know you'll be looking to make some changes. That's to be expected and it's all right with me. I don't care about niceties around the house, but you shouldn't have to put up with that. You've had a hard time, too, and you have Jeremy to worry about. I just want you to know, well, this is your home, too, and you have a say, that's all."

Eleanor stood up on her tiptoes and kissed Benjamin lightly on the cheek with her left hand on his shoulder for balance. As she did, Jeremy began to protest his hunger.

"Pa, thank you. I know Jeremy and I will be happy here. This was Francis' home."

Hiram returned carrying two small satchels and placed them on the floor.

"Thank you very much, Hiram," Eleanor beamed as Jeremy continued to fuss.

Flustered, Hiram could barely blurt, "You are certainly welcome, Miss Eleanor."

"Now, if you gentleman will please excuse me, it's Jeremy's feeding time."

"C'mon, Hiram. Let's give the lady some privacy," ordered Benjamin.

"Oh, yeah, sure," said Hiram as they both shuffled out of the room.

Benjamin closed the door and he and Hiram made their way to the kitchen porch.

"Whew, Ben," said Hiram when they were out of earshot of Eleanor. "Francis sure knew how to pick 'em. She's a beautiful woman. And that Jeremy is the spittin' image of Francis, no doubt about that!"

"Yeah, he is," Benjamin said. "No doubt." *Well, except for one thing*, Benjamin thought imagining what Jeremy's clubfoot must look like.

"Well, I've got to get back to my Sarah. She'll want to hear all about Eleanor and the baby. She'll probably give me hell because I didn't measure and weigh him," Hiram said with a laugh.

"All right then, I'll see you in the morning. Don't get lost on the way home," Benjamin said in mock sarcasm.

Hiram waved his response without looking back as he began walking toward the hollow.

Chapter 22

Preconceptions

Benjamin looked at the Regulator pendulum clock on the wall and judged it was time to do something about supper. Eleanor soon walked into the kitchen to find Benjamin moving among the pots and pans.

"Oh, please Pa, let me do that," she pleaded. "I may as well start earning my keep around here."

Benjamin stepped aside as the young woman swooped in and took over.

"I'm not sure what you're going to find in there," he said, motioning toward the icebox. "I guess I'll have to go into town tomorrow."

"Whatever there is, we'll make do."

Benjamin watched as Eleanor worked with swift assurance. She asked periodically where Benjamin kept the salt, spices, utensils, and other necessities. She wasn't behaving at all like someone used to being waited on by servants.

"I suppose this isn't quite what you're used to,"

Benjamin finally said to break the silence as much as out of curiosity.

"What do you mean, Pa?"

"Well, from what Jim Temple... ahh, Father Templeman said, your family up in Meadville is pretty well off. You must've had a cook and a maid."

"Hah! That's very rich, indeed! My parents were much too frugal for servants, Pa. No, we did everything around the house ourselves. Dad did hire tradesman to, you know, fix things like the plumbing or the roof. He wasn't any good at those things and besides, he was much too busy making money to be bothered."

"Well," replied Benjamin, "that sure explains why you seem to know what you're doing in a kitchen."

"I understand Father Templeman told you the whole story about my parents and their reaction to Jeremy?"

"Yes, we had a long talk about it. In the rectory, as a matter of fact. What did they think of Francis?"

"They liked him well enough, Pa, but they never thought our friendship - that's how they saw it - would go anywhere. They thought he was just another boy I brought home for Sunday dinner. They were pleased he was Catholic."

"That was his mother's doing," Benjamin responded.

"Yes, Francis told me all about his mother and how much you both missed her."

Benjamin nodded. "Yeah, that's certainly true. And now I miss him, too."

Eleanor put down a paring knife she was using to dice a carrot and looked at Benjamin.

"Pa, we both miss him. I loved Francis very much

and he loved me. We were planning on getting married after he came back from France. I know he hadn't told you."

"I think he wanted to, Eleanor, but I was too wrapped up in my own problems to listen to him."

"I know about his last night here and your talk in the cemetery. He told me in a letter. But your knowing about our plans wouldn't have changed anything, so there's no harm done, Pa."

"Did he write to you often?"

"Yes. I kept all his letters."

"Can I ask why you named the baby Jeremy? I mean, it's a fine name, but I'm curious why you didn't name him after Francis. That is, if you don't mind my asking."

"Of course I don't mind, Pa. You must feel free to ask me whatever you like. We have to get to know each other."

Benjamin nodded in acknowledgement of Eleanor's sentiment.

"Well," she began, "to be honest, Pa, I thought long and hard about naming the baby after Francis. When the chaplain at Allegheny College wrote to tell me Francis had been - killed, I decided immediately that I'd name the baby after him. Then, as time passed, I came to realize I couldn't spend the rest of my life calling him Francis. It would have been a constant, painful reminder, especially now that I know how much he looks like his father."

"I can understand what you mean. I think I would have felt the same way myself. I'd find it hard to call another little boy growing up in this house by my son's name."

"I'm so glad you agree. I confess I was afraid of how you might feel about the baby not being named for Francis."

"But why did you name him Jeremy?"

"My maternal grandfather was very good to me. He was a wonderful man. My heart broke when he passed away when I was 15. I was devastated. I decided then that when I had children, my first boy would be named for him. My grandfather's name was Jeremiah. That seemed a little old fashioned for today. Jeremy is a modern version of Jeremiah and I liked the way it sounded. Jeremy's middle name is Benjamin, Pa. He's named after one grandfather from each side of his family."

"That's nice. Thank you."

"Excuse me, Pa. This is as good a time as any. We obviously have a lot to talk about, and we will during the time ahead. But for now I just want you to know that taking me and Jeremy in is a very kind and generous act. After all, you never met me and knew nothing about me. What you've done is very Christian and I'll always be grateful."

Benjamin absorbed everything Eleanor said while looking directly at her. When she finished, Benjamin crossed his arms and pursed his lips. Finally, he said, "There's something you and I have to get straight right now, right from the start. I'm not a religious man, Eleanor. I'm sure Francis told you that. What religion he had, his mother gave him."

"Yes," Eleanor answered, not sure where this was going. "Francis explained how you feel about religion."

"I'm not saying I don't believe in God. I do, but I don't conduct myself according to what some priest or minister thinks God wants me to do. You said that my taking you and the baby in was a Christian act. It wasn't. It was the good and proper thing to do. Christianity had nothing to do with it. Francis loved you and you had his baby. That baby is my grandson. You would've been Francis' wife. Leaving you both to fend for yourselves would have been wrong, even cruel. I didn't take you in because it would make God, Jesus, the Holy Ghost or the butcher, baker and candlestick maker happy or to make sure I get to heaven."

"Pa, I...."

"Hold on, Eleanor. Frankly, what Delina and Francis would have thought of me if I hadn't taken you in means more to me than what God would think or what he'd do about it in the afterlife. But as much as I loved them both, what they would've thought of me wouldn't matter as much as what I would've thought of myself. Eleanor, I did what I did for two reasons and two reasons only: I did it because it was the right thing to do, not because it was Christian, and I did it because I'm selfish. I want my grandson, the last living part of my family, with me and in my life. You're his mother and my son loved you so you belong here, too. Frankly, I always thought 'God' should be spelled with two o's. People should do the *good* thing because it *is* the good thing, not to reap some everlasting reward or to avoid damnation. Frankly, if that's their reasoning, they can go straight to Hell, anyway."

Eleanor remained silent for a moment, then she spoke. "Well, Pa, that's plain enough. Francis also told me you're in a Masonic lodge, so I'm not surprised you don't care about pleasing God. To be quite honest, when I was deciding on whether or not to come here, I was concerned about how I'd deal with you being a Freemason. It's one of the things that worried me the most."

"What? Eleanor, you don't know anything about me or Freemasonry." Remembering his confrontation with Templeman in front of the altar of Saint Mary's, he continued, "Of course, most people don't, but they love to sit back and judge and poke sharp sticks at what they don't understand. Are you one of them?"

"Oh, Pa, no. I didn't mean...."

Benjamin didn't let her finish. "Most of the members of my lodge happen to be Christian and are church-going men. One is a Protestant Minister, believe it or not. Another one, the one who happens to have the worst voice in the lodge, is in his church choir. One is Jewish and I've even had Catholic lodge brothers. What goes on in my lodge has nothing to do with religion or the hereafter. It's got to do with the here and now. And by the way, there's a Masonic organization called the Knights Templar that *requires* its members to be Christian. Are you surprised?"

Benjamin paused. He saw that Eleanor looked confused.

"Is there a rule that for the like-minded to gather Jesus has to be nailed to a cross at the front of the room? We aren't a religion. Religion has a place and Freemasonry has a place, but they're different places. The only conflicts between them are in the imaginations of ignorant self-righteous fools who are looking something to attack to make themselves look important and feel big, at least in their own heads. It's easy to convince ignorant people of a conspiracy if you never have to prove your accusations."

Benjamin leaned against the table. "Didn't Francis tell you any of this? He heard Delina and I discuss it more than once."

"No, Pa, he didn't. We really didn't talk about it. He knew how I felt about being Catholic, and the Church is against Freemasonry, so I suppose he felt he shouldn't bring it up."

"The *pope* is against Freemasonry, Eleanor, but even I won't paint every Catholic with the same brush."

"Like Father Templeman? He knows you're a Mason, doesn't he?"

"Sure, he does. This is a small town and he was Delina's priest."

"Have you talked with him about this?"

"As a matter of fact, he and I just spoke about it recently." Benjamin remembered Templeman, infuriated, demanding he leave Saint Mary's. Then he remembered him stepping out of his Model T in the middle of a thunderstorm and later offering a toast to Francis before divulging his most painful secret. Benjamin remembered the man's trust.

"I've gotten to know him better lately. At first it was a problem, but now I don't think it matters to him. Not everyone who wears a crucifix marches in lockstep with Rome. The Catholic Church is no different than any other collection of human beings. There's always dissent, Eleanor, no matter what the faithful are told. Maybe that's why the conclaves that elect new popes are held in secrecy. They can't let the dues-paying members suspect one cardinal may be stabbing another one in the back."

Eleanor remained silent for a long moment and Benjamin was afraid he'd gone too far.

"Father Templeman didn't *label* you," Eleanor

said.

"What do you mean?"

"You said something before. You said even you won't 'paint all Catholics with the same brush.' Father Templeman didn't do that to you. Neither did Francis' mother, Delina. She didn't label you or your friends based on what she heard about Masons just like you didn't label all Catholics based on what the Church says about Masons."

"Well, Eleanor. At first Templeman did. Maybe the Church forced him to. But like I said, we got past that. Delina never did. So, yes, I suppose that's a good way of putting it."

"Perhaps you didn't realize it, but you refused to judge others by looking at just one part of the whole. It's like the old story about the three blind men and the elephant."

"You've got me there, Eleanor. What story?"

"The story has different forms depending on which culture is telling it. Essentially, it involves three blind men attempting to describe an elephant only by touching it. The first blind man examines the tail with his hands and pronounces that an elephant is like a rope. The second touches a leg and says an elephant is like a pillar. The third feels the trunk and describes the elephant as being like a tree branch. That's how some people see one another. They examine just one part and then pronounce judgment without considering the whole person."

"I never thought of it that way, but I guess you're right."

Looking past Benjamin and through the window behind him, Eleanor whispered, "Like I was judged."

Benjamin wondered for an instant if Eleanor was

talking to him or to herself. He sensed what she was about to say was significant to her and he didn't want to interrupt.

"You see, Pa, the people I love, my family, my mother and father, judged me because I became pregnant without being married. Everything that happened in our lives before then - all the good times, the joy, the love, all the memories - they threw it all away and replaced it with a label. I know what we did was wrong. I know I humiliated them, but I didn't kill anyone. I wasn't caught embezzling from the college or anything like that. Did I really deserve to be thrown out of my family? To have them turn their backs on me?"

"Eleanor, I hope one day they'll realize what they've done before it's too late. They're so lucky to have you. My child was taken from me and I'll never get him back. Your mother and father still have a chance. I'm not the most sensitive man around, but the way I see it, what you and Francis did, good or bad, may have saved my life. My son is gone, but I got part of him back when you stepped off that train holding his child."

"I can see why you're so adamant about your lodge. I judged and labeled you and you refused to accept it. You were right to do that. I'm so sorry, Pa. After what you've done for Jeremy and me I did to you what I hated having done to me. I didn't mean to be hurtful. I didn't understand about your lodge. Later, maybe you can tell me more about what it's all about and help me understand." She took out a handkerchief and dabbed her eyes.

Benjamin realized her tears weren't because of this confrontation, but were the result of a young woman having gone through an emotional sieve: an unexpected pregnancy; her fiancé's death; rejection by her parents who she thought she could trust. Now she had a handicapped baby, an uncertain future, and she'd been thrust into a new situation living with someone she didn't know. She was carrying around a lot of pain, disappointment, and frustration.

Hell, thought Benjamin, *the poor girl must feel like she has no control over her own life. I know that feeling.*

Finally, Eleanor's sobs faded. She wiped her eyes with a lace handkerchief and regained her composure.

"I'm sorry," she said. "I didn't mean to tear up like that. It wasn't your fault. You've been wonderful. I've been through quite a bit in the last year. It seems like I've lost my whole life. It's been a nightmare. Please don't think I was being ungrateful."

"Yes, you've been through a lot," Benjamin said. "No one would blame you for letting it all out."

Eleanor smiled and said, "Well, I certainly didn't intend to have that kind of conversation so soon."

"Neither did I, but now the air is clear, I hope. But since we're on the subject of religion, I guess you had Jeremy baptized?"

She shook her head as she dabbed her eyes. "No, Pa. That's another thing. I couldn't find a priest who would baptize a baby whose mother wasn't wearing a wedding ring. Their excuse was that since I wasn't married to Jeremy's father, regardless of the reason, there was no certainty that Jeremy would be raised in the Catholic Church. The priests I spoke with told me that if I were to marry a Protestant, he might insist Jeremy be raised as a Protestant. So, they refused to baptize my baby. Who are they to decide if Jeremy and I should be permitted to spend eternity together? He's my baby."

Thinking of Templeman, Benjamin said, "By now you can probably guess none of that matters to me, but you're the baby's mother. If he hasn't been baptized, I think we can fix that, if you want."

Eleanor was about to answer when she was interrupted by a loud noise. They turned toward the stove where the potatoes Eleanor had put on to cook were boiling over with an excited hiss as the water turned to steam.

CHAPTER 23

THE GOOD MAN

A few hours later, Benjamin remembered what it was like to have a baby in the house.

Awakened every two hours when Jeremy loudly announced it was his feeding time, he had no choice but to lie awake listening to Eleanor coo to her baby through the thin walls of the small house.

He would think about how many ways his life was changing and how he was being carried along with the current, powerless to alter events. Finally, he would fall into a fitful sleep only to be re-awakened by Jeremy's cries when it was time for his next feeding.

Benjamin was groggy when he arose at dawn to find Eleanor already in the kitchen preparing breakfast. Jeremy was wrapped in a blanket and sleeping in a wicker laundry basket on the table. Benjamin looked at Jeremy and thought of his own bed with longing.

"Good morning, Pa," Eleanor said with a smile. "I hope you don't mind about the laundry basket. I found it on top of the armoire."

"Mind?" he answered through a yawn, "I'd forgotten I even had it."

Benjamin and Eleanor made small talk as they ate breakfast, and were still talking over the last of the coffee when Benjamin began fidgeting with his coffee cup, slowly turning it in its saucer.

"Francis told me about that," said Eleanor nodding toward Benjamin's cup.

"Told you about what?" asked Benjamin.

"When there's something troubling you, you always stare into your coffee cup and slowly spin it around on its saucer."

"Oh. That. I didn't think anyone noticed."

"And there you are, acting just as Francis said you would. I'm ready, Pa, go ahead and ask whatever it is."

Jeremy remained asleep in the basket, only occasionally stretching, turning or yawning.

"Did you know that Bridgewater fella?" Benjamin asked. He didn't look up. He continued to examine the coffee grounds residing in the bottom of his cup. Regardless, he sensed Eleanor's hesitation.

"Yes, Pa. I did. Randy and Francis were best friends. Why do you ask?"

Benjamin nodded, still looking into his coffee cup. "Francis mentioned him once in a while in his letters," Benjamin said.

"Yes, he did with me, as well. They were close. They were very fortunate to be assigned to the same squadron. I think they relied on each other quite a bit."

"*Relied* on each other," Benjamin repeated, emphasizing the word.

"What's on your mind, Pa? What's troubling

you?"

"Eleanor, I'm just curious, he and Francis having been so close, and all. Whatever happened to Bridgewater? Did he make it? Did he get through the war?"

Benjamin noticed that Eleanor hesitated again. "I'm just curious, is all. Francis came here twice with Bridgewater in his flying machine, you know."

"Yes, Pa, I know about that. But I honestly don't know if Randy survived the war. He wrote to me after Francis was killed. You know, to express his condolences. We were all members of the same crowd up in Meadville. Francis and I and Randy often double-dated. Randy never had a steady girl. Each time we all went out together he was with someone different.

"That doesn't surprise me. What else?"

"Well, I answered his letter, but he never replied. I don't know what happened to him, Pa. Perhaps I should have found out, but you can understand I was a little overwhelmed with other things at the time."

"Of course. Sure, Eleanor. I don't really care if Bridgewater is alive or dead. I'm just curious, like I said. I don't personally know many people who were in the war. Did he happen to write what happened that day?"

"Yes, Pa. Randy described essentially the same details that were in the letter from Captain Card you showed me earlier."

"Card said Francis was trying to help another pilot. Did Bridgewater happen to mention who that might have been?"

"No, Pa. He didn't. Would it make a difference if he had?"

"I'm just wondering if the fella my son died

saving was worth it, that's all."

Eleanor looked down at her hands that were folded in front of her.

"Pa, Francis made the decision to risk his life for a friend. I suppose we have to trust in his judgment. What else can we do? Like the Bible says, 'Greater love hath no man than this, that a man lay down his life for his friends.' That's John 15:13."

"I suppose so, Eleanor. I guess you're right. That Captain Card quoted the same line in his letter. I suppose it must get a lot of wear and tear during a war."

They both suddenly became aware of a telltale odor wafting across the kitchen. Eleanor laughed at the look on Benjamin's face.

"It's been a while since I smelled that," he said.

Eleanor lifted Jeremy into her arms and took him to the bedroom to change his diaper. Benjamin returned to his own bedroom to finish preparing for his workday.

On his way out of the house to start his workday, Benjamin passed Eleanor's open bedroom door. She'd finished diapering Jeremy, but hadn't yet wrapped him in his blanket.

Jeremy was laughing and kicking his legs, as babies do. Benjamin, caught by surprise at the sight of Jeremy's inwardly twisted right foot, froze.

Eleanor looked up and saw the look on the face of her child's grandfather. She hurriedly hid Jeremy's legs and feet with a blanket.

"No, please don't do that," Benjamin said curtly.

He approached the baby and removed the blanket. Then he examined the child's crippled foot.

"This is my baby and your grandchild," Eleanor

said. "He's not an insect pinned to a specimen card."

Still holding the corners of the blanket aloft, Benjamin looked at her and said, "Yes. I know. I'm sorry. I just wasn't expecting to see - *it* - like this for the first time." He gently placed the blanket back over the squirming baby's legs.

Eleanor brushed past Benjamin and quickly snatched up Jeremy. She turned toward Benjamin with tears in her eyes as she held the baby close to her chest.

"What caused this?" Benjamin asked.

"What causes any birth defect? Who knows? According to my mother, it's my punishment for sinning. God is punishing both my child and me for *my* sin.

Your mother is an ass, thought Benjamin.

"What have the doctors said?" Benjamin asked. "What can they do?"

"In most cases, there's a device the baby can wear. The baby's shoe is attached to a brace that gradually forces the foot to straighten as it grows. We're lucky, because it's very common for both feet to be affected. Jeremy only has one foot that's affected."

"You said in *most* cases," Benjamin noted.

"In Jeremy's case, a brace will help to some degree, but I was told in St. Louis that his deformity is particularly severe and will require surgery and a long recovery period."

"And what will it take to get the surgery?" Benjamin asked, already knowing the answer.

"Money, Pa," Eleanor answers. "A lot of money I don't have."

"Your parents must know. They won't help?"

"Yes, Pa. They know. My mother came out to St. Louis when it was time for me to deliver. She held

Jeremy just long enough to see his foot, which she immediately declared to be divine punishment. When she was sure I wasn't going to die, she went home to Meadville. In her mind, she had fulfilled her maternal responsibilities."

She looked down at her son.

"As for paying for an operation, no, Pa, they won't help and I won't ask them. You see, I've shamed them and I've been cast out of the Garden of Eden. My father told me I've 'made my bed and now must lie in it.' Apparently, it's acceptable to punish innocent children for 'sins of the mother,' so to speak."

"What do you plan to do?"

"I plan to raise my baby one day at a time. When it comes time for him to walk, we'll take that one *step* at a time." She bounced Jeremy up and down in her arms to calm him.

"Well," Benjamin answered. "This ain't no Garden of Eden, but you and Jeremy won't be cast out. I just hope you understand that I just don't have the kind of money an operation like that would cost. I'm sorry."

"As I said yesterday, Pa, I'm lucky to be here."

You may not think so after a while, Benjamin thought, the image of Jeremy's twisted foot lingering in his mind's eye.

"Later today I'll talk to Templeman about getting Jeremy baptized. There shouldn't be a problem."

"Thank you, Pa. That would be truly good of you. By that I mean *good* with two o's." She smiled through her tears.

Benjamin turned and walked out not feeling very good at all.

Chapter 24

The Family Name

"Ben, it's just not that easy. You don't know what you're asking me to do." Templeman felt steeped in frustration as he tried to communicate with Benjamin. They'd been over this problem several times and were now going in circles.

Why can't he ever be reasonable? thought Templeman.

"I can't believe you'd refuse to baptize an innocent child," Benjamin countered.

"I never said I wouldn't baptize the baby, Ben. Don't put words in my mouth. I said it wouldn't be an easy thing to do. Stop being so damn angry and just *listen*, will you?"

The two men were in Templeman's office in Saint Mary's rectory. When he understood why Benjamin was making an unannounced and uncharacteristic visit, the priest had checked to make sure the gossipy housekeeper was gone.

The farmer's response was an impatient glare.

"I can't falsify a baptismal certificate. When Jeremy is baptized, I'll have to enter his name as Jeremy Benjamin *Bennett.* That's his *name*, for the love of God."

"His father's name was *Kyner,*" Benjamin responded angrily. "If you don't baptize him as Jeremy *Kyner*, Eleanor and the boy won't be able to show their faces in this town. How will he be able to go to school?"

"Ben, I am a *priest* and I'll conduct myself in accordance with my vows, which included a vow of obedience. If I were to willingly falsify Jeremy's baptismal certificate, it would be the same as lying, which would be a violation of that vow."

"How?" Benjamin demanded. "It's vow of obedience, not a vow of honesty."

Templeman sighed, thinking, *This test of wills is going nowhere.*

"Ben, when a priest takes a vow of obedience, he signifies his willingness to let God act through him. To knowingly and willingly lie would be to violate that vow. His promise to God would be corrupted. Do you understand?"

"What about keeping your background a secret from your congregation? Isn't it a lie to keep *that* truth a secret?"

Templeman looked at Benjamin with narrowed eyes as he thought, *"So, now you use something I told you in confidence against me?"*

"Ben, first, my bishop knows about my past and has agreed it would be in the best interest of my congregation for them not to know about it. Second, the only person who would be harmed if it became known I once had a family would be me. I wouldn't be able to have the same relationship with my congregation and would probably have to move on. On the other hand, falsifying a baptismal certificate would have all kinds of ramifications. Eleanor and the baby would suffer, the credibility of the Church would be diminished, and my superiors would justifiably lose faith in me. Frankly, Ben, I'm shocked and disappointed you would bring that up. I shared my past with you in confidence."

Benjamin's body went slack as he hung his head.

After giving his remark a moment to sink in, Templeman continued, "Besides, Ben, Jeremy's birth certificate lists his name as Bennett. What difference does his baptismal certificate make?"

"His birth certificate is in St. Louis. No one here knows him or Eleanor. The only ones who know the truth are you and Hiram. Hiram won't say anything and if you do, God will send you to Hell. I can tell people what I please. They won't know any different. No one will have a reason to ask for a marriage certificate."

Templeman rankled at the insinuation he needed the threat of eternal damnation to maintain a parishioner's confidentiality. He bit his tongue.

"Ben," Templeman continued, "there's another issue. Even if we conducted the baptism in secret then filed away the certificate in the back of a dark drawer, people would still know."

"How"?

"Because, when a child is baptized into the Catholic Church, he or she must have two sponsors who can answer for the child during the rite, since the child is obviously too young to understand what's going on. These sponsors are the godparents who are, in the eyes of the Church, technically responsible for the child's religious upbringing. They have to sign the baptismal certificate. And before you ask, let me say no, a child's parent may not also be the child's godparent. There's no getting around it. There would be no way to keep Jeremy's true last name a secret. I'm sorry."

"And I'm sorry I took up your time, Jim. I just feel so damn bad for both of them. For myself, too, I guess. The girl deserves a break and I wanted to make it happen for her. I can't even afford an operation for Jeremy's foot."

Benjamin turned to leave.

"There is a way, Ben."

Benjamin turned back and looked at the priest with surprise and hope in his face. "What? Why didn't you say something before? What is it?"

"I didn't bring it up because I'm not sure how you'll take it and I wanted to see how desperate you are, to be honest."

"Well, what is it?" Benjamin said, growing indignant.

"You can adopt Jeremy and give him the Kyner name legally. His name would then be entered as Kyner on the baptismal certificate. You would then, of course, become legally responsible for him, but you've already taken on that role, so it really wouldn't make any difference. Frankly, I'm surprised you didn't think of it yourself. After all, you adopted Francis and made him a Kyner."

Benjamin stood motionless. "But he's my grandson. Is that legal? I mean, to adopt my own grandson?"

"Of course it is, Ben. I know of similar cases where both parents are dead or out of the picture for some other reason and the grandparents are raising the child. I've never seen it happen when one of the parents is still alive and behaving responsibly toward the child, but I checked and, yes, it's legal."

"But Eleanor's name would still show as Bennett, wouldn't it?"

"Yes, she's too old for you to adopt," Templeman said in an attempt at humor. The situation had been much too tense.

Benjamin stared at him, his features motionless.

"Well, I can't falsify her name any more than I can lie about Jeremy's. Look, it doesn't happen very often, but it can always be implied - by you, not me - that Eleanor kept her maiden name upon marrying. I've heard of some of the women's suffrage people - the 'suffragists' - doing just that. I can't imagine a man who would tolerate it, but apparently some do. At any rate, it's your best option."

"Adoption. All right. I'll think about that. Thanks."

Templeman could see Benjamin was struggling with the idea.

"Ben," he said, "the baby has to be baptized. I know how you feel about those things, but it's very important to Eleanor and it's of grave concern to the Church."

"Let's keep this just between us," Benjamin asked. Then he turned once again and walked out of the rectory.

That night over dinner Benjamin explained to Eleanor what he had learned from Father Templeman. Everything, that is, except the priest's suggestion that

Benjamin adopt Jeremy.

"I don't know what's worse, Pa," Eleanor said, "not having Jeremy baptized or having everyone whisper behind our backs that he's a...a bastard."

"Anyone who says that will answer to me," Benjamin said with steel in his voice.

"That won't stop the whispering, and when he starts school...well, you know. Children can be so cruel."

After a few silent moments, Eleanor spoke up. "Actually, I do know what's worse. *Not* having him baptized. If anything were to happen to Jeremy and he wasn't baptized, I would never forgive myself. He couldn't find salvation and wouldn't be admitted into Heaven."

"I heard about all that from Delina," Benjamin said. "What kind of a religion is it that would punish an innocent child for something that's not his or her fault?" As he said the words aloud, he thought of Jeremy's twisted foot. He began to feel nauseated from self-reproach.

"Pa, I know how it must look to someone from outside the Church, but this is how it is. It's my Church and if I choose to be a Catholic, I must put my trust in the Church and those who God has entrusted with its safekeeping. I created this problem, so I'll just have to find a way to work through it."

Eleanor stood and began clearing the supper dishes. As she turned toward the sink, Benjamin looked at her back. Recalling his conversation with Templeman, he turned his eyes from her and looked down at his calloused hands. He could feel his face burning.

CHAPTER 25

TEA

"Oh, Sarah, if it weren't for you, I'd lose my mind," Eleanor said to Hiram's wife as she walked through the kitchen door. Sarah and Hiram made the walk from Black Hollow together. The men were now busy cultivating the corn.

"Honey," Sarah said while tickling Jeremy's chubby cheek, "I'm about to go stir crazy myself. Everyone's scared to death of this influenza and nobody's goin' anywhere. I'm grateful that I can come over here and help you with this beautiful baby!"

"After I arrived, I asked Pa to take Jeremy and me up to the cemetery so I could see Francis' mother's grave. I know Delina meant so much to each of them, but it felt almost like a pilgrimage. Pa was a different person up there; he was very subdued and thoughtful. Delina died so long ago, but I'm afraid he's not over losing her. It's like he's living in the past. Anyway, that's the only time I've been off the farm since I arrived weeks ago."

Sarah's expression hardly changed as she asked, "Have you given any more thought to having Jeremy baptized?"

"I'm a coward, I'm afraid. I'm hoping for some type of inspiration, so I've done nothing," Eleanor said as she put a kettle on the wood-burning stove to make tea. "I can't make myself allow Jeremy to be baptized with any name but his father's. Not in this small town. I just can't mark him that way. Yet, not bringing him into the Church is vile of me. There must be a solution, but I just can't think of what it is."

"Eleanor, you don't have any right to be so hard on yourself. You're not the first mother to feel torn about making the right decision for her baby. That's part of what being a mother is all about, honey. Making the right decision isn't always easy. If you weren't worried, *that* would be a problem."

Eleanor, who had never before been close to a colored person, was struck by the irony that she was now making tea for the only female friend she'd made since arriving in Athena; a negro woman. Regardless, she trusted Sarah to keep her secret.

"I keep telling myself Jeremy isn't baptized yet because the epidemic makes it too dangerous to take him into town."

"Well, you're right there, sweetie," Sarah replied. "It's too dangerous. People tell me the streets are almost deserted. No one wants to take a chance on dying from the flu."

"Actually, in a very odd way, it works out. In my family, babies are baptized when they're two weeks old. For those two weeks, the baby never leaves the house for fear that if anything happens, the baby won't be admitted to heaven. So, I keep him safe here with me until I can figure out what to do. The flu is the excuse I use, but it's hard to lie to yourself."

"You've got to do what you've got to do, Eleanor, but you know you can't keep him here forever."

"I know, Sarah. Like I said, I'm a coward. I can't make a decision. There has to be a solution. Pa discussed it with Father Templeman, but they couldn't come up with an answer. As if that isn't enough, now another problem troubles me."

"What problem is that? Is Jeremy sick?"

"No. It's Pa."

"Ben?" Sarah asked with a quizzical look. "What's wrong with Ben?"

"When he saw Jeremy's foot it was quite a shock for him. I know it was for me, too, the first time I saw it."

"And?"

"And since then he hasn't held Jeremy. As a matter of fact, he hasn't come close to him."

"I see what you mean, honey, but listen to me. Ben is a good man. He's as gruff as they come but there ain't no man more decent, except Hiram, of course." Sarah smiled.

"Of course," responded Eleanor, forcing herself to smile out of politeness. "Do you remember when I said that up in the cemetery, standing over Delina's grave, it occurred to me that Pa has never gotten over losing her and was stuck in the past?

Sarah nodded.

"Well, I've been thinking. Francis told me that after she died - in an influenza epidemic, by the way - Pa became totally devoted to him. Francis was his whole life. Francis was all Pa had left of his dead wife. He was really distraught when Francis joined the Army without discussing it with him first."

"I think you've hit the nail on the head, honey," Sarah said. "Ben was beside himself when Francis left. The day he got the telegram about Francis, Hiram came home and told me about it. The priest, Father Templeman, came out with the Western Union man. Ben just up and sent Hiram and Father Templeman away so he could be alone. That ain't natural. Hiram was so worried that he walked all the way back to the farm in a thunderstorm that same night to make sure Ben was all right."

"Was he?" Eleanor asked.

"No. He was standing in the middle of his field where Francis took off in that flying machine. He was just standing there in the dark and the wind and the rain with lightning crashing all around. He was crying. That field was the last place he saw Francis alive. When Hiram got there, he found Father Templeman trying to get Ben to go in the house. With Hiram there, he finally did."

"They *both* went back? In a *storm*? At *night*?"

"Yes, Eleanor. They did. I told Hiram not to go. It was too dangerous with the lightning and all. But he went anyway. Good thing he did, too. Ben could've been struck down by lightning any second. That storm was vicious."

"Pa certainly has two good friends," Eleanor said, "and one of them is a Catholic priest!"

"Yes, he does. He's a good man himself, Eleanor. You can see that, can't you?"

"Of course, but he was so devoted to Delina and Francis. It's such a terrible thing to lose the people you love, especially a child." As Eleanor spoke, she picked up Jeremy and hugged him, burying her face in his neck.

"Pa doesn't seem able to let go of the past. I wonder if he thinks that by accepting Jeremy, he'll finally have to admit Francis is gone forever? Sarah, do you think that could be it? Maybe, in Pa's mind, Jeremy's foot is just an excuse to push him away. You know, he never re-married after losing Delina."

"Sweetie, I said Ben is a good man. I never said he was easy to love. Delina was a Saint."

"I know, Sarah, but still, he ran a farm while raising a young son all by himself. He told me he didn't even hire Hiram until Francis was getting ready to leave for college. Any other man in that position would have tried hard to find a wife, out of necessity, if not out of loneliness. It's very odd. And he keeps going up to the cemetery to visit Delina's grave."

"Are you saying he didn't get married again because if he did, he'd have to say goodbye to Delina once and for all?" Sarah deduced.

"Yes. I think I am saying that. And now, with Francis and Jeremy, the same thing is happening again. Pa isn't allowing himself to get on with his life. Sometimes, very early in the morning before Hiram arrives or later when the day's work is over, I'll see Pa walking up and down that field where he last saw Francis. He almost thinks of it as Francis' grave or some kind of memorial. He's not letting go. It had to hurt Francis to be without someone who could fulfill the role of mother for him. This time, being ignored by his grandfather while he grows up will hurt Jeremy. Do you think I could be right?"

"Could be, Eleanor. Could be. You just give Ben

time. He has a lot of adjusting to do, too. He'll come around. You'll see," Sarah reassured.

"I hope so, Sarah. I don't think I can go on like this. What will happen when Jeremy gets older and begins to notice the most significant man in his life doesn't want anything to do with him?"

"It won't come to that, honey." Sarah replied, this time without smiling. She reached for the boiling kettle and poured the steaming water into the teapot.

As Eleanor watched steam rise from the teapot, her thoughts returned to the problem of having Jeremy baptized as a Kyner.

"Sarah, I can't allow Jeremy to be baptized with any name but his father's. He has to be a Kyner. There must be a solution and I have the feeling it's right in front of me. Why can't I see it?"

Sarah put the hot kettle back on the stove and looked at Eleanor. "Well, sweetie, maybe it would help if you spoke with Father Templeman yourself."

Chapter 26

BATTLEFIELD

The summer waxed and waned and the corn grew taller in the fields.

One warm evening after dinner, Benjamin was reading the newspaper while Eleanor pretended to enjoy a dime novel. Jeremy was asleep in his crib and a light breeze ruffled the new curtains Eleanor made for every window in the house.

Benjamin turned the page and his eye caught sight of an advertisement for Liberty Bonds and an accompanying text of a patriotic speech by General "Black Jack" Pershing titled "The Battlefields of France." In the speech, Pershing, who had actually given the speech from the French battlefields, exhorted Americans to "unflinching support" of the war effort. Pershing gave the speech on April 4, 1918, the day Francis was killed. "Goddamn it," Benjamin muttered as he turned the page.

Startled from her reading by Benjamin's unexplained anger, Eleanor looked at him with concern.

"Pa, do you mind if I ask you a question?"

With experience honed by years of marriage, Benjamin realized from Eleanor's tone of voice that he'd better tread carefully.

"Sure," he answered with feigned nonchalance, "what's on your mind?"

"Pa, please don't take this the wrong way, but I've noticed that since Jeremy and I have been here, you don't seem very interested in playing with him or holding him. Is something troubling you? Something about Jeremy?"

Well, there it is, finally, thought Benjamin.

"Eleanor, I'm not used to having anybody around except Hiram, and that's only during the day. I'm used to keeping to myself, that's all." *I'm a damned poor liar,* he thought.

"But we've been living here for several months now, Pa, and Jeremy is your grandson. I know having us here is a big change in your life, but surely enough time has passed for you to get accustomed to our being around. I feel you're treating Jeremy and me like temporary boarders rather than family. I'm concerned you may think you made a mistake inviting us into your home. If that's true, I need to know."

Oh, Jesus Christ! he thought. "Eleanor, I'm not sure what you're talking about."

"Ever since you saw Jeremy's clubfoot, Pa, you've been avoiding him. Does it bother you that much? His deformity isn't his fault. He's too young to even be aware of it, yet. Is that why you don't want to be near him?"

Can she really see I'm that much of a bastard?

"Eleanor, I don't know where this is coming

from. I've never been an affectionate person and I've never been much good with babies. I'd be acting the same even if Jeremy didn't have a problem."

Eleanor carefully examined Benjamin's face. He felt her gaze like heat from the wood-burning stove.

"Pa, that little baby needs you and you've been ignoring him. He responds more to Hiram and Sarah than he does to you. *You're* his grandfather, not Hiram. When he begins to play with other children, he'll discover he's different. It will be hard for him. They'll most likely be cruel. That will be bad enough, but if he senses rejection from you, the man in his family, it will be devastating. I wouldn't be able to bear it!"

Benjamin felt like a thief who'd been caught red-handed. Desperately searching for a way to escape, he said, "Eleanor, you've been through a lot. Maybe you're just being a bit over protective of Jeremy. On top of losing Francis you have a crippled child. It's an enormous burden. I'd say your imagination is running away with you."

"Pa, the fact that you turn your head whenever Jeremy's feet are uncovered isn't my imagination. The fact you haven't once held him since the day after we arrived on this farm isn't my imagination. And the fact that this has been going on for months isn't my high strung, over-active female imagination!"

"Christ, Eleanor, I worked hard all day and sat down to read the paper. I didn't bargain to be attacked like this!

"Pa, I'm not attacking you! I'm begging you to love and accept your grandchild!"

"Eleanor, I do love Jeremy."

"Perhaps, but you don't accept him. You don't

accept he's not like other baby boys - that he's not like Francis was."

"That's not true. His foot doesn't mean anything to me."

Liar!

With moist eyes, Eleanor slowly shook her head. "But Pa, don't you understand? That's not how you're behaving toward him. He's not a leper. He's Francis' son!"

"I know who he is, Eleanor. You keep going in circles. I know very well he's Francis' son!"

"And Francis is gone, Pa. Jeremy needs a father and that has to be you. You have to do what Francis can't. That chance was taken from him. You're the only one who can take his place."

"I know my son is dead, Eleanor. I told him not to go, but he didn't even tell me before he signed up. Now the irresponsible fool is dead and he's left you and that baby behind."

"And you, Pa. He left you behind, too. You keep walking up and down that field where he and Randy used to land just like you keep visiting Delina's grave."

Benjamin rewarded Eleanor's remark with an angry glare.

Eleanor ignored him. "Is that it, Pa? Are you afraid that by accepting Jeremy you'll be sending Francis away? That you'll have to finally say goodbye? Is Jeremy's poor little twisted foot only an excuse to push him away?"

"Eleanor!" Benjamin shouted.

She started. Never before had she heard Benjamin raise his voice.

"Listen Pa, please. Just because you have Jeremy

doesn't mean you have to give up remembering and loving Francis. I never will! You don't have to make a choice between them, Pa!"

"I've had enough of this. Francis said you were a librarian, not a damned psychiatrist."

He walked out of the house, letting the screen door slam behind him.

Eleanor buried her face in her hands and cried. It seemed to her that her world, though small, was on the verge of flying apart. She wasn't allowed to experience the luxury of solitary crying for long. The slamming screen door woke Jeremy, who began to cry.

Benjamin was confused and angry, but not at Eleanor. He was angry with himself. *You're a first class idiot,* he thought. It was too late to go to the cemetery. Instead, he walked down the hill toward the field. Looking westward, he could see the surface of the placid pond, pink from the reflected light of the setting sun.

Benjamin let his mind go blank as he watched the rays of the dying sun slowly fade. He found himself listening for the sound of a flying machine's rasping motor, a sound he knew would never come.

Francis, you young fool. You went and got yourself killed. You only thought of yourself. I hope you found what you wanted, because all the people you loved are paying for your selfishness.

CHAPTER 27

THE DARK CORNER

"Ben, I wasn't expecting you," said Templeman after opening the door of the rectory in response to Benjamin's knock. "C'mon in."

"Thanks, Jim," replied Benjamin stepping into the small hallway. "I guess I'll have to break down one of these days and get a telephone. Eleanor's been asking for one in case Jeremy gets sick or there's an accident."

Templeman closed the door after. Leading Benjamin into the parlor, he asked, "Are Eleanor and the baby alright?"

"They're why I'm here. Well, about Eleanor, anyway. Jeremy's fine."

A look of concern clouded Templeman's features. "What's the problem, Ben?"

"Eleanor's really been on edge lately. I think she's been cooped up too long on the farm because of the damned influenza. I'm beginning to feel like I'm back in Cuba. I thought it might do her some good if you could come out and spend some time with her. Can you maybe do a Mass or some other kind of service? She's complained a few times about feeling guilty because she hasn't been to church."

Templeman nodded. "A lot of people are too afraid of the influenza to go out unless they have to. Saint Mary's has developed quite an echo recently. To answer your question, I could certainly come out and give Eleanor Communion. It wouldn't be a problem."

"That might be just the ticket. Thanks. I'll let her know. It should cheer her up. How about coming for supper on Sunday?"

"Fine, Ben, but...."

Benjamin stood to leave and turned toward Templeman with a questioning look.

"Have you made a decision about adopting Jeremy? That would do more for Eleanor than a visit from me."

"No, I'm still thinking about it. It's not an easy idea to get used to, you know. It's not like when I adopted Francis. I married Delina. I barely know Eleanor."

"Ben, you know the boy has to be baptized. Adopting him won't solve all your problems, but it'll be a huge relief for Eleanor."

"Yeah, I know. Just let me think about it some more. So, we'll see you Sunday afternoon?" Benjamin asked, changing the subject.

"Tell Eleanor I'll be there."

"All right, then. Thanks."

Templeman stood in the open doorway watching Benjamin as he walked away.

I can't put my finger on it, he thought, *but*

something isn't right.

It was a sunny Sunday afternoon in late September 1918, when Father James Templeman arrived at the Kyner farm behind the wheel of his Model T.

Eleanor opened the screen door to greet Templeman. She was wearing the same white cotton dress she wore when she arrived at the Athena train station four months earlier. A cooing and gurgling Jeremy swaddled in blankets was in her arms.

After exchanging pleasantries, Eleanor said, "Father, I thought it would be best if I took Communion before we had supper. Lunch was a few hours ago, is that all right?

"Eleanor, you're a nursing mother. The rules about fasting before taking Communion don't apply in your case. You've waited more than long enough and in more ways than one. Where's Ben?"

"He's tending to a sick cow. He may be a while, which is another reason why this is a good time. I was thinking we could go down by the pond. There's a table and bench and it's such a lovely spot."

"After you, Eleanor. Please lead the way."

As they walked, Eleanor asked, "Father, according to the newspaper the influenza is getting worse. It should have run its course by now, shouldn't it?"

"Eleanor, it's actually very bad and yes, it's getting even worse. There are reports a more virulent strain has mutated and is spreading rapidly throughout the world. It's only a matter of time before we see it here. You had better not budge off this farm. Keep yourself and your baby safe. Just stay put."

"But this is all so strange. There have been flu epidemics before, but none like this. This is summertime, after all. Influenza is normally a winter disease. Do you think it's because of the war like the papers say?"

"Not the war *per se*, but there are millions of soldiers now, many times more than during peacetime. The medical people believe that their living conditions, especially at the front where they live in tight quarters with poor sanitation, etc., is the major factor contributing to the pandemic. They say by the time it's over more people will have died from this influenza than from the Black Plague."

"Oh, dear God, that's horrible."

"Yes," Templeman agreed. "It's worse than most people are aware. I just returned from helping with funerals in Pittsburgh. Not only are there more deaths than the churches can handle, but a good number of priests have been taken by the flu. They can't make coffins fast enough and many people are buried simply wrapped in sheets. It's quite hideous."

They arrived at the wooden table next to the pond.

Templeman looked around at the softly rippling water, the tall, uncut grass waving in the breeze and the puffy white clouds above. "This is a beautiful spot," he remarked as he placed a small black valise on the table. "Such beauty makes it hard to believe that at this very moment there is so much sickness and misery throughout the world."

"This is as close as I can get to the water without being in a rowboat. I can't swim," Eleanor confided.

Pointing to the wooden boat lying inverted further along the shore of the pond, Templeman asked, "Do you ever go out in that? Ben once told me there are fish here."

"Yes, I've taken Jeremy out for short excursions in the boat. It's a nice diversion since I don't feel safe to leave the farm. Not with the flu the way it is. I have to be careful with Jeremy, though. He's crawling now like a little rocket. If I turn my back for an instant, he's gone. The last time we were in the boat, he almost crawled out. I had quite a fright."

As Eleanor sat down and switched Jeremy from her right arm to her left, she looked at Templeman and asked, "Father, would you mind hearing my confession before Communion? It's been quite a while."

Templeman removed a gold embroidered stole from the valise. He kissed it, and then draped it over his neck. He then sat next to Eleanor and listened as she whispered her transgressions. When Eleanor was finished, he announced her penance and, finally, stood to give her Communion in the form of a blessed wafer of unleavened bread.

Afterward, Templeman sat again. "Has there been any progress toward a decision about Jeremy's baptism?" he asked.

Eleanor's features collapsed.

"Oh, Father, how can I baptize my baby when that would also brand him as illegitimate? I just don't know what to do." Her eyes began to glisten with tears.

"But Eleanor, you must know I've explained to Ben that I can't falsify a baptismal certificate."

"Yes, Father. Of course you can't and I would never expect that of you. But if Jeremy is given my name instead of his father's, the godparents would know and then everyone would. This town is just too small."

"Well, as I suggested to Ben, that can all be easily

avoided. He must have explained it to you."

Eleanor's face was a mask of confusion as she looked at the priest.

"Explained what, Father? There's a solution? What is it?"

"He didn't tell you? Eleanor, I suggested to Ben he adopt Jeremy just as he adopted Francis. Then, Jeremy would be a Kyner and that's the name that would go on his baptismal certificate. As for your name being Bennett, you could lead people to believe you wanted to keep your maiden name when you married. In this case, I don't think God would hold a white lie against you, or against me for suggesting it. No one would be the wiser."

Eleanor sat down on the bench. She was stupefied. "Father, you mean Pa can adopt Jeremy, his own grandchild? Even though I'm living in the same house?"

"Yes, Eleanor. I explained it all to Ben. It's perfectly legal, though I can understand why it took you both by surprise."

Eleanor's eyes moistened. "Father, Pa never said anything about adopting Jeremy."

"Come to think of it, he asked me to keep our conversation just between us, but I didn't think he was excluding you. I assumed he'd told you everything. Eleanor, I'm so very sorry. I spoke out of turn."

"No, Father, you didn't. You did the right thing. Actually, I should have thought if it myself, but I've been so - so overwrought." She buried here face in her folded arms and began to sob. "Why does Pa hate my baby so? His own grandchild! How could he be so cruel?"

Templeman was surprised and confused to hear

Benjamin accused in this manner. Still wearing his stole, he sat down next to Eleanor.

"Eleanor, tell me what happened."

CHAPTER 28

GUILT

When Eleanor was finished pouring out her heart to Templeman, the sun had drifted closer to the horizon turning the western sky a deep blue tinged with streaks of gold. The beauty of the evening belied the emotional turmoil roiling Eleanor's soul.

"Eleanor," said Templeman, "When Benjamin came to the rectory, I knew something was wrong, but I couldn't tell what it was. I never dreamed it was as you describe."

"Father, please promise me you won't tell Pa I know the truth."

"Of course, Eleanor, but don't you think one of us should confront him?"

"No, Father. I want Pa to do the right thing without being forced. Otherwise, we'll all be living a lie. I'll give him time, but I'm not sure how much longer I can stand this."

"Has it really gotten that bad for you, Eleanor?"

"Father, I've always thought of myself as a patient woman, but I don't understand what's going on inside of Pa that's making him behave this way toward Jeremy and I'm tired of guessing. I don't know what to expect and I'm afraid for my baby's future. If things don't change - if Pa doesn't change - the only way I'll feel safe is to act on my own. I'll have to go. I don't know how or where, but I will. I don't want it to come to that, but I won't raise Jeremy under a cloud."

During dinner, Benjamin sensed something was different. Both Eleanor's and Templeman's behavior seemed forced. They made small talk and laughed, but it was as though they were acting. His gut told him it was best to say nothing. He pretended to go along with them.

When it was time for Templeman to leave, he thanked Eleanor. Benjamin walked with him to the Model T.

"Thanks for coming out, Jim. I'm sure Eleanor feels better now that she got some religion."

"For Eleanor's sake, you're welcome, Ben. Maybe she does feel better, but she *could* feel a whole lot better. You know what I mean."

"Yeah, I know what you mean."

"Will you go through with it? The adoption?"

"Look, Jim, this will settle down soon. After this damned influenza has passed and people can begin moving around again, I'll drop her off for church on Sundays. That'll make her happy."

"Ben, Francis didn't fall in love with a simpleton. How can the woman go to church with an unbaptized child? People will want to get to know her and Jeremy. They're new members of the community and Saint

Mary's congregation. What happens when Jeremy gets older and starts asking questions? If that child isn't baptized, people will find out and they'll be curious as hell. They're good people, Ben, but they're people. They're no different than anyone else. If they smell dirt, they'll start digging - and talking. And if you let things 'settle down' as you put it, they may 'settle down' in a way you won't like."

"I hear you, Jim."

"I have to wonder if you do, Ben. I think I know you well enough to understand you're not an effusive person. You don't show your emotions and you don't like it when people around you show theirs. Rather than getting involved in a situation that requires you to interact with someone emotionally, you do nothing and hope the problem will just go away. Well, Ben, as a friend, I'm here to tell you there is such a thing as being too late. You have a problem and you have to handle it or maybe more than the problem will *just go away*.

Benjamin's eyes met Templeton's.

"That's right, Ben. *Now* you've heard me."

Benjamin crossed his arms and turned to look past Templeman toward the field. He remained silent while Templeman waited for some type of response.

"Maybe that would be best. Maybe they'd both be better off someplace else. I sure as hell don't deserve them."

Templeman's eyes widened. "What? What on earth makes you say *that?*"

"When you first told me about Eleanor and the baby, I told you I couldn't handle it. I told you I'd been through too much and I was dried out. I had nothing left to give. You should have listened to me. *I* should have listened to *myself.*"

"Ben...."

"I had real doubts, but I never guessed it would be like this, you know, this bad. I loved Francis and I want so much for this to work out, but every time I look at that little baby I see Francis at that age. What am I supposed to do, Jim, watch my son grow up again knowing it really isn't him? How can I do that without it tearing me up?"

Templeman listened. It was rare for Benjamin to expose himself like this. If he were going to be any help, he needed to know how Benjamin felt and what he was thinking.

"You'd think that because he reminds me so much of Francis it would be easier," Benjamin said, "but it makes it harder. It brings back all the memories - all the loss. I don't have the energy left to get past it. I'd have to push Francis out of my mind. How can I do that?"

Benjamin paused to gather himself. Templeman let him.

"Sometimes I ask myself, 'What would Delina say?' I know damned well what she'd say, but I'm not Delina. It's different for women - for mothers. They have all those maternal instincts."

Benjamin paused again, this time to wipe his eyes.

"And that pathetic little twisted foot. I don't know how to deal with that. There's nothing I can do to make it better. Every time I see it, I get sick to my stomach. There just isn't any money. So, he has to limp through his childhood as a cripple. Why? Because I'm so damned useless. My grandson is my responsibility and I'm powerless to help him. That's what I see when I look at him; a reminder that I'm worthless. I have no control over anything."

Benjamin turned from staring in the direction of the field to looking into Templeman's face.

"So, like I said, it'd be better if they left. Better for them and for me. I'm sorry Eleanor's unhappy with me. If she and the baby leave, at least she won't have to put up with me any longer."

Templeman waited to make sure Benjamin was finished, and then he took a deep breath.

"Ben, let's take a walk down along your field."

They walked in silence until reaching the field, they then turned eastward and begin walking along its length.

"Ben, I see your side of things. I understand that you believe it's your duty and responsibility to get Jeremy the care he needs. You're unable to do that, so you feel you aren't meeting your obligation to your grandson and you blame yourself. Having Jeremy around is a constant reminder that you're unable to fulfill your responsibility to him, which means having him around is painful for you. Do I have it right?"

"Yup. That's about it in a nutshell."

"Okay. I get it. I also get that you love Jeremy. Is that right, too?"

"Yup."

"And you want what's best for him and Eleanor?"

"Yup."

"And you think the best course for them is to leave because the situation here is so bad for Eleanor and you?"

"That's right."

"And what makes the situation so bad is that your inability to pay for an operation for Jeremy makes you feel guilty?"

"Yeah, Jim. You don't have to rub my nose in it."

"Hear me out, Ben. I'm not rubbing your nose in anything. I'm just laying out the facts logically so we can take a clear-eyed look at them."

"Okay. Now what?"

"Well, we've come full circle. You've painted a picture that begins and ends with *you*, Ben. Jeremy is crippled and *you* can't afford an operation that may cure him. That makes *you* feel inadequate and guilty. *You* feel like you have no control. *You're* reminded of that whenever you look at your grandson. *Your* sense of guilt causes you to withdraw from Eleanor and Jeremy and that creates a tense situation. Both you and Eleanor are miserable. The solution, as you see it, is for Eleanor and Jeremy to leave. Not only would they be better off away from you, but *you* wouldn't be constantly reminded you're powerless to help Jeremy."

Benjamin looked at Templeman.

"You make me sound like a real bastard, Jim."

"No, Ben, not at all. That's not my intention. But tell me, am I right? Did I just describe the way things are?"

"Yeah. You did. I guess that seminary training wasn't wasted on you."

"You're right. It wasn't. Neither was my experience as a husband and father whose family died because I wasn't with them. Ben, I have a great deal of experience at feeling inadequate, powerless and guilty."

"Okay. I understand what you're saying, but I still don't see any way around it. They'd be better off without me."

"Again, we go back to you. Ben, think about this:

you can't afford an operation for Jeremy, so you feel guilty. To escape your guilt, or at least lessen it, you withdraw from Jeremy, which means you must also withdraw from Eleanor. You've justified that, at least unconsciously, by convincing yourself Jeremy looks so much like Francis that you can't bear being around him. You'd have to 'push Francis out of your mind,' as you put it. You've wrapped everything up in a tidy little package called 'rationalization.' At the end of the day, everything would be easier for you if Jeremy simply weren't around. If the fire is too hot, you back away from it, right?"

Benjamin nodded.

"Eleanor, who can't read your mind, interprets your withdrawal in the only logical way she can. She believes you have rejected her son because he's deformed."

"But that isn't true!"

"Ben, Eleanor doesn't *know* that because you haven't explained your feelings to her. *Now listen!* The end result of all of this is the creation of an intolerably tense situation in your home. Both of you - you and Eleanor - are miserable. Your solution is to once and for all remove what you believe to be the source your guilt - Eleanor and your grandson."

"Well, she could have told me what she thinks!"

"How, Ben? You won't talk to her!

"I just don't deserve them. I think they'd be happier if they left."

"Would they, really? Or would *you* be happier? Where would they go? How would they live?"

Benjamin shrugged his shoulders.

"Do you think she really wants to leave?"

Another shrug.

"Let's think about that for a minute, Ben. Have you ever thought about what Eleanor wants? What would make her happy?"

"You don't have to be a scientist to figure that out. She wants her baby to be normal. I can't help her with that, so I can't make her happy."

"Ben, you keep bringing this back to you. Let's think about *Eleanor* for a moment. You were married. What is it that Delina wanted most? Think about it."

Benjamin remained silent and looked into the distance.

"Ben?"

"Look, Jim, I'm no good at things like this. I don't know what she wanted."

"Yes. You do. You just won't say it because you know Eleanor wants the same thing."

"Damn. To feel safe, I guess."

"Yes, Ben, in other words, *security*. Not *financial* security, at least not primarily. *Emotional* security. Delina didn't want *things*, did she?"

"No. She didn't. She never complained."

"That's right. She never complained because she knew you wanted to be with her and Francis and that gave her *emotional* security. *That's* what she wanted and *that's* what Eleanor wants."

"Jim, I can't pay for an operation to fix Jeremy's foot."

"Ben, stop making this about *you*! Do I have to spell it out? All right, I will. This isn't about *you*!"

Templeman's reward was a blank look from Benjamin.

"God, man, can't you get it? It's not about *you,*

Ben, it's about all *three* of you. It's about your *family*. Would Eleanor be eternally grateful if an operation corrected Jeremy's foot and he could lead a normal life? Of course she would, but that's not the main thing she wants. What she wants, Ben, what any normal mother wants, is to know she and her child are wanted and are safe, regardless of *everything* else. Eleanor wants the emotional security she feels she *doesn't* have now. She doesn't blame you or think less of you because you can't afford an operation for Jeremy. She *does* think less of you because she believes you're revolted by Jeremy's deformity and because of that you don't want either of them around. That young woman feels so unwanted and jeopardized in your house that she's willing to take her baby and walk off into an unknown future."

"Jesus, I never thought of it that way."

"Because you only thought of *yourself*, Ben."

Benjamin paused as he looked at the ground.

Looking up at the Templeman, he said, "You must think I'm a selfish ass."

"No. I think you have the emotional maturity of a 12-year-old."

Benjamin winced.

"No, Ben. I don't think that. I think you've been hurt so much and have spent so much time alone that you've forgotten how to let other people into your life. And you were right about one thing."

"What's that?"

"You were right when you said I should have listened to you back in the rectory. I should have been more astute to your situation. We should have had this talk back then, not now so close to the brink. I'm sorry, Ben."

"None of this is your fault. You've only tried to help."

"Ben, that time during the storm when I told you and Hiram about my past - about my family. You know, the day you received the telegram about Francis. Do you remember?"

"Of course I do, Jim. I'll never forget anything about that day."

"Well, I left out one detail. I left it out because it's particularly painful for me."

"Jim, it's none of my business, whatever it is."

"You're right, Ben, it isn't, but I think you need to hear it."

"All right."

"After I decided to join the priesthood, I began getting the house ready to be sold. I gave away all our belongings either to charity or to my wife's relatives, you know, things like her jewelry that I would have no use for but that they could remember her by."

"Sure."

"As I emptied her jewelry box, I found an envelope hidden at the very bottom. Inside the envelope there was an undated letter addressed to me. In the letter, my wife explained that she'd had enough. She was taking the children and she was leaving me. I guess she was just waiting until she was fed up enough to date the letter and actually leave."

They had walked up and down the field and were now back at Templeman's Model T.

"You see, Ben, my wife died feeling not just unhappy, but miserable. Our life together had become so painful for her that she knew it was only a matter of time before she couldn't stand it any longer."

"Jim, I'm really sorry."

"Ben, that's not the point. The point is that I was completely oblivious to her frame of mind. She was miserable and I was blind to it. I had it all backwards. I had given her *financial* security. She and the children wanted for nothing, except *me*. I had withheld the type of security she really needed. *Emotional* security, Ben. Now she and the children are dead and I have no way to make amends. I have to live with that every day."

"Jesus, Jim. That has to be hard."

"Yes, Ben, it *is* hard. When I told you and Hiram my story, I also told you I believed my purpose in becoming a priest was to help others avoid making the terrible mistake I made."

"Yeah, I remember you said that, Jim."

"Good, Ben, because now this is where I become a little selfish. You're helping me to fulfill my purpose. I'm here to tell you that in her soul Eleanor is where my wife was just before she died. She's written a letter to you in her heart if not with pen and ink. You're just as blind to her feelings as I was to my wife's. Eleanor is ready to walk out, Ben. Don't let her. If you do, you'll be putting Eleanor and your grandson at grave risk and you'll be one miserable human being. Take it from someone who knows."

Benjamin put his hands in his rear pockets and looked at the ground.

"Ben, there's something else I told you the night the three of us, you, me and Hiram, were sipping whiskey around your fireplace."

"Yeah?"

"I told you I knew Delina and Francis loved and respected you and your task was to honor that love and respect by living a good life - a happy life."

"I remember."

"You don't have to push Francis out of your mind in order to love Jeremy, Ben. By loving him, you're honoring Francis as well as Delina. By loving him, you're passing along their love to your grandson."

Benjamin nodded.

"If you push Jeremy and Eleanor away, Ben, you'd be dishonoring your wife and son. That would be a horrible waste for everyone concerned."

"I understand, Jim."

"One more thing. As I mentioned earlier, Eleanor didn't want me to say anything to you about the way she feels, or the fact I told her I suggested that you adopt Jeremy and give him the Kyner name."

"You told her that? I asked you to keep it between us!"

"Yes, Ben, I did tell her. I didn't mean to break a confidence. When you asked me to keep it between us, I didn't think you intended to exclude Eleanor. I was certain you would discuss it with her. But you're lucky I did tell her, Ben, otherwise she wouldn't have confided in me and I wouldn't be able to warn you you're about to make the biggest mistake of your life. I've broken a confidence with Eleanor, but at the risk of sounding arrogant, I have the advantage of being somewhat objective. I think telling you is a venial sin, at worst."

"You're right, Jim. I'm too wrapped up in myself, like the night before Francis left for good. I was blind then, too.

"Now what, Ben? What's your plan?"

"I have a lot of thinking to do. You've dumped a lot on me. I know I deserve it, but I've got a lot to sort through."

"Ben, all I can say is don't take too long. I don't think Eleanor will stay here much longer."

Templeman bent down and turned the crank under the car's radiator several times. After getting behind the wheel, he started it.

"Good-bye, Ben. Thanks for dinner. Jeremy is a beautiful child. Be thankful."

The farmer's eyes followed the Model T as it pulled away into the night, the beams from its headlights bouncing along the dirt track leading to Fairey Hill Road.

He watched for a time until the Ford was out of sight. He looked up at the soft glow of the oil lamp on the kitchen table and could see Eleanor's shadow as she moved about the room.

Returning to the field he paused to survey its length. Then he began walking eastward again.

CHAPTER 29

THE ROWBOAT

"Darlin,' I won't make excuses for Ben. I told you he's a good man and I still believe he is. Whatever is troublin' him runs deep. Francis' death hit him hard. Maybe you were right when you said it wasn't Jeremy's clubfoot that troubled him. Are you sure you don't want to tell him you know Father Templeman suggested he adopt Jeremy? Maybe you could try to work it out."

It was a warm sunny day in early autumn. Sarah Bolt had stopped by to keep Eleanor company while Benjamin and Hiram were in Athena having some equipment repaired.

"I've thought long and hard, Sarah. Pa lied to me. He knows the pain I'm in and he could have relieved it. He could give Jeremy his name and then Jeremy could be baptized without being stigmatized at the same time. But he intentionally refused to tell me. He'd rather see me suffer and his grandson go unbaptized than open his heart to us."

"So *talk* to the man, Eleanor. This is tearing you up. At least he might adopt the child and you can have him baptized."

"No, Sarah. I've tried and he won't listen. Pa has to do the right thing of his own accord. If I coerce him, he'll either ignore me and shrink further into his shell or simply go through the motions of being a grandfather to Jeremy so I'll leave him alone. No. He has to come to us freely. Otherwise, it will mean nothing and in the end everything will just get worse. At the end of the day, Jeremy will be the one who suffers the most. I told Father Templeman the same thing when he was here a few weeks ago."

"Honey, I'm so sorry. I just don't know what else to say. It's plain you're being worn down to a nub."

"It isn't fair, Sarah. Not for me and not for any woman in this situation. I have nowhere to go. What power do I have to control my own life and that of my child? When Jeremy turns 21, he'll have more rights than I, his own mother. He'll be able to vote. You and I can't even do that. I can't even get a loan at a bank to start a business or buy a house without a man co-signing for it. I'm at the mercy of people around me. I'm an American adult and I'm trapped. I'm a second class citizen in my own country, Sarah."

Sarah looked at Eleanor like a mother looking at child.

"Eleanor, do you think maybe you're preachin' to the choir?"

Sarah reached for Eleanor's hand and placed it side-by-side with her own. Eleanor's smooth pale skin contrasted dramatically with Sarah's own nut-colored hue.

"Take a look, honey. When it comes to bein' second class, I got you beat comin' and goin'. What do you think a bank would say to me if I went lookin' for a loan? When it comes to votin', sure, Hiram's a man and he can vote here in Pennsylvania, but what about our kin on the other side of the Mason-Dixon line. Ever hear of Mr. Jim Crow, sweetie? I don't expect you to understand, Eleanor. You come from a different world."

"Oh, God. I'm an idiot Sarah. I'm so wrapped up in my own problems, I can only think of myself. I'm selfish and un-Christian. Please forgive me!"

"Honey, like I said. I don't expect you to understand our problems. You can't put yourself in my skin. You have your own problems to deal with right now. Just think about this: no matter how bad your situation seems, there's someone out there whose situation is worse. Sure, you're stuck in a hard place right now, but you've got a beautiful little baby who loves you. I'd give anything for a baby like Jeremy, foot and all."

"Sarah, I'm so sorry to have burdened you with this. Please don't tell Hiram. He'd probably feel he should try and reason with Pa."

"I won't tell a soul, sweetie. You're right. He'd just jump right in and try to make everything all better and mess it up worse in the process, but don't you ever be sorry to tell me your troubles. We have to be here for each other. Besides, this influenza is getting worse. If it goes on like this, there won't be anyone left to talk to!"

The next morning, Eleanor awoke in an exhausted state. Between worrying about the situation with Benjamin and meeting Jeremy's demands, she got less sleep every night.

Had it not been for Benjamin's recalcitrance regarding Jeremy and then his outright deception, Eleanor believed she would have adapted well to farm life.

Though Sarah Bolt was being a good friend, Eleanor didn't feel she could confide in her about the extent to which her life had really changed. She had been the daughter of a wealthy and respected family and librarian at an upscale college. Now she was an unwed mother who spent her days rising with the sun, changing and washing diapers, using a smelly outdoor privy, feeding chickens, cleaning a rundown farmhouse, and cooking meals and doing laundry for a man who would barely look at her son. How could she complain about all of that to a granddaughter of slaves?

Eleanor would have accepted it all and been happy if not for Benjamin's refusal to open his heart and accept her and her child - his grandchild - as his family. She felt as though he were merely fulfilling an unwanted obligation, like paying taxes. She was nearing the end of her rope.

Well, maybe Mom and Dad are right. Maybe I'm getting what I deserve.

She threw off the covers and stared at the unpainted ceiling, mentally preparing for yet another day trapped on the farm. Sighing deeply, she finally found the strength to throw her legs over the side of the bed, stand up, and begin to dress.

Benjamin and Hiram were just finishing the lunch Eleanor had prepared for them.

"C'mon, Hiram," Benjamin said, "Time to get back at it."

As the two rose to leave, Eleanor turned from the sink wiping her hands on her apron.

"Pa, I was thinking. A little later I'd like to take Jeremy for a ride in the boat. I've been cooped up here for so long, I'm suffering from cabin fever that even a little diversion would help. I just wanted you to know where we'd be if you come looking for us."

"Sounds good to me," Benjamin said without looking at Eleanor.

Hiram, however, was obviously concerned. "You be careful now, Miss Eleanor. You don't float so well and I haven't had a chance to teach young Jeremy to swim!"

Eleanor's smile belied her thoughts. *Jeremy's grandfather should be the one to teach him to swim, Hiram, not you.*

"Thank you, Hiram. Jeremy and I promise to be careful," she replied, smiling.

Benjamin and Hiram let the screen door bang shut behind them as Eleanor cleaned up the lunch dishes.

As the sun slowly passed the zenith on its westward trek, Eleanor carried a giggling Jeremy toward the pond on the far side of Benjamin's field.

Eleanor felt drained, but she couldn't stand to be in the house another minute. A short excursion in the boat around the pond should revive her, at least to some degree.

She reached the shore of the pond and placed Jeremy on the grass. Keeping one eye on the baby, she struggled to right the inverted boat. Benjamin insisted the boat be turned upside down when not in use to keep rainwater from collecting in it.

Finally successful, she placed the oars in the boat lengthwise and pushed it partway into the pond. She doffed her leather ankle-length shoes and stockings, and then collected Jeremy, who was trying to capture a nearby butterfly skipping among blades of grass. She propped him in the bow of the boat while she hiked up her skirt to keep it from getting wet and pushed the boat into the water, jumping in just as the bow cleared the shore.

She adjusted Jeremy's bonnet to ensure it kept the sun out of his eyes, and then she placed the oars in their locks and began rowing.

As she guided the boat around the pond in a wide, gentle circle she surveyed the farm from this unusual vantage point. It really was a beautiful place.

Under other circumstances, it could be heaven.

She imagined what it must have been like to watch Francis land the flying machine up there on Benjamin's field. He had taken her flying in it - the "Jenny," he called it - a few times. He used to tease her that "Jenny" was the other woman in his life.

Well, maybe she was. Francis certainly loved to fly.

Looking down to check on Jeremy, she saw he had crawled to the side of the boat and was trying to touch the water.

"Hey you, mister," she pretended to scold, "you sit your little bum back down and be good."

Eleanor stopped rowing to return Jeremy to the safety of the bow. She then resumed rowing the boat in aimless, lazy circles.

How different it would have been, she thought, as the boat drifted toward the deepest part of the pond, *how different our lives would be if you hadn't died, Francis; if there had been no war. Right now we'd have a house in Pittsburgh - maybe in Shadyside - and we'd take the train to the country on Sundays to visit Pa.*

In her fatigue, she slipped easily into a hazy reverie. She was only vaguely aware of the gentle rocking of the boat. *Francis, if only you....*

There was a splash. Eleanor jumped straight up. Shaking her head to clear her senses, she looked at the spot where she'd left Jeremy. He was gone.

Eleanor was gripped first by denial, then near panic. She frantically scoured the unbroken silver ripples surrounding her. Nothing. Jeremy had slipped beneath the surface of the pond. She had no idea where.

"No, *No!*"

Benjamin was bent over a stubborn lever on a horse-drawn corn harvester while Hiram re-arranged bales of hay in the loft of the barn.

The piercing scream caused him to stand ramrod straight. He strained to hear.

It can't be!

A second scream.

"Delina!"

Benjamin launched himself in the direction of the screams.

Benjamin's long legs pounded the ground as he exerted every ounce of effort to eliminate the distance between himself and the source of the terror.

He could hear Delina screaming and Francis crying. He could hear the dog barking and snarling as it slowly advanced toward them.

"I'm coming!" he tried to scream, but only

incomprehensible gasps escaped his mouth.

These damned shoes! Willing himself to keep moving, he managed to reach down and remove the heavy work shoes that were slowing him; first one, then the other.

He was barely conscious of Hiram, far behind him, shouting, "Ben, I'm coming."

A vision of Delina with tiny Francis wrapped in her arms to protect him from the angry German Shepard danced in front of his eyes. He ran faster, lungs burning, his eyes streaming tears.

Something isn't right. The screams were coming from the wrong direction. As Benjamin passed the house he looked in the direction of the garden where the dog attacked his family. Nothing. *Francis?*

No! Jeremy!

Snapping back to the present, Benjamin raced in the direction of Eleanor's screams - toward the pond. He had wasted precious time running in the wrong direction.

He approached the edge of the pond.

Where are they? His eyes scoured the pond. *There!*

The boat. It was empty.

Benjamin plunged into the water and swam hand over hand toward the empty boat.

The boat was empty. Benjamin understood what happened. Jeremy must have fallen out. Eleanor, who couldn't swim, had hurled herself into the pond in a vain attempt to find Jeremy. She was thrashing around in the water as her soaked cotton dress tried to drag her to the bottom. He couldn't worry about her now. *Got to find Jeremy!*

He reached the boat and dove beneath the surface.

The pond water was usually cloudy, but Eleanor's frantic movements had stirred up mud from the bottom, turning the already limited visibility to zero. Benjamin was blind. All he could do was grope aimlessly in hope of somehow finding Jeremy.

He surfaced to gulp air and dove back under. Again. Then again. His lungs were on fire. How long had it been?

Up once more. He could hear Eleanor screaming for Jeremy. Hiram crashed into the water, but Benjamin was unaware of it. He was focused entirely on finding the baby.

His frustration and near panic were almost unbearable. Eleanor, fighting to breath and overcome by terror at loss of her baby, kicked him in the ribs. He ignored the pain and kept searching.

There was something in his peripheral vision. He twisted his body toward it. Several feet in the distance he could barely make out a small fuzzy white smudge contrasted against a dark gray-brown background. With outreached hands he kicked toward the apparition.

His outstretched fingers groped for the white blotch. After what seemed an eternity, he finally touched it. Cloth! A diaper! Benjamin clamped both hands on Jeremy's midsection and brought him to the surface.

Jeremy wasn't breathing. His lips were blue.

Benjamin wasn't prepared for this. This wasn't a battlefield. No one drowns on a battlefield. He didn't know what to do and was nearing panic as Jeremy's skin took on more of a bluish pallor. *His lungs must be full of water.* Benjamin held Jeremy almost upside down. Nothing. He squeezed the baby's chest and expelled some water. He squeezed again. More water. He was losing time. He was only barely conscious of Eleanor's screams. One more squeeze and that was it. He cradled Jeremy in his arms and looked at the still little face. *He can't breath. Do it for him!* Not knowing what else to do, Benjamin placed his own mouth over Jeremy's mouth and nose. He exhaled into his grandson's lungs.

"Please God! Not again! Don't let me lose this boy, too."

Nothing. He tried again. Nothing. As he pushed air into the baby a third time, he felt a warm fluid shooting into his own mouth as Jeremy's body jerked.

The baby had vomited. Then he began to scream.

Benjamin heard Hiram shout, "Sweet Jesus!"

Holding Jeremy tightly, Benjamin, who was between Hiram and Eleanor, heard Hiram say, "Ben! She can't swim. She's drowning!"

Benjamin looked to the side to see Eleanor struggling to stay above the surface of the pond while trying to call Jeremy's name between gasps of air, "Jer... Jere... Jeremy!"

"Eleanor!" Benjamin shouted at her, trying to get her attention. "Eleanor, *stand up!*

Eleanor, who was nearing complete exhaustion and believed she was drowning, stared wide-eyed at Benjamin as Hiram tried to get to her.

"*Stand up*, Eleanor! The water here is only four feet deep!

Just as Hiram was about to reach for her, Eleanor's feet found the bottom of the pond. She managed to stand up with help from Hiram.

"Jeremy!" she gasped as she struggled to get to her child. Jeremy was screaming. Eleanor could see Benjamin was holding the screaming baby tightly with

his face buried in his neck.

"Not again," she heard him say. "I'm not going to lose you, too. Not ever."

Eleanor, her wet hair plastered to her head and face, reached for Jeremy. Benjamin looked at her with tears streaming from his reddened eyes.

"I've been such a fool," he said. "I'm so sorry. Can you ever forgive me?"

Eleanor answered him by taking Jeremy and then folding herself and her baby into Benjamin's arms.

Two days later, Benjamin took the wagon to the Calvary train station for the trip to Deutschburgh.

Entering Harmonie Lodge No. 924, Benjamin's eyes searched the room before alighting on one particular Freemason.

Approaching his lodge brother, Benjamin said, "Judge Rapp, I wonder if you can give me a few minutes after the meeting?"

"Brother Ben! Of course I can. Don't tell me you're having legal problems?" Rapp answered with a wink.

"No. I just need some help doing something I should have done a while ago."

"Anything for a brother, Ben. As long as it's legal!" he said with a grin.

Late one day not long afterward, Benjamin again made the walk to Delina's side.

The light of the lowering sun was pushing the shadows of the stones into long narrow lines, like the fingers of a giant dark hand stretched out on the green grass.

"Well, Frenchie, I don't know if you had anything to do with what happened down there at the pond, but I recall that when you thought I was confused, you could always make things clear to me in a jiffy. I guess you still can."

He put his hand on the headstone and collected his thoughts.

"You know we have a grandson now. He's becoming quite the little scamp and really gives his mother a run for her money. I think they need me to spend more time with them on the farm, since Francis is with you. I won't be able to come up here quite so often, but I think that's the way you want it. I love you, Delina."

As he turned and walked away, the farmer could feel the warmth of the bright sun on his face. It seemed to pass through him, making him feel alive.

CHAPTER 30

THE NAME OF THE FATHER

The winter air was frigid, but the sky was a cloudless bright blue backdrop for the brilliant sun on this Sunday, January 12, 1919.

"Jeremy Benjamin Kyner, I baptize you in the name of the Father, and of the Son, and of the Holy Spirit. Amen." While speaking those words, Father James Templeman poured holy water over Jeremy's forehead three times. Jeremy's godparents, members of the Saint Mary's congregation, were holding him above the baptismal font as Eleanor, Benjamin, Hiram and Sarah looked on.

As one of Benjamin's lodge brothers was a judge, the legal process had moved swiftly. It might have been even faster had it not been for the influenza pandemic that kept fearful court employees at home. Regardless, Benjamin had adopted Jeremy and he was now legally a Kyner.

Jeremy's new godmother returned the eight-month old baby boy to Eleanor. "It's such a shame your husband will never have a chance to hold such a beautiful child," she said. "The war took so many, and then there was the influenza. It's quite understandable why you didn't want to risk taking little Jeremy out in public to be baptized or for any other reason."

"Thank you for understanding, Cheryl. It was so kind of you to step in at the last minute. I really do appreciate it."

Benjamin watched as Eleanor resumed custody of Jeremy. Before the small ceremony, Eleanor expressed privately to Benjamin how thankful she was that Jeremy would finally be baptized, but she didn't want to dwell on the war or the flu, nor did she want to discuss why she waited to have her baby baptized until he was eight months old. What she didn't mention to him was that she also wanted to keep her deceptions simple and to a minimum, better to more easily remember them later and not contradict a previous lie.

Benjamin, for all his gruffness, understood the important thing was for Eleanor to focus on making it a day she'd be happy to remember.

For her part, the irony of what made the day possible wasn't lost on Eleanor. She'd almost lost her son due to her own inattention and negligence, yet it took a shock of that magnitude for Benjamin to finally realize what was really important and to look past what wasn't. Once that happened, Benjamin had truly become Jeremy's grandfather.

When they rose that morning, the day was frigid, but bright and clear with air that stung noses and caused eyes to water. The roads and fields were covered with several inches of new snow, so Benjamin left the wagon in the barn and hitched the horses to the sleigh and they set off to Saint Mary's, the three of them bundled under a bright red sleigh blanket in the front seat.

Less than an hour after they arrived back at the farm their guests began to appear. The small group - the farmhouse couldn't hold many - consisted of Templeman, Hiram and Sarah Bolt, Jeremy's godparents, and a few neighbors and members of Benjamin's lodge and their wives. After a couple of hours of socializing, which included passing Jeremy around, the baby finally let it be known he had had enough and Eleanor put him in her room for a nap.

Gradually, the guests began to make their goodbyes until only Templeman, Hiram and Sarah were left. Sarah, who had helped Eleanor prepare for the party, was now helping her clean up. The three men stood by themselves in front of the blazing fireplace. Each had a glass holding a small amount of dark liquid.

Benjamin said, "A lot has happened since the last time the three of us were in this particular spot. I want to thank both of you. I know I wasn't always easy to tolerate."

"You ain't ever easy to tolerate, Ben," said Hiram, "but you're welcome just the same."

"Ben, we're just happy everything has worked out as it has," Templeman said after Hiram's jibe. "Now that both the war and influenza have ended, maybe we can all get back to some kind of normalcy."

"Things will never be as they were," Benjamin said looking at the framed photograph of Francis, "but there's nothing I can do to change it. I'm just grateful for what good there is left now that it's all over." He punctuated this statement by motioning toward Eleanor's room where Jeremy was sleeping.

"You've been through a lot, Ben," Templeman said, "but you made it. A lot of people have suffered great loss in the last few years and got nothing in return. You've been blessed. I think a toast to Eleanor and Jeremy is in order."

The three men raised their glasses and swallowed the contents.

Hiram grinned after sipping from his glass. "Hmmm… That Irish whiskey still packs a wallop."

Sarah emerged from the kitchen untying an apron from around her waist.

"Sweetie, I think it's time we got back home."

"Yes'm," responded Hiram. "Thanks for the hospitality, Ben."

Benjamin took his glass and Hiram and Sarah put on their coats.

"Why don't I give you two a ride back?" offered Templeman. "You'll freeze to death in this weather, otherwise."

"That would be very much appreciated, Father," Sarah said.

Eleanor, hearing Father Templeman, walked over and hugged him.

"Father, thank you so much for everything. We're eternally grateful."

"Eleanor, no thanks are necessary. I'm just sorry you have to take care of both Jeremy *and* Benjamin!" he said to the amusement of everyone but Benjamin, who he then punched in the shoulder. Benjamin couldn't help but smile.

After Eleanor exchanged hugs and good wishes with Hiram and Sarah, they followed Templeman out.

Benjamin and Eleanor watched as Hiram cranked the starter and Templeman started the Model T. They turned away as the Ford trundled toward Fairey Hill Road.

After leaving the farm and turning northward, Templeman glanced in the car's rearview mirror and saw a large, late model touring car turning into Benjamin's drive. The diminishing sunlight reflected off the automobile's highly polished dark blue paint and massive, brilliant radiator grill. The car's canvass sides had been hung from the roof against the cold air.

"That looks like a Pierce-Arrow, a new one. Now, who on earth would be driving something like that to visit Benjamin and Eleanor?" Templeman wondered aloud. Both Hiram and Sarah turned to look as the Model T continued toward Black Hollow.

The mysterious Pierce-Arrow continued to wend its way toward the Kyner farmhouse. Upon arriving near the porch, the motor went silent and the driver's door opened. A glistening ebony cane appeared from the car's interior and crunched into the new snow, its tip nudging the ground repeatedly as it sought firm purchase on the frozen soil. With careful and deliberate moves, a figure stepped into the chilled air and leaned on the cane, squeezing its silver grip with a hand gloved in calfskin. After surveying the property with an intense eye, as though becoming re-acquainted with it, the figure limped toward the house and, with obvious difficulty, climbed the steps. There was a small lever mounted in the center of the door. It was connected to a bell on the other side. Hesitating for a moment, as though having second thoughts, the visitor finally turned the lever and the bell within chimed.

With her guests gone and the house back to

normal, Eleanor was about to relax with a novel. Hearing the bell and assuming it was one of her recently departed guests who had forgotten something, she rushed to open the door without a thought.

She swung open the door expecting to see Templeman, Hiram or Sarah. "Well, did you forget…oh, my dear God!" Taking a step backward, her hand flew to her chest as she gasped. Her heart pounded. Eleanor could not have been more flabbergasted if Jesus, Mary and Joseph had been standing on her threshold seeking refuge from the winter cold.

"Hello, Eleanor," said Randolph E. Bridgewater, III.

CHAPTER 31

THE BAD PENNY

"Please, please, just call me Randy. There's no need for the religious formalities," Bridgewater said, still sporting his trademark mustache curling past the edges of his mouth. The mustache was split with a wide grin.

Eleanor could only stare at Bridgewater in the open door.

"Eleanor, it is quite cold. Would it be possible for me to come inside?"

Eleanor caught her breath. "Of course. I'm... I'm sorry, Randy," she said and stepped aside to allow him to enter the kitchen. "You gave me such a shock!" She put her arms around Bridgewater's neck and hugged him.

Eleanor took a step back to appraise her visitor. Bridgewater, who had never been heavy, appeared to have lost about 15 pounds. He had crows' feet around the corners of his eyes and his temples had a touch of gray. Yet, he was only 26. He looked 20 years older.

"Randy! I didn't know what to think when I

didn't hear from you. I thought you might have been killed!"

"Well, I would have called but you don't have a telephone," Bridgewater said glibly as he stuffed his calfskin gloves into the pockets of his ermine fur coat and slid it off. Eleanor hung it on a wooden peg by the kitchen door.

Bridgewater watched, noting it was the same place where he had hung his kit bag after he and Francis first landed the Curtiss JN-4 "Jenny" on the farm an eternity ago.

Turning back toward him, Eleanor saw the cane and noticed his limp.

"Randy, your leg. What happened?"

"Oh, that. Well, as luck would have it, just before the armistice I got wrapped up in a quarrel with a Hun. We flailed away at each other without doing much damage, or so I thought. We each got low on petrol and went our own separate ways, he east and I west. It was quite disappointing. Sadly, upon attempting to land I discovered my worthy opponent had shot up my undercarriage. Sneaky bastard. The whole thing collapsed when I landed and my machine rolled up into a tidy little ball, with me in the middle of it with a nicely smashed right knee."

"But the armistice was signed over a year ago. Your knee's not healed, yet?"

"The doctors tell me it's as 'healed' as it's ever going to be, I'm afraid. So, it's me and the stick from now on," he said tapping the cane on the floor. "The women seem to love it. It makes me look rather dashing, I think." His mustache widened into another grin.

"I haven't heard from you since…since you were

in France," she said. "How did you find me?"

"Well, Eleanor. I first made the monumental error of visiting your dear mother in Meadville."

"Oh, no. I wish I could have warned you, Randy."

The two were now sitting opposite each other in front of the fireplace.

"Oh, yes, indeed. I thought the weather was brutally cold until your mother opened the door and I asked for you. Dear God, the woman almost froze me solid with her look."

"What did she say?"

"That you didn't live there anymore and she didn't know where you were. Then she slammed the door in my face."

"I'm so sorry, Randy, and humiliated."

"Why? *You* didn't slam the door in my face."

"Well, I…."

"Forget it Eleanor. It's not important. I found you. That's what counts."

"After I hit that dead end, I asked for you at the college library. One of your former co-workers referred me to the chaplain. He told me where you were."

He reached over and gave her hand a brotherly squeeze.

"Before we start to catch up, please let me say how very sorry I am about Francis. I was there and saw everything. Eleanor, it was the worst moment of my life and I felt absolutely helpless. Francis was my best friend and there isn't a day that goes by that I don't wish it had been me instead of him. Please believe me."

Of course, it was your stupidity that killed him. Tell her, you coward. Tell her it was your fault your best friend and the father of her child is dead because you relaxed in the middle of a battle.

"Oh, no, Randy. Don't say that. What's happened has happened. I know you must have done everything you could to save Francis."

Eleanor's attempt to soothe Bridgewater had the opposite effect, but he managed to keep his tortured conscience concealed.

"Well," he said. "You've obviously had the baby. How is the little tyke?"

"You know about Jeremy? Francis must have told you."

"Yes, he did. He was concerned for you. He worried about how your parents would take it. It goes without saying that he was correct to be concerned."

Eleanor simply nodded.

"Jeremy? A little boy? Where is he? Come to think of it, where is Francis' father?"

"Jeremy's asleep. He was just baptized today. If you had gotten here sooner, you could have joined the party. Pa is outside checking on the animals. He should be in any minute. Oh! Where are my manners? We have all sorts of food left over. I've only just finished putting it away. Some is still warm. Can I get you something? Maybe something to drink?

"Oh, perhaps something to drink, if it's no trouble. Thanks. But wait, the baby was just baptized today? I'm not Catholic, but isn't this a little late?"

Eleanor took several minutes to fill Bridgewater in on everything that happened since she discovered she was pregnant, everything except how Benjamin had behaved after their arrival on the farm. That was no longer important. She got him a cup of coffee and a slice of cake as she talked.

"Well, it seems as though I'm not the only one who's been in a war, Eleanor. Francis chose well. You've come through like a trooper."

"Randy, I received your letter after Francis was killed. I answered, but I never heard back from you."

"Ah, yes. Well, I did receive your reply, Eleanor, and I'm sorry I didn't keep in touch. I thought you had your own problems to deal with and I only would have written about the war. Frankly, the war was really having its way with all of us over there. Regardless, I should have written," Bridgewater lied. *You didn't write to her because you were ashamed.* "At least on this farm you were safe from the damned influenza."

"Yes, that's one good thing," she answered. "We were spared."

"Well, I wasn't. I got it just as I was about to leave France. Obviously it didn't kill me. A good number of the fellows weren't so fortunate. They say more than 50 million people around the world died, with 600,000 of those being right here in the States.

"Oh, dear God."

"That's right. We used to say, 'If the Hun doesn't get you, the influenza will.' At least we could shoot the Hun."

Just then Benjamin opened the kitchen door. "Eleanor? Whose fancy car is that out front?" he asked as he closed the door behind him and began removing his hat, coat and gloves.

"It's mine, Mr. Kyner. It's a 1918 Pierce-Arrow Model 66." As he spoke, Bridgewater rose with the aid of his silver-tipped ebony cane.

Benjamin froze at the sight of Bridgewater standing in the middle of his house. Over Bridgewater's shoulder, sitting on the fireplace mantel, was Francis' framed photograph. To Benjamin, Francis seemed amused at the scene unfolding before him. Bridgewater followed Benjamin's gaze. He hadn't noticed the photograph before now. With some effort, he ignored it and looked again at Benjamin. He was just about to speak, when Benjamin regained his composure and said, "I didn't think President Wilson had dropped by with a baptism gift for Jeremy," Benjamin said dryly, "but I'm surprised to see you. I guess that answers my question."

"What question is that, sir?"

"You're alive. You made it. I wondered if you had."

"Mr. Kyner, I understand you were never pleased Francis and I were friends. Regardless, I am here, sir, to offer my sincere condolences on the loss of your son. He was my best friend and I feel his absence keenly, though not as keenly as you and Eleanor. I'm very saddened that his own son will never know him." *And it's my fault.*

Benjamin responded with a quick nod and a curt "Thanks."

Jeremy began to stir. Eleanor excused herself and went to check on him.

Pointing to the cane, Benjamin asked, "Souvenir from France?" He waved Bridgewater back into his seat.

"Actually, yes. I was just telling Eleanor about it."

He repeated the story he'd just related to Eleanor.

"Oh, speaking of the car, it's borrowed from a business associate of my father's. I have to get it back to him this evening. I return to Boston by train tomorrow. So, I won't be able to stay very long."

"Oh, what a shame," Eleanor said as she emerged from her room with Jeremy. "You just arrived and it's been so long!"

"It really can't be helped, I'm afraid. Beggars can't be choosers, you know. Hah! How ironic!"

Inwardly, Bridgewater was relieved. Being in the presence of his best friend's family wasn't something he was looking forward to and he wanted it to end as quickly as possible.

Eleanor emerged from the bedroom with Jeremy.

"Well, hi ho, there he is!" Bridgewater said. "May I hold him?"

"Of course you may, Randy," Eleanor answered. "I just changed him, so he's nice and fresh."

Jeremy squirmed as she passed him to Bridgewater.

"My, my," said Bridgewater as he took Jeremy, "look at the way he's wrapped up. He must be warm enough in this swaddling. He can barely move his legs."

Jeremy ceased struggling and gave Bridgewater a look of confusion. Then, as Bridgewater brushed his cheek with his finger, he flashed a bashful grin.

"I did not come empty handed, by the way."

Carrying Jeremy and using his cane, Bridgewater limped the few steps to where his coat was hanging. Leaning the cane against the wall, he fished in one of the coat pockets. His hand emerged holding something quite small.

Bridgewater turned to display the carved wooden model to Eleanor and Benjamin.

"One of the boys in the squadron used to whittle these out of pieces of wrecked fuselages. He made quite of few before it was his turn to 'go west,' as we used to say.

"It's lovely," Eleanor commented as she admired

the model. "Go west?"

"It means he was killed," Benjamin said dryly.

"Oh, my." Eleanor looked shocked at Benjamin's blunt remark.

"Quite right, Mr. Kyner," said Bridgewater. Then, noticing the look on Eleanor's face he adds, "One old soldier to another, Eleanor. It just makes it easier to say it that way."

"Anyway," he continued, "after returning home to Boston I painted this to resemble Francis' machine. It's an S.E.5a. It has the same color, markings and insignia. I thought the child might appreciate it when he's older."

Bridgewater handed the model to Jeremy who clutched it clumsily in his little fingers then tried to put it in his mouth.

Eleanor gently removed the model from Jeremy's mouth and pried it from his fingers. He whimpered in response.

"He's teething, Randy. Everything he touches goes in his mouth to get gnawed," Eleanor said with a smile, "But he certainly likes it. It really is beautiful and very thoughtful. Thank you ever so much. We'll have to keep it safe until Jeremy's old enough to not want to devour it!"

Holding the wooden replica in her hand, she asked, "Is this really it? It really looked just like this?"

"Yes. They are identical. Except for their size, of course."

Bridgewater could see Benjamin's eyes practically drilling holes in the little wooden model flying machine.

Eleanor handed Benjamin the wooden creation.

"Isn't it lovely, Pa?"

Benjamin examined the model and then returned it to Eleanor, who walked to the mantle where Francis' framed photo reposed. She reverently placed the little winged creation next to the photograph.

"It looks good there," Bridgewater said quietly.

Looking down, Eleanor opened a drawer and removed a white envelope.

"Pa, do you mind if I show Randy the letter?"

"No, go ahead, Eleanor."

Eleanor crossed the room and sat next to Bridgewater. The baby was trying mightily to yank on the ends of Bridgewater's mustache, which jiggled temptingly whenever he spoke.

Eleanor handed Bridgewater the letter and took Jeremy so he would have both hands free.

Bridgewater first examined the envelope, and then extracted and unfolded Captain Card's letter.

"Ah, yes, Bobby Card. He was always very diligent about writing these. Not an enviable task, by any means," Bridgewater said as he began to read.

Finishing the letter, he said, "Yes, that's about it. As I said, I was there and saw it all. Bobby got it just right."

"Did he survive the war?" Eleanor asked.

"Who, Bobby? Yes, as a matter of fact he did, although he went down in the same engagement in which Francis was lost. His engine was shot up, but he managed to put his machine down on our side of the lines and Canadian infantry picked him up. Very fitting, since he's from Nova Scotia. His family is in shipping, I believe. They own several vessels. I believe he said he's a licensed ship's master. He used to brag about being a Nova Scotia 'Bluenose' sailor. One wonders why he didn't join the navy."

In an effort to ward off questions, Bridgewater went on to tell several anecdotes of the adventures he and Francis had on the ground in England, Scotland and France.

Benjamin, who had been silent as he watched and listened carefully to Bridgewater, finally spoke.

"You said you were there. If you don't mind my asking, what exactly were you doing when Francis was killed? You can understand we'd like to get as many details as possible about what happened to him."

"Absolutely, Mr. Kyner. You and Eleanor have every right to know everything. Please, don't hesitate to ask whatever you wish," he said, inwardly wincing at the thought.

"As for what I was doing at the time, I was trying to maneuver my machine into position to shoot the German who was after Francis."

As he spoke the words, Bridgewater could feel his pulse begin to race.

"But how did it all start? Card said Francis had been trying to help another pilot who was being attacked by a German."

Yes. That pilot was me, Mr. Kyner. I stupidly got myself into trouble and your son died saving me. How exactly does that make you feel, sir?

Bridgewater recounted to Benjamin and Eleanor almost exactly how the aerial battle that claimed the son of one and lover of the other unfolded. *Almost* exactly.

"Okay, but the guy Francis was trying to help. Who was he? What was his name?"

Bridgewater was ready for this. He had anticipated the question and had practiced his lie until it could roll off his tongue like honey.

"Winters," Bridgewater responded with a well-practiced note of remorse in his voice. "A really good kid, but nervous. He always vomited before a patrol, just as he was about to climb into his cockpit." Bridgewater noted the uncomfortable look on Eleanor's face. "Oh, I'm sorry, Eleanor. There were many of us with the same or similar afflictions. It was caused by nerves."

"Don't mind me, Randy. Please, go on."

"Well, during the encounter he apparently failed to remain vigilant and allowed himself to be jumped by an ambitious Hun."

The face of Winters, who was actually the first to die in the melée, appeared for an instant in Bridgewater's mind. *God, I'm such a bastard. Winters, forgive me.*

"This Winters. He was a good man?" Benjamin asked.

"Yes, sir. The very best. I'm sorry to say, however, he didn't survive the engagement."

So he can't come back and call me a liar.

"Do you mean Francis' sacrifice was wasted?" Benjamin demanded.

"Pa!" Eleanor exclaimed. "What do you mean?"

"No, Eleanor. It's quite all right. Mr. Kyner, you were in the service and saw combat. Francis told me. No, Francis did not waste his life saving a comrade. You certainly realize that combat is smoke, noise and confusion. That is no less true in the air than on the ground. One functions not minute-by-minute, but second-by-second. You do what you must do when you must do it. The next second is in the future and known only to God. The right thing for Francis to have done was come to the assistance of a squadron mate. Should he have said, 'No, I won't help my friend. He's a dolt and is likely to get himself killed anyway?' No, of course not. What would you have done, sir? You would have risked your life to help a fellow soldier without having any way of knowing if that soldier would survive the battle. Am I correct?"

The practiced words that flowed from his mouth didn't reflect those going through his mind, *Actually, Francis, you did throw your life away - on me.*

Benjamin looked at Bridgewater, and then at the floor as he ran his hand through his sparse hair.

"Yes, I suppose you are. I'm sorry if I implied something improper. I just don't want to believe my son threw his life away. I wouldn't want Jeremy to ever think that, either."

"Mr. Kyner, I assure you that Francis' death was not in vain. What he did was noble. The King of England himself, who authorized the Distinguished Service Order, recognized his actions. Francis is credited with seven kills. He was an ace who flew so adroitly that he forced that Hun to shear off his own wings. It was truly an amazing feat to witness."

"You know, it would be nice to write to - is it 'Lieutenant?' - Winters' family. It might be comforting for them. It would make me feel better, too," Eleanor said.

Oh, Christ, Bridgewater thought. *I didn't anticipate that.*

Bridgewater cleared his throat. Benjamin noticed and gave him an odd look - a look of suspicion. Bridgewater saw the look in Benjamin's eye and fought to ignore it.

"Well, Eleanor, I actually don't believe

Lieutenant Winters had a family, I'm sad to say. He may have talked about it at some point, but come to think of it, I don't recall that he ever received mail."

I'm truly a bastard.

Benjamin said, "Being young, away from home, and in combat every day is tough. Getting letters from family makes a soldier's life a little more bearable. It must have been hard on the young man not to receive any letters. No wonder he was throwing up."

Not missing Benjamin's implication and hoping his hosts didn't notice the beads of perspiration he felt forming on his forehead, Bridgewater thought, *Good God. I've survived repeated encounters with men who wanted to kill me. Never have I wanted to turn tail and run more than now, sitting here in this farmhouse. Jesus, old man, get off it!*

"Well, I don't know. Perhaps he did receive a few letters from friends at home. We relied on one another, Mr. Kyner. Winters was a good sort. We were all volunteers and he held up well. Regardless, it's in the past now."

Desperate for a change in subject, Bridgewater guided the conversation back to what life in France was like for Bridgewater and Francis. He managed to avoid any inferences that would give rise to questions about the day Francis died. Benjamin said nothing but didn't take his eyes off Bridgewater.

For Bridgewater, the hands of the Regulator clock on the kitchen wall crawled with agonizing slowness.

After a while, Benjamin lit the oil lamp that sat in the middle of the kitchen table and Bridgewater thankfully took that as his cue to make an honorable exit.

"But Randy," Eleanor said, "you haven't told us

anything about yourself. What will you be doing now that you're home? What are you plans?"

"My academic career is over. After France I don't think I could stand all that college drivel. My father found me a place in his firm, which I suppose is really no surprise. So, I'm going from cockpit to boardroom. Well, at least there I'll only have to dodge hot air, not Huns. Of course, I may be bored to death. Well, dear, I really must get the car back before it turns into a pumpkin."

"Will you try to fly again?" she asked.

Bridgewater limped to the door and slipped on his coat.

"No, Eleanor. This knee notwithstanding, I've had quite enough of that. I'm afraid flying has been tainted for me. Every once in a while, I'll catch a whiff of leather or gasoline or something else that reminds me of the smell of a cockpit and I get queasy. Oh, brilliant white clouds in a pristinely blue sky are still beautiful as long as they stay up there and I stay down here." As Bridgewater ended his sentence, he diverted his gaze from Eleanor to Benjamin, as though to say, "*You know what I mean, don't you?*"

"And I still prefer rainy days. I find them relaxing. We never had to fly in the rain. When it rains, 'no one flies and no one dies'."

Bridgewater noticed that Eleanor looked like she wanted to say something, but couldn't think of what. After donning his coat, he gave Eleanor and Jeremy pecks on their cheeks.

"Please come back soon, Randy," said Eleanor, "and be sure to write."

Making a polite, non-committal reply, Bridgewater extended his hand toward Benjamin.

"Good-bye, Mr. Kyner. At the risk of sounding self-serving, I really do wish it were Francis visiting my parents instead of the other way 'round."

There, I've told the truth for once.

Shaking hands with Bridgewater, Benjamin replied, "If it had happened the 'other way 'round,' Mr. Bridgewater, Francis would probably say the same thing to your parents. But before you go, is there anything else you can tell us about how Francis died? Anything you might have forgotten?"

"Pa," Eleanor interjected. "*Forgotten?* They were best friends. Randy couldn't forget anything about…what happened that day. I'm certain he's told us all there is to tell."

"That's right, sir. You have the whole story."

Damn! He knows. I have to get out of here.

"Sure. I hope you don't think I meant anything else," Benjamin said, apologizing for the second time during Bridgewater's visit.

"Not at all, Mr. Kyner. In your place, I would be asking the same question. Now, I really must be off."

A final good-bye from Eleanor followed Bridgewater out the door. Due to the frigid temperature, she watched from the warmth of the kitchen as he limped to the car, got in, and started it. As the headlights came on in the early January darkness, she turned to face Benjamin.

"Pa? What was that all about? You were beginning to make me feel uncomfortable."

"Take a good look at him, Eleanor. You won't be seeing him again."

"What? Why on earth would you say that, Pa?"

"Because he was lying," Benjamin said while

looking Eleanor straight in the eye. "There's something about what happened that day he's not telling us. He's ashamed and he's frightened. He won't be back. Francis died saving another pilot and I'm willing to bet it was Bridgewater. My son, the father of your child, is dead and that arrogant lying fool is alive. How is that fair?"

Rarely had Bridgewater felt as relieved as when he was again alone and maneuvering the big Pierce-Arrow along the uneven track leading to Fairey Hill Road. Driving across Benjamin's field where he and Francis took off in the Jenny so long ago, he grimaced in painful recollection. That had been a different and very naïve world.

Stopping at the end of the lane, he put the car in neutral and set the parking brake. Bridgewater was oblivious to the fact that just down the road to his right was the one-room schoolhouse where his best friend spent eight years studying, among other things, the geography of the place where he would one day trade his life for Bridgewater's own.

"Dear God, I am grateful that chore is done with," he said aloud as he reached into a coat pocket with his gloved right hand. "I have to hand it to you Francis. Of the two of us, you got the better deal."

He extracted a sterling silver flask and unscrewed the top. Looking at the open spout and then toasting his reflection in the windshield, he said to the empty space around him, "Ah, sweet refuge of the weak-willed coward."

He swallowed deeply from the flask.

Looking at the gleaming container, he said, "Don't you worry about the 18th amendment, my darling.

Prohibition be damned. I have lots of your brothers and sisters hidden away."

He screwed the top back on and replaced the flask in his pocket. Then he released the parking brake, shifted the transmission into first gear, and pulled out onto dark and empty Fairey Hill Road, where he drove into the darkness toward his future.

CHAPTER 32

CHOICES

Benjamin had been waiting for this day. He was finally able to do something for his grandson.

Jeremy laughed as the young woman attempted to slip his twisted right foot into the new brace that had arrived from Pittsburgh.

"He thinks it's a game," laughed Eleanor. "Jeremy, be good!" Then she laughed again.

Benjamin stood behind them. His eyes narrowed in concentration, accentuating his already perpetual squint. He wanted to know how to do this.

As Allyson Rochelle, who had been a nursing student when Benjamin first met her almost two years earlier, tried to capture Jeremy's flailing foot, his diaper slid from its intended location. The change in temperature had the usual effect and a narrow golden stream suddenly arced upward, drenching the front of her nurse's uniform.

"Ahhh!" she cried to Jeremy's delighted laughter.

"Whoa!" said Benjamin in surprise.

"Oh, I'm so sorry!" Eleanor said loudly as she covered her mouth to stifle her own giggles.

"Damn!" said Allyson as she finally got the shoe in place. "There, I win!"

Jeremy began to express his unhappiness that the game was over and that he was now wearing a very uncomfortable contraption that kept him from kicking his legs.

As she dabbed the front of her uniform with a spare diaper, Allyson said to Eleanor and Benjamin, "Well, you see how the brace goes on. We can take if off now, but he has to wear it every night while he sleeps. At first he'll hate it, but he'll get used to it over time."

"But this won't cure his clubfoot," Benjamin said with disappointment.

"No, the deformity is much too severe. Jeremy will need at least one operation to correct it. Maybe more."

"Well, that won't be happening soon," Eleanor said, "but thank you so much for coming out here."

As Allyson prepared to leave, she said, "The brace would have been ready months ago, but the influenza was the priority. Almost all non-critical medical care was suspended."

Eleanor said, "We're very fortunate you were able to stay on with the doctor after you graduated. I know you were a big help during the flu outbreak."

Allyson continued, "Bring Jeremy by for his checkups and we'll adjust the brace slowly. This will be a very long process and it will accomplish only so much."

Allyson said her goodbyes and left.

As they heard her car pull away, Benjamin looked at Eleanor, who was holding Jeremy.

"I noticed when Bridgewater was here you didn't tell him about Jeremy's foot. You kept it pretty well hidden by that blanket."

"That's right, Pa," she said, looking at him solemnly.

"It was because of me, wasn't it?" he asked, though he already knew the answer.

"Pa, we both know how you feel about Randy. If he had learned about Jeremy's foot, he would have asked questions and that would have led to his insisting on helping. If I allowed him to pay for an operation I'm afraid your resentment would be more than I could bear. It would have made our lives miserable."

"Even if it meant the little kid would be able to walk normally?"

"Pa, please don't make this worse for me, but yes. I chose what was best for our *family*, Pa. You and me and Jeremy. Randy would have meant well, but it wasn't worth it. Anyway, I don't want Randy's charity. I think it would have scarred us. I used to hope my parents would soften. I could have accepted their help because they're my parents, after all. But now, after all this time, I don't think I'd take their money. I've thought a lot about this and I believe finding a way to help Jeremy is something we have to do as a family. Something else will come up. I pray every day and I'm certain the Lord will not forsake my son."

Benjamin put both arms around Eleanor and Jeremy and drew them close.

Now what the hell do I do?

THANK YOU!

Dear Reader,

I sincerely hope you enjoyed *Benjamin's Field: Rescue*, the first book of the *Benjamin's Field Trilogy*.

I hope you will go on to read the second book, *Benjamin's Field: Ascent*, and learn what happens to the characters in book one, especially Jeremy Kyner. Why did I title it *Ascent*? Hmmm.... There must be a reason!

Please consider leaving a review on Amazon or Goodreads. Reviews are critically important to authors and I would very much appreciate yours, good, bad or in between. Not only do reviews help others decide about reading a book, but your feedback is important to me. You can post a review on Amazon by visiting my author page at https://authorcentral.amazon.com/gp/books and selecting *Benjamin's Field: Rescue*.

I also invite you to visit my personal website at www.jjknights.com.

If you do post a review, please let me know at jjknights@jjknights.com so I can thank you personally.

Thanks again,
J. J. Knights

Made in the USA
Charleston, SC
30 June 2016